DARK CURRENTS

DARK CURRENTS

Edited by Ian Whates

NEWCON PRESS

NewCon Press
England

First edition, published in the UK April 2012
by NewCon Press

NCP 044 (hardback)
NCP 045 (softback)

10 9 8 7 6 5 4 3 2 1

ISBN: 978-1-907069-34-5 (hardback)
978-1-907069-35-2 (softback)

Cover art "Conflagration" by Ben Baldwin
Cover layout by Andy Bigwood

Invaluable editorial assistance from Ian Watson
Text layout by Storm Constantine

Printed in the UK by MPG Biddles of Kings Lynn

CONTENTS

Dark Currents: An Introduction

Ian Whates

In many ways *Dark Currents* represents a return to NewCon Press' roots: a genre-straddling collection of stories produced by a diverse group of talented wordsmiths writing to a common theme. After a number of anthologies that have focused on one specific area of genre – *Conflicts* and *Further Conflicts* (science fiction), *Anniversaries* (fantasy), *The Bitten Word* (vampires), *Hauntings* (uhm, would you believe… ghosts?) – I was keen to again oversee a book that encompasses science fiction, fantasy, horror, dark fantasy and slipstream all under the same cover.

Inspiration came when artist Ben Baldwin approached me regarding his work. I looked at Ben's website and needed no further persuading. This man has *talent*! One image in particular caught my eye and I immediately contacted Ben to discover that yes, it was indeed available.

An evocative image of fire, water, ships ablaze, with a seated figure watching on.

Dark Currents/Dark Tides: that's all that any would-be contributors were given. The rest was up to them.

As ever, I was seeking a mix of familiar names and the less familiar, of writers I'd worked with before and those whose work I admired but hadn't yet had the pleasure of publishing. I began to approach authors at Eastercon, 2011, and the first two I spoke to were Aliette de Bodard and Nina Allan; two exceptional writers who are already making names for themselves and whose careers can only go from strength to strength. I also met Sophia McDougall for the first time that weekend, and our paths were destined to cross several times in the following months, notably when we were both guests at a massed signing event at Heffers in Cambridge. Sophia was another natural to approach for *Dark Currents.*

I first encountered Adam Nevill when we were on a panel together at a literary event in Lincoln a couple of years ago. I was deeply impressed by his writing ethos; even more so when he produced the superb *The Ritual* in 2011. We bumped into each other at the launch of China Miéville's *Embassy Town*, where I took the opportunity to talk short stories. Adam's was one of the first submissions to arrive. He had clearly embraced the theme as his tale fitted to perfection. Only subsequently did I discover that Adam had finished the story shortly before we spoke and was wondering where to send the piece when I offered it the perfect home. Serendipity in action.

Adrian Tchaikovsky is an author who has already made a significant impression with his novels, but not perhaps with his shorter work. I've a feeling this might soon change. I recall attending a reading in which Adrian treated us to a new story; it was witty, entertaining, and clever. I loved it, and immediately invited him to submit for the anthology.

Una McCormack is an author I have a great deal of respect for. Una has appeared in two previous NewCon anthologies and never fails to deliver something memorable. She is part of a cabal of us authorly types who gather from time to time in a Cambridge pub… to, ahem, discuss genre literature. It was Una who first introduced Rebecca J Payne to the group: another emerging talent. Rebecca's first ever story submission was accepted by *Interzone* and subsequently came third in that year's readers' poll; not the worst of credentials.

I first discovered Neil Williamson's fiction via his excellent collection, *Ephemera.* It's been far too long since Neil appeared in a NewCon Press volume – not since 2008's *Subterfuge* – and I didn't hesitate in approaching him regarding *Dark Currents.* Another author I was pleased to invite is Andrew Hook – whose Elastic Press, coincidentally, published Neil's *Ephemera.* Andrew's observant and inventive brand of slipstream brings an added dimension to any book.

Lavie Tidhar has to be one of the busiest writers around; his short fiction seems to pop up all over the place and is always worth reading. It seemed inevitable that NewCon Press would publish Lavie at some point, and *Dark Currents* struck me as the perfect opportunity. Lavie is a writer from whom it's always best to expect the unexpected, and the same can be said of Tricia Sullivan. This is the fourth story of Tricia's I've been fortunate enough to commission (three for NewCon Press and one for the recent *Solaris Rising*) and each has been very different from the others, having in common only their quality. Tricia's piece here is short but packs a real punch.

Emma Coleman is something of an enigma: tall, slender, quiet… you'd think that butter wouldn't melt; yet a dark corner lurks somewhere deep within. When Emma first joined the Northampton SF Writers Group a few years back, we were all impressed by the strength of her writing, but also by its inherent darkness. I was disappointed when circumstances prevented Emma from contributing to 2010's *Shoes, Ships and Cadavers* – the volume launched to showcase the group – but I'm delighted to now put that omission right by publishing a story from this very talented writer.

I received more unsolicited approaches for *Dark Currents* than for any previous anthology. Presumably this is an indication of the growing reputation (or perhaps infamy) that NewCon Press is garnering. The result is that I've had a wider pool of stories from which to select the final book than ever. Amongst these unsolicited pieces were Jan Edwards' rumbustious ectoplasmic naval tale and Finn Clarke's near-future dystopia – two stories that just couldn't be ignored – as well as Rod Rees' deft intertwining of alternative history and genre tropes. Rod's story arrived via his agent, the estimable John Jarrold, who had heard of the *Dark Currents* project and enquired whether I'd like to see a piece from one of his authors that might just fit the theme: Rod. Of course I would! And I'm delighted that I did.

I've always resisted the inclusion of poetry in any NewCon Press anthology (okay, a couple slipped into the *Now We Are 5* booklet, but that was special circumstance and intended as a one off). I have little knowledge of the field and reckon such things are best left to those more qualified. Then Vick Linde – a multi-talented lady with impeccable taste in reading – approached me for three words from which to build a poem for her blog. The result was "George"; a poignant piece that I felt would make a perfect coda for the *Dark Currents* book… It just goes to show: never say never; those currents are strong.

Ian Whates
February 2012

THE FALL OF LADY SEALIGHT

Adrian Tchaikovsky

Each night, in dreams, she still flew through the green-blue dappled vastness of the Void. The dim-lit chasms arched and wheeled around her. A space that is no-space, greater than the mind can conceive, immeasurable, ineffable, nowhere and nothing.

In her dreams she could still soar through the infinite sea-lit halls that her mind made of the Void's awful nothingness; dance amidst the motes of sifting dust; soar unbound and untethered as man has always yearned to do, and never done, save there.

In her dreams, most nights, no others were there. She could not hear the static buzz of comrades in her head as they looped together through an abyss that each flier saw differently. She did not see the memory-shapes her mind had once conjured: shapes giving space and distance and form to the mere bundles of thought they were all rendered down to.

Nor were there enemies in her dreams. No sharp darts of motion as Commonwealth soldiers arrowed in for the kill. No mental daggers lancing into her brain. No feel of resistance, of sudden shattered release, as she turned the weapons of her mind upon the enemy.

Only sometimes, in her dreams, there was Isender, who had

loved her – whom she had shared her inconsequential body with, whom she had shared her mind with as they flew together. Sometimes she dreamt of Isender, whose real name she had never known.

Her name was Eleanor de Witney, of a family whose every generation gave at least one son or daughter to the service of the Crown. In the vastness of the Void they called her by another name. Once they had seen the world her mind constructed in that matter-less vacuum, they had called her Lady Sealight.

She woke to the unbearable prison of the flesh, dropping out of the dream of flight that was now denied to her forever: into her leaden, lumpen body, her wounded, broken mind.

Where am I now?

There was nothing to suggest a yesterday to her, as though the dreams had taken not only her hope but all her history. She was left as vacant as the Void she had once sported, loved and fought in.

Was I here yesterday?

Had she used the Prod yesterday? Something told her that she had not. Some indefatigable internal clock told her: one more day and it is charged again. She must have triggered it, must have come here, the day before last.

I can no longer deal with a material world.

Even as the thought tore at her, memory began dropping back into her hollow brain in fragments and shards. The island republic: tropical paradise; tourists and loungers and the larcenous poor; police on street corners, young as schoolboys with machineguns tucked under their arms like books; the hotel. She had been so tired, more tired each time. She could not even remember paying for the room.

Just another place that is not my place.

How many had there been? Her clock struck inside, telling her: *thirteen. There have been thirteen places now that have not been home.*

Hunger was waking inside her now. Lady Sealight had not eaten, save as need be. Her body had been fit, thin, trained, and largely irrelevant. Her mind had disdained it. Like all the Abyssonauts she would have spent her life free and unfettered in the Void, had she been allowed. If duty and the Crown had not tied her down she would have danced off into the sea-murky gothic grandeur and never come back.

Now the prison of her body wanted food. She was aware that she was rebounding from her loss of the infinite, falling back into the crass and the material. She knew the hole she tried to fill with food was the unbounded Void, and that she would eat herself to death before she could plug it, and yet she ate. She ate to emphasise the misery and the degradation of the flesh that held her in.

She called room service. Her fingers remembered how. The empty cartons and bottles on the floor beside the bed gave solemn testament. She recalled none of it. Her memory seemed to skip, to shudder over things as recent as yesterday.

It's just because I'm tired.

She hoped it was because she was tired.

"Peanuts," she told the telephone. "Beer. Sandwiches. Meat. Chocolate. Ice cream. Food."

Tomorrow she would fire the prod again, before things became too bad here: groping for home like a blind woman scouring the streets of London for a lost pin.

Once the British Empire had the world in its hand, there was nothing for it but to turn inwards. Parliament bucking at the reins of a King who hauled them in all the harder at the resistance. Englishman spilling English blood as had not happened since Richard's triumph at Bosworth Field. Whilst the conquered world looked on and held its shackled breath, the Crown and the Commonwealth fought like sleepwalkers. Spies but no armies. Scientists but no bombs. The Empire's leaps of technical might, that had humbled a world from pole to pole, made all the old wars obsolete, impossible. Only backward, third-world places had any use for the massed infantry, the tanks and guns. The field of combat for the civil war was the Void.

They tested all children, nowadays. They subjected them to the terrible vacancy of the Void at five or six, seven was late, eight too late to train. This was cruel, and everyone knew it, but the safety of the Crown was at stake and the Empire needed soldiers. They recoiled, those frightened children. They screamed and cried and begged to be taken back into a material world their senses could grasp. Some never recovered. There would be scars on most, nightmares of a cavernous lack of being, that would stretch from infancy to senescence. Some would lose their minds in that first touch. It was cruel. It was necessary. The Commonwealth did far worse.

Some children, confronted with a dimensionless space, a senseless abyss of non-information, painted a picture for themselves, splashed colour across the invisible, called light into the eyeless gulf. Perhaps one in ten thousand could make that mental leap, like seeing the other side of an impossible figure, inverting a line-drawn cube. They were the motive behind the cruelty, the ends that justified the means. For every soldier of the Crown, a handful of minds were destroyed and others would never sleep easily again.

It was a personal thing, the Void: along and behind and within the physical world, without end, without measure. That Void had no distances or landmarks. It had no material existence. To fly the Void was to have your body made into nothing, to vanish from existence entire and be remade on your return, whole, or almost whole. It was the mind that vaunted in the Void.

It was not dark, not silent. That implied that light, that sound could come there. The Void had no medium that light could navigate. No sound. No scent. No touch. The vacuum of space was bursting with energy and life against the Void. The madness of those children was rooted there: the human mind withering and dying in the conscious, shocking absence of stimulus. Only those gifted few could colour the Void and, if they could give it form, then they could *fly*. There would be no limits to them. They would be little gods.

For most of those so gifted, that first brush with the Void was yet a horror that would stay with them all their lives. Their minds made of it an infinite personal horror. They saw twisted, spiralling towers of bone; filled the sky with malice-ridden idiot faces; trembled in terror before vaulted cathedral cloisters wreathed in dark smoke, or louring jungles peopled with bright pinprick eyes. Still, they found the service of the Crown. It was an honour and a duty, and the war was too fierce to leave them a choice. They were condemned to fly in their own nightmare.

For just a few, though, that first forced entry into the Void was something else, something wondrous and strange. Their minds reached out into the infinite and smiled. Isender, when he flew, cast himself through a golden sky as beautiful as he was.

Eleanor crammed chocolate into her mouth, bitterly trying to escape a sea-blue, sea-green, coral-limned space where she had moved like a dolphin and, even when the sharks of the Commonwealth had pressed close, known no fear.

The television channels of the hotel featured imported soap operas in foreign languages; staticky game shows where poor picture quality gave human skin the colours of cheese; newsreaders carefully picking around the gaps they were forbidden to illuminate. Eleanor knew the pattern. She had seen the angry men in nondescript clothes eyeing the police with loathing, heard the slogans the students shouted across the square. The island was brewing revolution.

One day until the Prod was charged and she could exchange this hell for another, no better, no worse. Would she get out ahead of the guns this time? She thought not. The newsreaders looked strained, as though they needed a holiday anywhere but here. Mechanically she checked her hardware. Everything in poor shape, but holding. Everything low on power. The Assumptor was still bending causality around her, hiding the armour and the weapons and the Abyssonaut's three-lobed helm, making people see what they wanted to see. Sick of it, she let it die for a minute, in the privacy of her own room. She looked down without its haze to confound her, saw the eroded plates of her mail, scarred and pocked as though her eruption from the Void had been re-entry from space. An Abyssonaut's kit had to survive being unmade in the baptism of nothingness that was entry to the Void, had to survive being remade in the tumbling, system-wrenching return to a physical world. Her return had been more wrenching than most. Everything had suffered, herself most of all.

She examined her hands, which of all things marked her trade. The webs between the fingers were delicate but obvious. Mutation was part of the package. Bodies came back from the Void in all states, viable and non. It took the strongest mind to rebuild perfectly. Eleanor was good, but nobody of her generation was that good. Isender's body was crippled, a lop-sided spine and buckled legs like an accident victim. Who cared? Bodies came back deformed but minds returned stronger with each voyage.

Recently, the last three worlds or so, people had started to notice her hands even through the Assumptor field. The machine was failing, she knew, and soon she would not even be able to walk amongst her own kind without being a freak.

Home, she thought, but what were the chances that she would ever get home?

She had flown a score of skirmishes against the Commonwealth before that fatal mission. In the Void, freed into her own sea-lit world, she had loved to fight, had taken chances that her instructors railed over, that her peers admired and tried to emulate. She had coasted on the wave of an adrenaline that touched only the mind, as she shifted and soared and stooped on Commonwealth soldiers, lancing with her brain against the shields of theirs, shearing past them with outstretched claws to drag at their minds. She had never been freer than dogfighting across non-space, turning and corkscrewing and doubling, confounding them, outmatching them – knowing, in the moment when she shattered their minds, that even her enemies adored her.

Three times she had received the call to drop out of the Void for a land assault, and those she hated. The sudden, angry wrench as her body was shuffled together, the hostile sight of a Commonwealth control room or hangar or mess. Her webbed hands would fumble for her kit. The Particle Spear to disrupt their electronics or their nervous systems, the Jung-Saffer cannon to madden their minds, the Strife Gun to set friend against friend, even a plain knife for the most desperate corners. A moment's work, with Commonwealth Chasmonauts closing on her position every second, and then the blessed disintegration. Re-entering the Void to see their dark, arrowhead flecks twisting and homing, sounding out for Isender and the others to cover her retreat.

She was a veteran. Only nine other Abyssonauts had ever lived as long in active service. New recruits spoke in hushed tones of the beautiful Lady Sealight.

She looked at her face in the mirror. Flat, heavy-browed, heavy-jawed, the eyes dull and murky brown, the hair lank, almost colourless. It had never mattered before.

In the hotel's restaurant she had a huge meal, which she put on the tab. Her mind scattered over the last two days, found no details concerning money. It didn't matter. In a hotel, on an island, at a moment of local crisis, national tension, what were the odds the currency would last long enough to make any payment worthwhile? And tomorrow she would be gone.

The restaurant was crammed with foreign nationals trying to get out. There was no way out. She heard no ships were docking at the port, that planes were being diverted from the airfields. Embassies were barring their doors. The island Eden readied itself for the wrath of God. She was crammed in, sharing a table, wolfing down her meal. She tried to make small talk with a spiky-haired musician who talked in high, strained tones of famous names he had once played with; with a calm-mannered government man whose grey eyes flicked once a minute to her hands.

Outside, a demonstration was shouting out for revenge. If she looked past the musician's bony shoulder she could see placards showing a Hispanic face dashed with red, with hand-painted logos. The police were at the fringes, in nervous clumps with their safety catches off.

"I mean, they gotta let me on the plane," came the shaky voice of the musician. "I got a gig in Montana, man, and they ain't gonna let me miss that for anything. My agent, she'll get on the blower to the embassy, you watch, and they'll all just smooth the way, know what I mean?" She looked once at his red-rimmed eyes and knew there was no gig, no agent. The government man knew it too. She wondered which government he was with.

That one fatal mission. The Minister had called them in, all the best Abyssonauts. There was an emergency. The Crown was at stake. The Commonwealth scientists had made an advance.

The Minister had outlined the situation in steady tones, but behind them had clamoured the musician's same nervous fear. The Commonwealth had found, or made, a prodigy: their secret weapon to end the war.

"This man," she could hear the Minister saying, "this new Chasmonaut of theirs, has a power. With the aid of a machine of theirs he can transport others through the Void."

"Others, Minister?" came the flat sound of Isender's voice.

"Soldiers, Captain," the Minister clarified. "Warriors. The Commonwealth has trained a force of old-style soldiers, expendable killers, and this new man of theirs will carry them through the Void, right to us. Think! Not six or a dozen men materialising in the base, firing once and melting away, but a hundred or more surging through our command. They'd not leave a man alive and, if we beat them off, this man of theirs could ship a new load in. They call him Icarus, their new man. He will change the face of warfare forever."

There were cries of horror, of disbelief. The Minister nodded, and there were tears in the corners of his eyes.

"I know, I know. Even the Commonwealth… Our spies assure us that it's true, however. This civil war, the burden of which has rested on your shoulders only, and those of your counterparts on the other side, will now be opened up for every man, woman and child in the nation. This will be an old-style war, with innocent men and women being armed, being sent helpless to their deaths. Instead of a duel of experts it will be a massacre of amateurs."

"What can we do?" She remembered herself saying that, although perhaps it was someone else after all.

"You must prevent Icarus from reaching us. You must cut through his escort and destroy him in the Void, *at all costs.* It is our one chance."

He turned away from them then, so that they could not see his pain. *At all costs.* They were all expendable then. The cream of the Commonwealth Chasmonauts would be defending Icarus. This would be the greatest battle of the war. If they lost, it would be the last.

By the time the Minister had turned back they had walked or run or been wheeled from the room, already preparing for transit into the Void.

When she passed back through the lobby people were talking in panicked voices of two men who had been shot dead in the tourist quarter. They had been spray-painting anti-government slogans, some said. They had been foreigners. They had been carrying a bomb. Feeling full, unwell, Eleanor trailed for the lifts, making her way through the conspicuous gaps that had opened between natives and visitors. As she flapped at the lift call, a government soldier came in and stood on the reception counter. There was nothing to worry about, he announced in harsh English. No people had been shot. It was all malicious rumour put about by a minority group. Nobody had been shot and nobody should worry. Distant gunfire underscored his speech but he did not seem to notice.

The lift attendant, who had been dressed up like a performing monkey in red and gold, was absent. Perhaps he had gone to wave a gun and join the revolution, to charge into death like last century's toy soldier. Eleanor fingered the buttons, reaching for her floor. She found it hard to focus on the numbers, or anything else. As the lift doors closed she was already thinking of food again, needing *something* to stop the Void within clawing at her. She felt sick, stuffed. She wondered if she made herself throw up, whether she could force more food in.

I'm going mad. There must be something else.

A bath. She would have a bath. She would fill it right to the top and float there, and pretend…

Her door clicked locked behind her and she let the Assumptor's field die, casting off the images that had hidden her. She released the buckles of her armour and let it fall backwards off her onto the bed like a corpse. Her body, seeming heavier, more ungainly when naked, slumped itself to the bath and fumbled with the taps. For one brief, unbearably bright moment, she considered taking a razor to her wrists as she lay in the water. She had been exiled from the Void, her wings had been torn away, what else was there to live for?

She could not see a razor to hand, and her own knife was still scabbarded with her armour. The thought passed her by, leaving only the acid aftertaste of *Would I really have had the courage?*

She could feel the hotel around her. It was a latticework of fear, stacked anxieties. People lying to themselves about their futures and their chances. Through the walls she could dimly hear prayer, weeping, a couple making love. The thought made her hurt and sad. That was what people do, she supposed. That was what the flesh did. Raised in the Void from the age of four, what would she know about how to live in these meagre dimensions?

She had discovered, once, whether Isender was physically capable of that act. It had been more an exercise in genetics than anything else. A duty they had towards the next generation of the Crown's soldiers.

Twenty-seven of them had vaunted into the Void. Every Abyssonaut not already flying had been sent into the aether to stop Icarus.

Lying back in the bath, water sloshing over the sides, she remembered with a clarity she could not apply to anything more recent.

Isender was calling muster, stringing out their company name by name at his command, and she had thought *We are nothing but names here, in the Void.* At the far end of the line (and "end" and "line" had no meaning there, outside of the mind), Chertsey Vaults opined that Icarus was just a myth, that this was just training, keeping them in shape.

Her voice, as Lady Sealight's mind constructed it, had the same raw edge as the musician in the hotel bar, as the Minister at the briefing.

There was no distance in the Void, but they plotted a course that would make them be where the Commonwealthers were, driving through the chaotic densities like men hauling hand over hand up a rope; falling through its vacant expanse like high-divers waiting for the water's iron impact. The Lady Sealight soared and danced through the green-blue abyss bounded at each infinite edge with twisted walls of coral. None of the Minister's speech had been lost on her but she knew no fear. She was home. She had been born to this. She could feel Isender laughing with her as he sped through his golden heaven towards the foe.

The mind's hemispheres colluded, spinning lies. They calculated and guessed their way across layers of tissue-thin reality, aiming themselves at the null-point where the waveform would collapse and they would be instantly amongst the enemy. Their minds and eyes judged the odds, the time remaining, and gave them dots to home in on, gathering stormcrows in Isender's heaven, sharks in Sealight's sea.

In the mind it had been eleven minutes. In reality there was no way of measuring time nor time to measure. They were upon the enemy like hawks.

Memory broke apart, shards all that remained of the Battle of Britain.

She was strafing down on a Commonwealth man who had been arrowing in on Chertsey Vaults. Her mind slammed into his, unguarded and unwary, like a sledgehammer. He dissolved away into the non-stuff of the Void, leaving a cloud of dark in the sea of her mind. Chertsey made half of a panicked vote of thanks before someone else, something else, got her. Lady Sealight doubled back, circled, looking for Icarus. The name of her slain opponent bobbed once in her mind. She had clashed with him twice before.

Isender was storming through, golden and beautiful, the very force of his motion scattering the Commonwealthers every which way. One dogged him, tried to pin him down. He reversed instantly: they wheeled and spun around each other, fighting ace to ace, minds trading thrusts and parries with the dexterity of fencing masters.

The game of Abyssonauts and Chasmonauts, the civil war to date, had been a formal duel of gentlefolk, respect and quarter given on all sides. No more. Icarus had changed all that. Now they were knife-fighters in a street brawl, mad for blood. All around the Lady Sealight, pairs and trios gyred and danced and tried to kill each other. She had lost track of friend or foe, of Isender, of all. Someone plunged past her, clawing wildly at her brain, and it was only after her lacerating riposte that she was sure it was an enemy.

Then it was before her. The thing that was Icarus.

The Void bent around it, buckled and warped with the unnatural gravity. Icarus and his five hundred. Her eyes, which for two decades and more had read the Void as seascape and sunlight, could not interpret it. There was no precedent. There was just a towering blot, a hideous, bloated mass of wrongness. And somewhere at its centre, a man. Icarus.

No hesitation. She was at him before she even knew. She took the might of her mind in both hands and lanced the monstrous boil through. Instantly she felt his defences steel themselves. He was strong, massive, armoured with the fragile minds of his cargo. He reached out for her, and ten of his people gave up their souls to fuel his brutal assault. She was sent reeling, ringing with the force of his near-miss. *Power, but no finesse*, she had thought then. And Icarus gobbled up another dozen hearts and minds, and his reaching hands filled the sky in his attempt to swat her.

He will catch me, now or the next time. She had been calm. Always, in the Void, she was calm. Time loved her and slowed for her, so she could think. She saw the gaps in Icarus' attack that would let her slip through, another close call. She saw the other gap, too, at the heart, where the twisting coils of his assault were landing lights letting her know exactly where he was. Follow the tentacles to the brain.

One single slice of no-time in which to make the decision that was no decision. She dived for him, the spear of her mind held out before her and. as his grasp closed on her. she pierced his mind and knew that she had won.

In her sight, then, he was a kraken, with the obscuring cloud of his ink ripped away. A kraken with its eyes transfixed by her lance. She felt, individually and collectively and in great detail, five hundred Commonwealth soldiers die in terror, each one alone.

Icarus' coils convulsed and crushed her then, and flung her far away. She was falling through the Void, suddenly, a hundred tiny voices in her ears as her equipment screamed at her. She reached out, but the Void betrayed her at last and she could gain no purchase on it.

She felt herself blink in and out. It was touch and go, in that moment, whether she would exist at all. *Would it not have been better if that had been the end?*

And then she was in another place and it was cold.

Through the floor, through the bathwater, she felt a vibration, more mental than physical. A stuttered shudder that stopped almost as soon as it had started and left her in no doubt. Gunfire. The thought brought a strange calm to her, in knowing that the stormclouds had broken open at last, that the guillotine had dropped.

The flesh surprised her. She found it standing before the bed, naked and dripping, staring down at her armour. With careful, practised speed she shrugged into it and clasped the buckles together.

She would not get involved, she told herself. She would leave by the most direct route. None of this was her fight. Her fight was on another Earth, beneath unreal and unbounded skies.

She could barely concentrate on the solid things around her. *The stairs*, she decided. *Down the stairs and out.* Only at the head of the stairs did she realise that she had no mental image of the hotel, where the fire exits were, where the stairs came out. Her mental map had been shattered and she could not piece it back together in the time she had. For what could have been a whole minute she stood at the stairwell's top, mouth open, feeling her grasp of the situation slipping further and further from her.

This is it. I'm going. I've lost myself. I can no longer cope.

A heavy-footed woman in khaki shorts and shirt blundered into her from around the corner, pug-nosed face pink with annoyance. Tourist khakis, not soldier khakis. The woman rebounded from her, stared at her sharply. Her eyes were dragged to Eleanor's hands, back to her face. She had a detached look, like a woman calculating the savings at a sale, as though she, too, had lost touch with events.

The stranger thumped down the stairs grimly, armoured in the assurance that some tourists have, that whatever is going on is somebody else's problem. Eleanor staggered after her, caught up in the other woman's blind purpose. She had, in that moment, lost all track of what she had intended to do.

A man with a beret and a gun waited for them at the foot of the stairs. Beyond him was only the lobby, a dozen other gunmen looking out, hostages crouching on the floor, facing the great glass doors and windows of the hotel. There were other soldiers beyond the doors, government soldiers. They had a tank.

One man stood on the hotel's reception desk, shouting "Nobody move! This hotel is now under the control of Revulotionary Moderist Party! Nobody must move."

The revolutionary facing Eleanor and the tourist barked something, too swift to follow. Eleanor's mind flickered over the weapons in her suit. She had never had to face guns in her right and proper place. They belonged to the past and to this twisted hell she had found herself in. Even as she recoiled, her companion from the stairwell tried to march across the lobby, and a revolutionary laid hands on her. She slapped the man across the face indignantly. It was a move of such practicality and simplicity that it left Eleanor, too, reeling.

The chief revolutionary atop his reception desk pulpit time, chose that moment to declare, to no one and everyone, "Alright! They asked for it." One tanned hand lifted high to give a signal to his men.

Eleanor felt time begin to fragment again, felt the future-echoes of the upcoming tragedy wash over her.

There was a sudden burst of activity from the bar, as some of the staff, or the tourists, began their desperate bid for freedom. The chief revolutionary calmly directed his gun at one of the hostages, aiming for the centre of the suitcase she clutched to herself.

Eleanor began her long walk out into the lobby. *I will leave now*, she decided flatly. She activated the Ravless field in her suit and felt her feet leave the floor slightly as it pushed away the molecules of the carpet. She hoped it would be enough.

She saw the government man from dinner with a phone to his ear. Perhaps he was going to call in, to tell the soldiers and the tank not to respond. Eleanor already knew he was too late. Shots had been fired, hostages were being killed. The government would have to act. She threw the Ravless field into overdrive and felt her feet leave the floor altogether, dancing up into the closed space of the lobby like an angel.

If she closed her eyes she could almost believe she was home.

She felt, rather than heard, the tank gun thunder, imagined it recoiling back, rocking the whole square before the hotel. She was walking forward in air. She opened her eyes as the shell struck the hotel's glass front and shivered it, all at once, into a thousand million shards of flying glass that spun and bounded around her, caught momentarily in the Ravless field and then flung away. With time running slow as treacle she knew the rifling dot heading towards her, now coin-sized, now fist-sized, head-sized, was the tank shell. She reached out for it, palms forward, and it rebounded from her hands like a leaping salmon. She watched herself do this, and wondered, and watched on as she glided forwards through the ruined, glass-toothed maw into the open air. The Assumptor field was gone. She hung above the government soldiers in full armour like the ghost of Joan of Arc. Some part of her observed the looks of rapture, of terror, on all their faces. She passed on, alighted on the ground behind them, skated away over concrete made slippery by the Ravless field. It would not do to miss her footing, not with both sides of a civil war staring after her in awe.

Any technology sufficiently advanced will be indistinguishable from magic. Some scientist had thought that up years ago, but how true, how true.

The cold place. From the untemperatured Void she had found herself in the cold place. Blinding white when the sun shone on the snow. Blinding white when the snow obscured the sun. The heater units in her armour had strained and buzzed and fought and still she had been cold. Here was a world that never saw the positive end of the thermometer. If they had not found her she would have been killed by that cold.

They had been a dozen in number. Squat, hairy, encased in the hides of dead animals. Their weapons had been bronze and iron, which should have told her there and then what had happened. They had treated her with a grudging reverence, as though fulfilling some unwanted but unavoidable duty. She never knew what they thought she was.

Their faces were craggy, secretive, heavy-browed. There was a word for them, in historical texts, a word for a casualty of evolution fifty-thousand years old.

She spent a long while thinking she had been sent back in

time, although she knew from her classes that this was impossible. It was the metalworking that told the contrary tale, of course. This was not the vanished past of the Neander valley and its doomed souls, but a present where the ice age had never left, where the Cro-Magnons had never come. Fifty-thousand years of harsh weather and stunted growth to bring the world into a fragile iron age.

When the Prod was repaired and charged she had activated it at once, confident in her return to the boundless sea-blue skies of the Void. There had been other places. Other presents. She scattered herself sideways through the universe like a mountaineer sliding inexorably off an ice ledge. There had been the European super-state where Mongolian was the Lingua Franca. There had been the silver city of the scientists, where she was laughed at as a primitive. There had been a world held in the clawed fist of the sabre-toothed cats, where men rode against beasts with mace and chain, and feline eyes held too great a depth of knowledge and understanding. There had been thirteen presents, now, in her past, and none of them was home.

And in each world a violence had been brewing. Whilst the Neanderthals knuckled down before the anger of the elements, clinging on for the sake of lost humanity, the scientists plotted clinical wars against distant worlds and the cats unsheathed their claws and stalked human prey. There were wars, gangfights, regicides and uprisings, and each world was worse than the last. Three of the thirteen were wastelands, where place and people bore mute witness to a history of war that the final bombs had not ended, only made more local and more petty. The universe Lady Sealight travelled through chewed at itself like a mad dog, with more blood at every baring of the teeth.

And now here she was, in some self-destructing island republic with the sands of her mind running ever faster through the hourglass. The next present, or the next, would find her a war that all her machines and trickery could not win through, and that would be the end of Lady Sealight.

She had no mental map or plan of the city she was in. She simply walked away from the stilled conflict, and nobody called her back or made any move to stop her. She would never know whether her intervention, unintended and unasked, would make any difference.

Her feet were searching for something. They had quietly taken over after declaring her mind unfit to govern, an internal insurrection. She walked on into the vacant streets because something was amiss – something other than all the things she knew to be amiss. From behind shutters and curtains the natives watched her pass: an apparition in battle-armour, face blank and eyes almost closed.

With some determination, her feet led her to a square with a fitful fountain coughing up dirty water, and left her there, staring at the display on her bracers. Lights, red and green and white, winked on and off. Some were simply chanting the same mantra of damage and uncertainty that she had heard every day since her exile but there was a new voice in the mechanical chorus and it had news. This was what her feet had seen, whilst her eyes had been on other things.

A power signature.

The words fell into the sterile ground of her brain and lay there, stillborn. She turned them over, examined their shapes, as a dark-age savage might have handled the works of Plato.

Realisation charged her, grabbed her ears and shook her until a grain of understanding fell into place. A power signature. *Someone else's* power signature. Her suit had detected a sibling nearby. Some other with technology to dazzle the locals.

She turned around and the woman was standing at the edge of the square. How long she had been following was beyond guesswork. When she saw she had Eleanor's attention, the woams she walked forward and the walk betrayed her instantly.

She was a slim, trim woman dressed in a local's nondescripts but there was an ungainly awkwardness to her walk that screamed to Eleanor that she, too, felt the prison of the flesh, that she was born for the soaring Void and not this clumsy matter.

"Lady Sealight," the woman said slowly, hesitantly. She stopped walking after half a dozen paces, the fountain between them.

Eleanor did not recognise her, but the woman was patently too old to be a new recruit. Even her crumbling mind could solve that particular equation.

"Commonwealth," she said wearily, feeling relatively little actual ire. "How did you find me?"

"I do serve the Commonwealth of Great Britain," the woman acknowledged. "We have been searching for you for some time. When you fought Icarus you... damaged the Void somehow. You fell through it, left a trail. I was sent to discover whether you had survived. To recover you."

Eleanor's face had no expression, but some small song of battle was starting behind her eyes. This was better than madness and slow decline. The enemy had found her at last, as she knew they must. She had been cornered and brought to bay. Now at last she could fight and die and, even if the battlefield was gross matter, she would still die as an Abyssonaut should.

"You are here to stop me returning to aid the Crown..." she breathed, and felt all the controls of her weaponry beneath her fingertips. How much of this island, she wondered, would be standing and sane after two such warriors had battled. She would show the government and the revolutionaries what a war was!

There was a long, awkward pause before the woman replied. Eleanor could see the fear in her eyes. A poor warrior, this one.

"I want you to listen to me," the Commonwealther said. "The war..." She steeled herself visibly. "The war is over."

Eleanor stared at her blankly. The words had passed through her brain without catching on anything.

"Britain is at peace once more," the woman told her. "The

forces of the Commonwealth have deposed the Crown." She was tense, ready for the explosion.

It never came. Eleanor's face was blank as a newborn's. "I don't believe a word of it," she said, conversationally. "Commonwealth tricks. You must have a very low opinion of me."

"We have a very high opinion of you," the woman told her. "You are something of a legend amongst our Chasmonauts. Listen to me, I thought that you would have trouble believing me. Were our positions reversed… well, I'd think just like you do. Which is why I didn't come alone. Now don't do anything rash. I'm going to bring someone else out here. A good friend of yours."

Emotion or expression had yet to touch Eleanor. She made a noncommittal gesture that the Commonwealther took for assent. The woman beckoned into the shadowed alley from which she had stepped and something wheeled its way into view and, at last, brought life back to Eleanor's face.

It was a mechanical chair, and she knew it almost as well as its occupant. She could have written a book on the distant breath-noise of its motors, the red velvet of its upholstery, the gilded owls that stood silent vigil atop the back. She could have written many books on the owner's lop-sided shoulders and withered legs, his sunken cheeks and huge eyes and battle-weary smile.

Something broke inside her, and it felt like dying. "Isender," she said.

"Hello again," he told her, as he always did. "You've no idea what we've been through to find you."

Eleanor took at step towards them, and the Commonwealther started visibly. "Listen to me, before you come any closer, you've got to do something. You've got to power down all your weapons."

Eleanor shook her head irritably. "I won't fire on you. I won't fire on *him*."

"It's not that. Listen to me. Haven't you noticed the places you move through end up in chaos? You've noticed that? Your equipment is malfunctioning. Everything's leaking power. Your Strife Gun is doing all of that. Setting up the violence around you. You've got to turn them all off."

"*I'm* doing that?" Eleanor was taking too many hits, too much damaging information impacting on her. She felt control slipping away again.

"I'm afraid so," Isender confirmed. "We've seen the damage caused. Believe me, it's for the best."

Numbly, shaking inside, Eleanor stared at her hands. Of their own accord they were moving through the power-down sequence, shutting off her weapons one by one, sending them into a stand-by from whence they could do no more damage. The armour felt abruptly heavy on her, the ground suddenly coarse and hard beneath her feet.

She thought of the deaths, the pointless, wasted deaths, all the worlds she had ruined. The magic of her technology that had become Pandora's Box.

She walked slowly towards Isender, and the Commonwealther stepped back to let them talk.

"What happened?" she whispered. "How did they win the war?"

Isender shrugged his mangled shrug. "We fought as well as we could," he said softly. "What could we have known? We stopped Icarus, but they still had a Daedalus. We thought that secret weapons only came in ones. It was brief, that's all. By the time we rematerialised, it was mostly over."

She stared at him. "You…"

He looked up at her without embarrassment. "There was nothing left to fight for," he said. "Besides, I wanted to do this. I wanted to find you. The Commonwealth was my only chance."

She nodded, simply. Everything had all fallen into place. How foolish she had been. It was a grand foolishness, in fact, one that soaked back through recent events to colour all her life. What had it all been for? What a colossal waste from start to finish.

She looked down at Isender again, feeling wretched, helpless, naked.

"Come back to us, Eleanor," he told her. "It's been too long. Come home." The promise of the Void danced in his eyes.

"Yes..." she said, but it was in response to a proposition made in her mind only. Her hands had found something at her belt that interested them.

With detached dignity she watched as they drew the simple knife from its scabbard and, with an observer's sense of wonder, buried it in Isender's chest. The face she knew so well, had loved so much and yearned for constantly, gave her one agonised, betrayed look and then crumpled in upon itself. It swirled, creased and finally dispersed into the aether, leaving behind only the shell of a man in Commonwealth armour, his face self-disgusted, his breastplate and ribs neatly pierced by the plain blade of the knife. The chair still looked like Isender's chair, though, for the Assumptor field had survived the death of its occupant.

Eleanor looked around for the Commonwealther woman, her hands already powering up her weapons. Her quarry was at the edge of the square, backing and backing, her face the horrified rictus of a woman who discovers that the avenging demons of Commonwealth infamy are worse, far worse, in the flesh. Even as Eleanor brought her Jung-Saffer cannon online the woman backed into nothing and thin air, activating her own Prod to make her getaway.

Her brain still trying to piece it all together, Eleanor stared down at the dead man in the chair. Later she would deduce that whilst Commonwealth spies might have reaped the prize of her real name, Isender himself never knew it, as she had never known his. She would tell herself that his "Eleanor" had sealed his fate and that was how she had unmasked him. Some deep part of her would always know, however, that as the knife pierced the man's armour (made for the Void and modern weapons, not to ward off the toys of primitives) she had understood none of that. She had known nothing but that Isender had betrayed her, and that the Crown had betrayed her, and that she had nothing left to care about at all.

In the dawn of a new day the city was eerily still, and Lady Sealight sat on a rooftop and stared into a sun still wet from the ocean. There had been occasional gunshots during the night, but nothing she would class as a revolution. She had kept the Strife Gun powered down, just in case.

She supposed that the civil war probably still raged, back home, and that the real Isender and the others still fought it. She supposed that there was no Daedalus, and that Icarus had taken his secret to his insubstantial grave. She supposed that the Commonwealthers had come for her because she had been the one to strike Icarus, and they did not want her to return like King Arthur and save the nation in its hour of need. She supposed all of these things, because she had no information to the contrary.

She had taken components from the dead Commonwealther and repaired some of her systems, but it had done little good, would do less good in the long run. This was the thirteenth world that was not her own, and there would be more.

And yet, what choice did she have? After all, her country needed her.

She sighed and stood, letting the dawn wind rustle through the food wrappers that kept her company up on the roof.

"Once more into the breach," she mouthed, that famous line from Shakespeare's triumphal *Richard III*. Her hands found the switch that activated her Prod.

She vanished into air with no witnesses or apologies and no one to mourn her leaving, gone to another battlefield that was not her home.

THE AGE OF ENTITLEMENT

Adam Nevill

At dusk, when all about us faded, we walked in silence down the deserted street called *Rue du Sous-Lieutenant de Loitière*, that neither of us knew how to pronounce. Ahead of us, even though we could not see its surging beyond the white stone and slate-coloured buildings on *Quai du Canada*, we knew the sea was going black. That street was closest to the ocean and appeared more than empty. It was dead.

The streets of Arromanche were not ruined. Not so much as a window was broken. Nor were they all yet derelict; though I was never sure which were and which were still occupied. The flags had been taken down; the tanks and field artillery preserved since the Second World War were rusted, the cafés and museums had closed, and the veterans who once visited here were long dead. But more than the desolate and sombre inland reach of the town, huddled into itself and shuffling away from the seafront, the buildings facing the ocean were completely lifeless; spent, somehow, as if they had already been overcome.

We could sense the ocean's swallowing of the watery light, and we could hear the endless tumult of its cold choppy heaving, the great restless sighs. Insensible, timeless, it pulled us down to the shore and into a terrifying orbit. To think I once regarded the sea with fondness; its fragrance and bird calls producing a sense of comfort. Now the mere thought of its existence as we are erased, nation by nation, made me shudder. And that morning, right after we arrived at Le Havre, while standing before the great expanse of water, my inner world was suddenly crushed to a thing insubstantial. As with my perception of the black infinite depths above the earth, the water's unbreathable immensity felt closer to the land than it ever before. Too near, somehow. In Arromanche this very feeling was acute.

My heart beat fast. Panic swelled up my throat. I gulped at the cold air. "The sky is closer. The sea is closer. The light is going out." When I said this to Toby on the street called *Rue du Sous-Lieutenant de Loitière*, he smiled with no warmth and too many teeth. I desperately wanted reassurance, but he was delighted by my discomfort.

Our relationship had always been an unbalanced thing. I amused Toby, and took care of the practical matters he required to make these journeys. I think they were the only reasons he tolerated my fretting anxious presence at his side. Like an old relative, or servant, deferring to someone younger and more powerful and spoilt and knowing: that's how he made me feel. I despised him.

"It's good shit." He was referring to the contents of the little brown glass bottle he kept inside the breast pocket of his tatty Gore-Tex waterproof. I had barely touched it; earlier that day, in our room at the guest house, I had taken a sip of the bitter syrup before we began exploring Bayeux at noon. But Toby had filled his mouth with it, until his teeth were filmed with the old blood colour of neat iodine. Which is why his eyes were still glassy, and why he had lain down in the wet overgrown grass of the War Cemetery beneath the abandoned *Musée Mémorial de la Bataille De Normandie* and stared at the dismal grey sky, all afternoon, in silence. He was content to lie among the unkempt graves of five thousand dead soldiers; who no one has the energy to honour after all that had happened so quickly in this world.

Toby had no interest in recording the *experiences* anymore; or of talking about them; or relaying them to me; or making sense of them. He was content merely to *have* them, in silence, over and over again. He said nothing to me besides, "But are they willing to be forgotten? That is the question, my dear." And he had giggled like an infant after tempting the fallen so brazenly.

And as was its wont, close to the shore in Arromanches, my fear pulled things in at me on that vacant street; and all at once too. My gaze was drawn to the grey stone walls bordering the weed-wretched gardens at the rear of the once grand hotels on our right. Then my vision groped to the windows above, set within bricks seared by salt and lashed by wet winds for centuries. And in the second storey window of the building neighbouring the derelict church I saw a figure.

I stopped suddenly. Inhaled so sharply I unleashed a tiny scream that turned and fled back down my throat.

The figure's scrutiny had alerted me to its presence; it had been watching me and then suddenly turned away the moment I looked in that direction. It had not vanished but merely turned its back to me. Which I could still see, robed in something long and smooth and pale; keeping with the chalky-white-grey light the Impressionists adored here once, so long ago. The head of the figure was cowled. And upon the hooded face both hands clutched so that I would not see its expression.

"Jesus," I said, and the word trembled before leaving my mouth.

"What?" Toby said, looking at me and frowning with a tired indifference.

I swallowed, unable to speak; was clenched into the cold paralysis of a short and powerful shock.

Toby turned and followed my eyes. "What?" he said again.

I pointed at the window. "There."

He shrugged. I stepped up beside him. "There!" I jabbed my finger toward the window in which the figure still stood, exposing itself and yet pleading with us not to stare, not to see it in such grief. This was not mourning, this was desolation; I knew so at once.

"What am I looking…? Oh, yeah. But what?"

"It moved when I saw it. Turned away. Covered its face."

"Let's go look," Toby said as he strode across the road to the garden wall.

"No. No," I cried out, and I marvelled at his complete insensitivity. This figure at the window required a respectful distance; was to be looked at quickly and then moved away from. I knew this instinctively. But Toby was so brash. With the feelings of others, if I am to be honest, he was a vandal and a trespasser. His incessant seeking of sensation, of the esoteric, of the weird, of visceral experience delivered in full glare, of risk and danger, troubled me at that moment on that road more than anything else I had watched him do in all of the twenty-three years I had known him. But I could not rationally account for why his leering intrusion here shocked me sick. This involved no swallowing of unidentified pills, no deliberate losing of oneself in strange places, no camping in extreme landscapes with unsuitable gear, no going in through dark windows, or provoking the unstable with alcohol and rude cleverness; his intrusion here would carry a heavier penalty. To impose and interfere would be sacrilegious. How I knew this I cannot tell you exactly. Suffice to say this was a place in which a multitde died so horribly in a forgotten war. And as Toby and I have seen in those places where so many ended their days through violence in great swathes, their desire to remain can *invest* where they fell. Because they reach, I tell you; and they clutch forever at where they sense the light once was. I have warned Toby of this realm that is only ever sensed or glimpsed in certain places at certain times. But sometimes this region, which I suggest is a kind of parallel non-existence, is thrown wide open. Like *here.* Which accounted for my extraordinary nervousness since we had alighted from the one ferry each week that still ends its line on this abandoned Normandy coastline.

Of course, that is precisely why Toby had wanted to come here, with me as his guide. He had heard *things* about the place.

And I was a golden Labrador to a blind man. I took him across things. I led him around obstacles. He would have walked directly past the figure in the window had I not been at his side suffering an anxiety attack; the very peak of my seizure resulting in the drawing out of… of what, I do not know.

"Statue," he said, his voice dropping with disappointment, and contempt for me as if I had failed to entertain him enough with the sighting. Then, his tone buoyant with excitement, he added, "But it's still pretty amazing."

I felt some relief that it was only a statue, but not for long. This carving in stone of a women wretched with grief, turning inward and away from the world, covering her features and clasping her terror and despair right back upon her own face, made me wither before it; shrink before all it symbolised in this dark and dying place. And I bowed my head and closed my eyes at the mere thought of who the sculptor had modelled this figure upon, or from what the weary yet untiring yearning from beneath the waves had *invested* into stone. I wanted to scream at Toby again, that 1807 bodies eviscerated within the salty shallows and between the neat hedgerows had still not been found. That we had to tread lightly and soundlessly, and keep our eyes and our voices down. What we had stirred up out of the derelict trenches at Vimy Ridge Memorial the previous year had made him vomit on to his own shoes. And I had fainted.

But Toby had no such concerns here, no such interpretation, as he stood before these cold, wet and mostly abandoned buildings of scoured stone, only yards away from the ghastly sea that slapped down upon the shingle and drowned the light.

The sea. Vast. Senseless. Monotonous. Dreadful. Nullifying, like the expanding freezing abyss above us, indifferent to this blue grain of life we stood upon. Specks upon a speck. The sea and the sky were almost touching here; *could he not feel it?* Here was extinction.

The sudden roaring of my imagination nearly put out its own light with a hiss. I squeezed my nails into the palms of my hands and said the words; the invocation. Said the words over and over again to evoke myself back into myself. Then I relaxed my shoulders, exhausted.

Toby stood at the wall, staring, enthralled by the distant stone figure behind glass. The room around the figure was completely lightless. Not a single feature suggested itself from out of that space. And then he spoke without any emotion, but his words made my bones ache with cold, and the skin around these bones prickled. "There are others. Look."

I joined him at the old wall. And I looked into the neighbouring house. A similar figure stood alone, cowled and robed with the head turned away from the world, the face clutched. This one stood immobile too, a sentinel at a second storey window. On the other side of the church, a third stone figure filled a side window in a miserable concrete building, the blue metal roof peeling. It must once have been a garage.

"Wonder why they are there?" Toby asked, his query sincere.

To me, the figures seemed to be sealing the empty buildings, or marking them as condemned, or as unstable, as *invested.* It was a way for the dead to rise as the living made room: they *invested* into things, into places. "Let's get back."

"This is so cool."

There have been times in our companionship when I dearly wished to destroy him, physically; this was another of them.

As soon as we were back inside our room at the guest house, he stretched out on his bed. Still wearing his coat and his muddy boots, which were soiling the bottom of the bedspread that the withered and yellowing old lady who owned the *pension* would have to scrub, he closed his eyes and was snoring within a minute.

Hunger, sitting in the cold cemetery watching him all afternoon, and the recent episode in the street, had weakened me. Quietly, I made my way over to the little table upon which we had placed the remainder of our lunch for the car journey down from La Havre. Inside the plastic container, I made the discovery that he had eaten, without my knowledge, the last two sandwiches, the last bag of crisps and my uneaten chocolate bar. I looked across at the tray that bore the kettle and hot drink materials that came with the room. I remembered seeing two small packets of complimentary shortbread biscuits. These too he had eaten. The plastic wrappers were discarded beside the little broken television. He had not even put the wrappers into the bin.

When I realised I was risking a broken tooth from grinding my teeth, I unclenched my jaw and rubbed it. I looked at him on the bed; his snoring vibrated through the walls and filled the chilly air. His thin face was pale, his pinched mouth open. His curly white hair seemed too youthful for his face. An old man in a girl's wig. I wanted to kick him off the bed and stamp and stamp and stamp on his curly-bitch head.

I looked away. Beyond the window the sea and the sky were black, as if existence had ended outside the glass. The sudden intense heat in my body abated and left my head aching. There was still some tea and coffee in sachets, but boiling the kettle might wake him.

I cursed myself for such an act of consideration; a human instinct he knew nothing of, because he had never displayed it once in our long friendship. Toby immediately placated any impulsive appetite he experienced with no regard for anyone else's needs. He was a snatcher, a grabber; or he expected everything he needed to be provided everywhere, all of the time. He was entitled. And his contempt for me was reaching epidemic proportions. Though now I knew exactly *why*; now it all made sense. Now, *he* made sense. But, even worse than his revelation in the car about his family background, was the fact that we cannot change our natures.

In the dark, I sat my drained and tired body down upon the end of my bed. It had gone eight.

I thought of what he had said to me in such an offhand way in the car. It had numbed me to the core. And I had been poor company thereafter. In the passenger seat, he had read my shock and merely adopted a half-smile upon his face that had lasted for the remainder of the day. I had been too proud to lose my temper; and had been too upset to speak anyway. I was betrayed, and betrayal is a powerful emotion that shuts down most of the mind besides the ability to sustain misery, at least until rage takes over. And this was no lover's tiff, because we were not lovers. But we had shared a bond that only lovers share. Or rather I realised, with a cold trickle of terror and shame in equal amounts, that what we had shared for twenty-three years was the devotion of a dog to its master; a master that considered his own needs as superior to those of the dog, and was soon to abandon the trusting hound too.

In that dim and fusty room in a boarding house on the shore of a relentless tide, I could not bring myself to list all of the things I had sacrificed and missed in life, due to my misguided attachment to this man, this *friend*. But the listing of my grievances would come in time. There was always time for the listing of grievances in these long dark days. Toby would soon return to a comfortable world full of potential and opportunity and promise that I had known nothing of in the last two decades. A world he had deliberately kept hidden from me and had retreated to during his enigmatic disappearances over the years.

This was to be our last journey together: without a trace of remorse, he had informed me of such in the car on the French side of the channel. After the trip's conclusion in two days, I would be left with so many silent hours of contemplation on wasted time and youth. And the memory of him and his deception, that would become viler in my mind, would always be there to accompany me as I sank back into directionless, debilitating, and wretched poverty. He did not state this, but we both knew it to be true.

What did any of it now mean: these uncanny experiences of ours, in the abandoned and derelict corners of Great Britain that had hurtled backwards to the social inequality of Queen Victoria's reign? And so quick was the regression it had taken everyone by surprise and gone even further back to feudalism, and now was becoming the new dark ages with a population to match. It was even worse in France, because even the French were but a fraction of the sparse population in their own countryside, and only the dead of ages now remained behind en masse.

Toby and I had thought ourselves unique and above the disintegrating world. But what music or poems or writing or films or art had our collaborations in the esoteric, and our explorations of psychic geography in a dying world, ever produced? Those creative ventures we had planned and incessantly talked of, through the long hours in the squats and grim flats we had shared together, smoked in together, in which we had withdrawn from the fallen world together, had degenerated into recreational drug use and a perpetual staring into space. We had become degenerate. Hopeless, like most of what remained of the world.

I thought of those inexplicable stone figures in this town with their faces turned away. Without Toby their fate would become mine: cold as stone, an installation planted in isolation, paralysed with despair, waiting for the darkness to finally take everything away, to drown it with aeons that have been drowning futility for aeons.

But if I protested too much, he would shrug and smirk and merely tell me that I was being 'dramatic'. And then he would be gone forever into the light of comfort, into a grazing of pale female flesh, into vast warm rooms, and into so much money it would only cause anxiety at the prospect of it being shared. And I would be left behind, in a place like this: a dead corner. My existence beyond whatever tiny grim space I occupied would amount to nothing more than him saying, 'I knew a chap once…' That would be my epitaph, lost in the fragrant air of some noisy party in Paris, or South Kensington, or Edinburgh, where the privileged congratulate themselves on still being privileged despite all that has happened.

Better for me, and for all those he and his kind have

exploited, if I had smothered him right then in that guest house. With one of the musty pillows as he lay snoring like some sated king upon the faded candlewick bedspread. Over his thin pointy face I should have pressed down hard until his vigour was stoppered.

Instead of murder most just, I abandoned the unlit room; leaving the curtains open to the darkness, to the immensity that made an even greater mockery of my foolish trust and my pathetic hopes. I went down and through the silent fusty house and into the cold night roaring with ocean.

Some place, somewhere in this dim town, must have still been serving food. Maybe hot food would make me feel better for a little while. But I would bring nothing back for him; I would sate my own hunger. For was I just to wait for him to awake from his drugged stupor and then set about finding him nourishment, as I had always done? As he would doubtless expect me to do, and at my own expense. He was *entitled* to what I could do for him. That was the foundation of our relationship. And what one group of people can do for another has been revealed as the foundation of civilisation now that all illusions of fairness have been doused. Now that nearly everything is in ruins. Perhaps it is the very foundation of our species and always has been.

I walked down *Quai du Canada* and avoided looking out at the great imploring sea, idiotic in its surging. I did not want to be pulled into it. To my left, the long line of empty hotels and bars had unlit windows, many covered from the inside with blankets nailed to sash frames or old newspapers taped to the glass. Before I turned inland, I saw another stone figure at a window. It had drawn itself further back inside the room, but, in the ambient glow of one of the last working street lamps, it still showed the black ocean its stone head, covered with a cowl and clutching white fingers.

I walked along *Rue du Mézeray* and *Route de Ryes*. Here too everything was closed, shuttered, derelict. But in the weak yellow light of the lamps and the occasional lit window above street level, I caught glimpses of stone figures in the distant gloom of the empty gift shops, or crouching in despair behind the dirty glass of bankrupt estate agents, cafés, and shops. Each of the figures made me start, and I made sure not to stare for too long, in case my appalled scrutiny would draw me inside an empty shop front, to stand in horror in the darkness, in the dust with them, among the litter of fliers advertising pizza restaurants long gone.

I walked along the wider thoroughfare of *Rue Marie-Rose Thonnard* and saw not a soul. The restaurants were shuttered against an indifference sustained by time for long enough to fade their hoardings and signage; the coaches had long departed and left no trace; the shuffling tourists were less than a memory of a distant time when holidays were taken by any but the few. The darkness came in from the sea and filled the places in which human antics had once occurred.

On both sides of the channel what remained of us drew together in greying cities, clutching at charity thrown from the back of lorries; or we stood in long lines, day after day, hunched toward the distant promise of something of colour. This country was also being closed down village by town, as if the villages and towns were little lights on some great grid that winked out on the *Grande Retraite* towards Paris and left the rest in darkness. On the epic grid, the coastline was almost entirely black now, as if the sea was coming over the rim; thick and salty and toxic.

But in the abandoned places, other regions were either opening or had always been open but obscured by irrelevance. Without clutter and noise and traffic and so much electricity, strange flowers were opening to the moon, and curious doors and windows were being left carelessly agape and uncovered. There was no life to be had in such spaces now revealed; just a silent staring at what has *invested* itself, until an unrecorded end. But that had done nothing to dim Toby's fascination with such things in such places. Until now, because now he was saying goodbye to it all; bidding farewell to the places where those left alive were outnumbered by the dead.

Back to the sea. Toward the seaward side of Arromanches I found an open restaurant. And I studied its yellowing menu intently through the brown glass while my stomach gaped and burned. The broad windows were tinted to protect diners from the heat; many years ago someone had thought it a good idea. In the seventies perhaps. This town seemed to have known nothing of the brief peaks of prosperity that had come and gone since the decline. Like everywhere else, the people left when the tourists left, or the factories closed, or the fields became overgrown, and the jobs vanished.

I checked the prices rather than the items on the restaurant menu. Vanity possessed me to casually withdraw the coins from my pocket and to count them; I knew exactly how much money I was carrying. Along with the crisp brown sheet of a treasured ten euro note, that I could not bear to part with, was the last of my benefits in coinage: three euros and thirty-four cents. It had been thirty-two cents, but I had found two greening one cent coins close to the cemetery and had polished them into a serviceable lustre while Toby stared at the sky from the amongst the weeds and tombstones. My half of the guest house bill, five euros, was buried at the bottom of my rucksack. That five was gone, dead to me; and was to become the property of the yellowy woman soon enough.

There was to be no rib-eye steak or bourguignon for me that night. It would have to be soup of the day and a cup of coffee. When I returned to Wolverhampton, whatever remained of my money would have to last for two weeks until my next benefit payment. The length of time was staggering; recalling it made me lightheaded, and I needed to lean on the glass of the restaurant for a moment to regain my balance. Inside the restaurant I saw a woolly head, hunched over a table, feeding.

The restaurant was warm. The walls were brown and tatty and peeling. The furniture municipal. The carpet hard under my feet. I could see no staff behind the counter with the curved glass sneeze screens and little golden lamps shielding empty hot plates. Despite the scores of tables, there was only one diner: what appeared to be an old man in a bad wig and a maternity dress, gobbling at soup. I kept my eyes away from him. Beside his table was a wheelchair and a plastic supermarket bag full of children's books.

I walked alongside the broad counter, peeking over and muttering 'Hellos' towards the dim suggestion of a kitchen beyond a fire door. No one came out.

I sat at a table by a window; there was nothing to be seen through it beside some smudges of building exteriors and the odd globe of a street lamp. I could still hear the sea. For all I knew it was black as oil and welling up the glass outside the restaurant.

A meagre old woman with a man's haircut eventually shuffled out of the dim kitchen and approached without looking at me once. She dropped a menu encased in a heavy binding on the table before me and then retreated back behind the counter where she busied herself with things out of my sight. I felt awkward and underdressed; had not washed in three, no four… no, at least five days, and I was pungent and rubbery beneath my waterproof and knitwear. Stupidly, I envied the disabled man his ghastly floral maternity dress; at least he was clean. What had possessed me to think I could come in here and eat?

I raised the leatherette menu, which was the size of a stamp album and tasselled. I affected a poise and nonchalance that filled me with a hot self-loathing; as if I, a scruffy man with soiled canvass shoes on his feet, ate in French restaurants as a matter of course. I was ridiculous.

I added the price of soup to the price of coffee and then counted my own money again inside my head, to make sure I had enough.

The waitress came back; she knew I was English. Who else would visit here now the Americans stayed within their own borders with their own dead? "No steak. No stew. Just lemon sole, potato gratin." She barked more than she spoke.

"Soup?"

She nodded.

"Soup. And to drink, I'll have… a cup of coffee. White. Sugar."

She snatched the menu off me.

"Bread with the soup?" I asked, and tried to keep desperation out of my voice.

"Extra."

"How… How much?"

"Furty cents."

"Great. Thank you"

She was already walking away from the table as I thanked her. I fretted that she had not taken my order for bread. I felt that I would die without it. I had only eaten two sandwiches at eleven, and had been rationing the crisps and chocolate, that Toby had eaten, for later.

But I think the soup was the best thing I had ever eaten, and there was plenty of it. I soaked it into the two slices of white bread and then crammed them into my mouth. When I had finished, I sat back and sipped at my coffee. Feeling magnanimous, expansive, a man of the world, I pondered the tip.

And left without giving one; the meal consumed most of my change, and I deducted points due to the abrupt service. Thoughts of money had also spoiled the second half of the coffee, which I had swallowed without any memory of doing so. I had left my room in Wolverhampton the previous morning with forty euros to my name, but the ferry, petrol, guest house, the soup and the lunch I paid for, left me with only ten euros to live on for a fortnight. A miserable prospect, but I had done so before, many times over the years, having eschewed a material lifestyle as had Toby – 'because what is the point now?' – or so he claimed.

Hunched over, I plodded back toward our lodging. I kept my head down to avoid the stone figures and my instinctive gaping at the sea; the horrified astonishment that I felt it wanted of me. But I was quickly consumed again by my petulant thoughts about paying for our lunch. It was not an unusual train of thought; spending what little I had on Toby inevitably began an interior discourse on the unfair division of *our* limited resources. But considering what Toby had so recently told me about his father's directorship of a major surviving industry, and his parents' purchase of a large flat for their son, in South Kensington in London, where he would now reside while working for his father's cremation empire, would it have been unreasonable for me to raise the matter of half of the fee I had spent on our lunch provided for the ferry and car journey?

This line of enquiry soon had me gasping for breath and slapping at the stone walls I passed on my way back to the guest house. I even paused to scream "Jesus Christ!" at the black and utterly featureless sky. Cascading through my mind came specific memories, phrases of his, and a terrific welling sensation of betrayal.

Toby had always pleaded poverty for the twenty-three years I had known him. I recalled his habitual rent-free living in my dismal flats and rooms. He always claimed to have no home address; to have successfully crafted a possession-free existence that involved living on the sofas and floor space of 'friends', and sometimes in a tent on beaches and in verdant parks that no one used anymore. And I had admired him for this; had even recounted his exploits to anyone who would listen in the long aid queues. What had attracted me to Toby in the first place was his calm, his confidence, his refusal to worry, his aversion to any anxiety about money. And now I knew how such an attitude was sustained.

Back in the days when I could find work, how many jobs had I lost due to his insistence on my dropping everything and embarking on a journey? A journey that I inevitably funded. And during that time when there was, at least, some work available to the educated but semi-skilled, how often had I called in sick for just the same reason, when some new adventure was announced upon Toby's return into my life? And what of his curious and inexplicable golden suntans that were not endowed by any British sun? They were a result of what he claimed were holidays provided by affluent friends, or merely 'friends of friends'. And he may well have been sunning himself on the decks of 'friends'' yachts while I collected tickets at the dispensary, and handed boxes of powdered milk over the counter to single mothers who shouted 'Dat's mine, innit,' while pointing long finger nails at the hundreds of parcels behind me, on the shelves holding the boxes that awaited collection.

Not once had he ever invited me to his parental home, which had sounded excessive during his confession in the car – the home in Suffolk, I am referring to, not the one in Spain. In fact, he had always dismissed his parents as tyrants, as bullies, and claimed to have had no contact with them; for all of the years I had known him he had practically passed himself off as an orphan to engage my sympathy. And it was a lie; it was all lies. He was a lie. Utterly inauthentic while claiming his life was a penniless search for the sudden emergence of the authentically weird. He was a *Trustafarian* and had been slumming at my considerable expense for twenty-three years.

Lies. Liar. Lies. Liar.

I ran down to the water and fell to the freezing wet sand and clutched at it with my hands. I shuddered with a rage so powerful I became blacker than the terrible sea.

And he was getting *married*. Married: how was that even possible? There were no women in our lives.

I walked into our room a little calmer, but still intent on confrontation after a gradual build. I would have something of his fortune. I had decided this while sobbing into the stones on the beach, the rocks reduced to dust by so many waves for tedious millennia. It would not be inappropriate for him to now provide for me; to return the favour, so to speak. I also felt triumphant about eating independently while he slept, but Toby merely said "I'm not hungry" when I asked him 'what are you going to do about food'. So my little victory was dashed.

I found him slouched upon his bed smoking a joint that I had been able to smell from the ground floor of the guest house. He'd been inside my rucksack to find the little baggy, containing enough skunk for two joints, that was to have been a treat during our visit to Normandy. The baggy was empty; he'd put all of the weed into one joint for himself. His eyes were red and heavily lidded.

"I want to see the gun emplacements at Longues-Sur-Mer," he said.

"What? Now?"

He nodded. "They're the only remaining guns of the Nazis' Atlantic wall."

I didn't want some drug-impaired activity at night to distract us from what we needed to discuss. "But it's pitch-black out there."

"So?" he said with such ironic force, it made me blink and swallow.

He looked at the end of the joint, now just a butt. "There's a fortified observation point up there too. In blast-proof concrete. They could hit targets twenty kilometres away with those guns."

Why had this not been mentioned before? It was so typical of his selfishness; to have designs on visiting something that he would only share with me moments before he actually wanted to see it. "It'll all be broken or locked up." Which was a futile thing for me to say, as those very facts would make him want to see it more.

He looked at me and frowned. "Was that not the entire point of the journey?"

My anger closed my throat down and made my blood hiss through my ears.

"And the fact that is will be pitch-black" he said, "makes it all the more worthwhile. And I'm really fucked now, so I want to be up there before I straighten out."

His teeth were brown and gleaming with liquid too, so he had taken yet another hit from the bottle. So was I to experience it all *straight?* As he'd taken all of the drugs, it appeared that was to be the case.

He stood up. "Coming?" He said this with such a weary disinterest, he really didn't care if I went with him.

"My, my, how things have changed."

"What? What did you say?"

I swallowed; it was hard to keep my thoughts straight because I was so angry and upset and feeling rejected. If I spoke my voice would have been full of tears.

He shrugged and made his way to the door, stepping over my open and discarded rucksack. It was on the floor at the foot of my bed, where he'd left it after rummaging for the drugs.

We drove to the cliffs in silence. He asked me to park near the old cliff walk. He wanted to climb up to the guns from the sea, in the dark, like the American Rangers had done at *Pointe du Hoc* in 1944.

"No way," I said.

But from the car I followed him down a cliff path to the shore, where he then began moving around to the area below the gun emplacements. I trailed him along the crunching shingle, and up and over a stone groin, and then up the side of some wet rocks to the foot of a steep grassy cliff face that would have to be scaled as a scrabble, on our hands and knees in the dark. The sign on the fence at the foot of the grassy cliff forbade access and warned of avalanches. In parts, the sea-facing side of the hill formed a sheer rock cliff face, dropping into angry waves smashing into the black rocks. But I was to follow him and his feeble torchlight upwards? It was too dangerous. "No way, Toby."

Without a single word of advice or encouragement, he set off on his hands and knees. I dithered at the bottom, then followed his sounds ahead of me. I stopped after a few minutes and shouted at him to slow down and to direct the torch down at me. He turned the torch off and laughed. But I had gone up too far to start back down the cliff again in the dark, and he knew this. He was forcing me to follow and I was already nearly in tears with fear.

I had nothing else to guide me; his red waterproof and his pale curly head were consumed by the lightless night. Where they clawed at the slippery grass on an almost vertical hill, I could barely see my own hands. At one point, I made again to go back down; but so steep was the gradient, I was sure I would just plummet into the darkness below if I slipped. Descending the same route was impossible. In a breathless voice, I pleaded with him again to stop, but he didn't reply. His sounds just accelerated ahead of me, as he went higher, alone. Swallowing a panic that wished to become hysteria, I too continued upwards, slowly.

A terrible universe of thin cold air reached out into the darkness behind my back and above my head; it seemed to suck at me. A cold breeze then slapped against me as I clung to the grassy rock face like an insect. Beneath, so far down, was the thunder of the sea, rushing in to smash itself against the land. It was as if I were climbing into the sky; as if I had gone through the very atmosphere and was entering the deep frozen gases of space. There were no lights at the top. A slither of moon. No stars.

It took me over an hour to haul my trembling body up that incline. By the time I reached the top my mind was witless with vertigo and agoraphobia; fatigue had turned my muscles to warm water.

I stumbled through the shrubbery at the summit, and then climbed a wire fence to a mercifully level surface beneath long grass. In which I came across the derelict observation post. It was like a featureless mausoleum with a thin slot in the front for the dead to peer through. I called out to Toby and received no answer.

It took me another twenty minutes to find him up there in

the darkness.

"Would you be fucking quiet," he said at one point, from somewhere to my left. Squinting into the inky absorbing nothingness of the cliff top, I followed the sound of his voice. By this time my breath was sobbing out of me, and my fear of how we would get back down was close to paralysing. And something terrible was up there with us. Not an individual or a shape this time. But something above us that had no form or end. I felt I could have just fallen upwards, into the sky, at where the stars should have been. This was a night that would have once wrecked ships. There was no bottom to it, no horizon, no sides or ceiling. It was a vast absence that did not end. It was not paranoia that had made my climb unbearable but a justified caution at climbing over the edge of the world.

Where the fence was broken, Toby was standing on the cliff edge, staring up and outwards to sea. "Can you feel it?" he said.

"Too much," I cried out, and fell to my face and grasped handfuls of long grass. It was too dark to even see the gun emplacements. A terrible sensation that my feet were then rising from the earth and moving upwards into the cold black infinity overcame me and I screamed.

"What is fucking wrong with you?" he snapped at me. "You are ruining it."

Whatever blackness was attempting to wipe my presence, my very existence, off the face of the earth upon that cliff top, whatever it was we had climbed upwards and right into, withdrew momentarily from around my unravelling mind as if a tight hat had been snatched off my aching head. And within the lightless air I became red and I burned wild and hot with fury.

I stood up. I walked right at him. "Ruining," was all I could release from behind my clamped-together teeth. And then he came into focus suddenly as he turned around on the very edge of the cliff. He was actually angry with me.

I punched both hands into his chest. Hard. My elbows locked tight.

And Toby fell backward, and was then yanked straight up into the air.

There was a whisk of nylon sleeves as his arms wind-milled. In raking torchlight, his mouth opened and his eyes went wide behind his silly little spectacles, and then the details of his shock and fear were gone from me as his body surged even higher and further out too, like a kite caught on some sudden upward draught of fast moving air. His coat flapped.

And then I heard him drop like a stone down and into the darkness.

I stood still and listened to the silence for a time that began to feel preposterous. Until, so far below the cliff top, I heard a distant puncture as something struck the rocks, and surely came apart down there too. And then I heard no more from him.

Silence thickened all about me on the cliff top. Far away and below my feet I heard the rush and hissing retreat of the ocean waves. There was no other sound.

I looked at the sky in awe. There was nothing to see besides forever. And what had once been the lightless canopy of the universe was not only closer than ever to the surface of the Earth, it was touching the Earth.

I dipped my head and clutched my hands across my face. And I shouted out into the lightlessness, cried out the inscription upon the memorial for the Commonwealth soldiers: "We, whom William once conquered, have now set free the conqueror's native land."

After the incident on the cliff top, I walked inland and eventually found a road that led down to the car. I drove back into the town whose name I will never speak again, and nor will I countenance its name spoken in my presence.

Inside our room, I ransacked his scruffy rucksack and found more than I bargained for. His address book contained details of a vast life that I had no knowledge of. It was a thing filled with names and numbers and email addresses on every single page and

I will always treasure it. I now possessed his secret world. His mysteries were mine to explore whenever I wished to, if I wished to.

Inside his toiletry bag, I found his money and his drugs. He had an ounce of weed in a baggy, and some pills. The little waterproof wallet bulged with over five hundred euros. Pin money for Toby, but I could live on less for years. I pocketed the money and drugs, his iPod and his smart little camera. I wondered if there were pictures of his fiancée on there; if so, I intended to masturbate over them.

The rest of his things I stuffed inside his rucksack and then jammed his effects deep inside an overflowing skip at the corner of an abandoned building site on the outskirts of the town. I left the guest house before dawn, leaving ten euros on the front desk with the room keys on top of the money. I drove out of town and headed for Dunkirk to catch a return ferry at midnight. The whole thing was very exciting, I can tell you. With the *Wet-Wipe* tissues he had in his toiletry bag, I even wiped everything of his I had touched and then abandoned.

I called Toby's parents three weeks later and inquired after him. His mother answered the phone. She was very posh. "He's off" – which she pronounced *awf* – "on one of his escapades. Who can I say called?"

Despite the fact that I had killed her son, I gave her my actual name. In the phone box, I nearly fainted with excitement.

She'd never heard of me.

He'd clearly never mentioned my name to his own mother in all of the twenty-three years we had known each other. Again, he managed to spoil a small moment of triumph. He was a natural.

But the strangest thing of all is that even now, when I ponder the fact that I have killed, I can feel no remorse at all. The sentence, I feel, fitted the crime; and his was a crime that no vestige of a criminal justice system would recognise, and yet the damage of such a crime had blighted a life: my life. His death at my hands made me feel renewed, invigorated, awoken and awake, if that makes sense. I felt that some small act of fairness had finally been *invested* into an unfair world that had left billions dead. I felt entitled. And the craziest thing is, had he paid for our packed lunch on that final trip, he would still be breathing now.

ELECTRIFY ME

Tricia Sullivan

"Art," says my maker, "You really must stop this power fucking. You're going to lose all your teeth."

I can't help it. Crossing the cow field, climbing the pylon, embracing the wire like the dude riding the bomb at the end of that movie, Dr. Derangedglove.

You can't even call it pleasure, it's more like the ghost trick or illusion of pleasure, the expectation of pleasure. A placebo-gasm.

"My needs are hard-wired," I tell him. "Like humans being attracted to pairs of round things. Like plants turning toward light."

He waves his robot arm in the air. "This is hard wired. Get a job."

My maker's arm is a hot toy, but it wasn't a fashion choice for him. Losing the original arm goes back to my conception in an accident that killed my maker's sister and was his fault. In some attempt at redemption he had me made from her parts and tendencies. We never talk about this. I found out by snooping and deduction.

Before anybody starts thinking that the powerfucking is some kind of result of me being mentally damaged by my Greek-tragedy origins, may I say: no. It's a result of a confusion of terms.

Powerfucking for the original Art would have involved dating men who keep yachts in Marbella and exude controlfreakery. Or, considering she wasn't that cute, it might have meant some kerfuffle with the local rugby team. She'd been bright but would have turned down life with a well-balanced geeker type in favour of sexual adventures with mercenaries and crocodile-wrestlers. After all this fun I reckon Art would have been pissed off to know that she'd die due to her brother's bad judgment in passing an IKEA lorry.

I don't do Dangerlove like that. My reproductive parts are only Barbie genitalia and unlike the original source of Art I can't be convinced that a guy with a Rolex in a Ferrari has got something to offer me.

Give me the straight juice.

I find a skydiving company called Electric Blue. The ground-level work is boring, but I can feel the droning tug of the buried cables that power the airport. They're calling me.

First jump. The new assistant instructor is a Made man. We recognise each other..

"What's your MO?" I say. "Me, I'm into power. Trying to wean myself off the National Grid."

He laughs. "Oh?"

So I tell him about the wires. He isn't shocked. Haha, get it? Anyway:

"Nothing to do with evolutionary psychology," he says. "Nothing to do with sexuality. Or dopamine or D4DR. Nothing at all."

I laugh. I stare..

"We all do it," he tells me. "We try to find our way home, but we don't belong in the same places they do. We're made half of ideas. It's like the thoughts aren't sunk deeply enough into our flesh. We're not grounded."

"I don't think you get what I'm saying." I am trying to be polite in the face of the total shite he is talking. "I go for the actual current."

"Oh, I get it," he says. And like the image on an old

Polaroid, a kind of a mad leer develops on his face.

My maker keeps a Polaroid of his baby sister in a box with some other old junk. He had everything else digitized but this one picture of my maker's mother and her pink bean of a newborn. It lingers in the dark box. Light will make it fade.

We're moving through a cloud. The wind's stronger, and rain starts to fly sideways into the hold. The head instructor has the class in a huddle, but he doesn't seem to notice me and the Made man. That's not unusual. People tend to skip over us, like movies they've seen before.

"You're doing the right thing," he tells me. "It's just that the power lines you're using to hack open the face of reality are lacking in mythical resonance. High-voltage lines are too industrial and shallow."

"They almost killed me twice," I say. "How weak can they be?"

He gives me a pitying look. "Artemis. The purpose of the exercise is not to go to A&E. It's to break through."

"Break through... to where, mate?"

"To the place where you're whole."

The wind blows his words across his face. I can see their cartoon bubble. The air is alive with loose ions that clutter and bounce, looking for partners, fulfilment, a place to belong.

"You need an integrating source with mythical resonance. That's how you'll find the seam that takes you to the world that would have been, if only you were intact. Watch this!"

And he throws himself out of the helicopter and into the crash of clouds. I see the lightning come for him like the fractal root of some cosmic tree.

Fucking shit. He's just incinerated himself. The smoking ruin of his body twists and he opens the chute.

The head instructor grabs for me too late. Lightning meets me as I leap. In the mythical resonance available to us courtesy of

Back to the Future Parts I-IV, the possible and the actual are inseparable.

I can feel her all around me. All 157 years of her, clogged arteries, baggy neck, arthritis in the left knee. Head like a bass drum. Knowledge in her flesh, memory in her bones, DNA beavering away to keep her alive even now.

The arthritic knee screams in pain as the ground rushes up and bodyslams us. Can't breathe. Rolling in the hay with myself & myself, tangled in the chute lines. She is astonished. The scars on her cervix where there would have been children. The air in her lungs, residuals from the other possible destinies of nitrogen and oxygen in their other lives. The slightly-peeved surprise at not having been warned.

No one ever is.

We stagger off the field together, hair smoking. This is the best day of her life.

ALTERNATE CURRENTS

Rod Rees

So the question I pose to you is this: what is a genius?

I'll wager that, like me, you will proclaim a genius to be the man who can understand things that ordinary mortals can't, who has a sharpness of intellect that separates him from the common weal. Those Yankees amongst you might cite the late, and much unlamented, Abraham Lincoln's belief that genius disdains a beaten path and seeks regions unexplored, but being of good Confederate stock I shy away from the musings of that son-of-a-bitch. Besides, I can beat any definition dreamt up by Abe-nigger-lover-Lincoln with both hands tied behind my back and a rooster crowing on my head and I can do it in two words.

Nikola Tesla.

Trump that, Abe.

By any measure and by any definition, Nikola Tesla was a sure-fire, copper-bottomed, genius.

And I knew that he was of that persuasion the moment I first clapped eyes on him as he strode across a snow-decked Central Park back in March 1895, but now, when I think on it, it's difficult to quite figure why I deemed him to be special. Sure, he was tall – over six foot, easy – but not *peculiarly* tall. Sure, he was slender as a reed but not so thin as to be in any way out of the ordinary. And sure he was dandified, with his sharp cut broadcloth coat, his fancy waistcoat, his silk top hat and the silver-knobbed cane he delighted in twirling, but nothing that would make him stand out from the other New York swells striding up and down Wall Street like they owned the world…

which, of course, they did.

No, I guess the thing that signalled Tesla as being an oddity was his eyes. Soft, light-grey and set deep they might have been, but they were eyes that didn't so much look at you as *into* you. I knew from the get-go that Tesla saw things a mite differently from the rest of us.

It was Teddy Roosevelt, bumptious blowhard that he was and bursting with pride after being made Police Commissioner, who attempted the introductions. "My dear Tesla, thank you for attending us so promptly and at such an ungodly hour..."

Tesla raised a hand to interrupt and then took a step beyond where Roosevelt and I were standing and breathed, "Nine-hundred and thirty-nine."

As best I could judge, Tesla had been numbering his steps across the Park. It was, as you might reckon, a touch unsettling, this not being an activity I'd recommend for a full-grown man, but I comforted myself with the thought that genius is often sauced with madness.

Counting completed, Tesla turned and nodded an acknowledgement. "Good morning, Commissioner, and think nothing of requesting my attendance. I am always intrigued by occurrences of a singular nature and ever eager to utilise my talent in the service of the city of New York. So where is this meteor of yours?"

Got to tell you it takes a lot to nonplus Teddy Roosevelt, but Tesla did it easy. He spoke softly, so that you had to listen hard to grab hold of what he was saying, pronouncing his words in that over-exact way foreign types are apt to do, with just the slightest sibilance betraying his antecedents. But though he spoke quietly there was steel in his words that warned you to take heed of them, which is just what Roosevelt did.

He blinked back his surprise and then smiled. "Want to get straight to the meat of the problem, eh, Tesla? But you must allow me a moment to introduce my colleague." He took me by the arm and urged me forward. "This is Major Henry Arnaud, of the Military Intelligence Division, who is here… well, I ain't quite sure *why* he's here, but he is. Major Arnaud, this is Mr Nikola Tesla, the world famous electrician."

To describe Tesla as an 'electrician' was to do him a disservice, but then Roosevelt was always uncomfortable around those more able than himself. I held out my hand and Tesla took it a mite reluctantly, as though he wasn't fond of touching his fellow man. He didn't remove his gloves. Closer to, he was younger than I had first figured – shy of forty, for sure – but looked prematurely aged; his skin had a grey cast to it and there were deep shadows under his unblinking eyes suggesting that he rarely slept.

No matter: that is how I now found myself shaking hands with the man who had revolutionised the production of electricity, had tamed the waters of the Niagara Falls and was being proclaimed as 'the new Edison'.

I decided that a few words were necessary to commemorate such an occasion. "I have read much about you, Sir, and deem it an honour to have you consulting on this matter."

"One of the New Orleans Arnauds, perhaps?"

"How …"

"Your accent is your betrayal."

"You have a good ear, Sir."

"Indeed, but all polyglots are thus blessed. And the meteor, Major?" asked Tesla again, obviously impatient to get down to business now that the common courtesies were over.

"This way, Sir."

The three of us crunched our way over the pristine snow – the sun was just coming up and the overnight snow hadn't yet been desecrated by promenaders – in the direction of the crater formed by the meteor when it had landed. It was a bitingly cold morning and I hunched deeper into my great coat better to avoid the wind. Tesla noticed, but then, as I was to discover, Tesla noticed everything.

"You must find the cold of a New York winter somewhat

bracing after your service in Cuba, Major."

Now *that* was a straightener. My mission on behalf of the US government to survey the Spanish defences in Cuba was of the utmost confidentiality, so it was a fine how d'ya do to have a man I had never met in my life so blithely unmasking this most secret of undertakings. I decided to prevaricate. "I am sorry, Sir, but I have never been to Cuba."

Tesla chuckled quietly. "Oh, come now, Major. You are in 'Intelligence' so please do not deny that faculty's possession by civilians. It is obvious to me that you have recently returned from Cuba where the US military made much use of your fluency in Spanish and your familiarity with Havana. You spent a great deal of time there when you were a child, did you not?"

Tesla's perspicacity was becoming decidedly unnerving. "No, you are mistaken, Sir. As I say I have never been to Cuba."

"Remarkable," observed Tesla.

I made to change the subject. "We have had Arthur Ruskin, Professor of Astronomy at Columbia College, make a preliminary assessment of the meteor, Mr Tesla, and he has opined that, though somewhat more regular in appearance than those normally seen, it is nothing out of the ordinary."

"Nothing out of the ordinary except for the electrical phenomena associated with its manifestation," Tesla corrected.

"Indeed," noted Roosevelt as he pulled a notebook from his pocket. "The meteor's arrival at five o'clock this morning was observed by a musician returning home from participating in a concert. He stated that the meteor 'glowed with a brightness that exceeded even the arc lamps illuminating Broadway', that it was 'circled by ribbons of fire' and that it 'gave off a strange keening sound, akin to that emitted by a howling dog'."

"Did your witness happen to describe the key this keening sound was rendered in?"

Roosevelt's left eyebrow arched upwards signalling his amazement regarding Tesla's insight. "You are something of a mind reader, Tesla. He noted that it was in 'F sharp in the sixth octave'." Roosevelt stopped and pointed down to the hole drilled in the snow. "Here we are. This is the latest of New York's immigrants."

Tesla ignored Roosevelt's attempted levity. He stooped down to take a closer look at the meteor embedded in the frost-hard ground, prodding at it with the toe of his galosh. In truth the meteor was quite nondescript, spherical in shape, perhaps six inches in diameter, and coloured a flat black. It looked like a second-cousin to a weather-worn cannonball.

"Professor Ruskin was of the opinion that this was of natural provenance?" enquired Tesla.

"He was. He believed it to be formed from carbonaceous chondrite," replied Roosevelt.

"Remarkable," muttered Tesla as he made a number of measurements the purpose of which was quite beyond me. Finally he turned back to Roosevelt. "I would like this object taken to my laboratory on South Fifth Avenue where I have the facilities to examine it more thoroughly."

"I must be present when these tests are conducted," I interjected hurriedly: my orders were that I should take the greatest of care regarding the safe-keeping of the meteor.

Tesla nodded as though he had anticipated my stipulation. He then used his cane to point to the lines in the snow running straight as a rule away from the crater in the direction of Columbus Circle. The lines, two inches in breadth, resembled the wake a toy boat might make on the surface of a pond, rippling and snaking as they did over the snow.

"Did Professor Ruskin make any assessment as to this phenomenon, Commissioner?" Tesla asked.

"He advised us that it was the result of the disturbance made to the snow's surface by the backwash of the meteor when it crashed to earth. He considered it to be a consequence of atmospheric turbulence."

"Remarkable," pronounced Tesla, in the way he always did when confronted with stupidity, and then he strode off in the direction of the striations which ended abruptly one hundred yards distant at the edge of the Circle.

"Tell me, Major, do these marks extend beyond this point?"

"No, Sir."

"Excellent." Again Tesla crouched down to make a more particular examination of the snow and the footprints and strange circular patterns embossed in it, then, seemingly satisfied with his perusal, he looked towards Roosevelt, "Commissioner Roosevelt, would you apprise me of the number of constables you have under your command in the New York police department?"

"We have ten thousand sworn officers comprising New York's finest."

"Then you must mobilise all of them." Tesla scribbled in his notebook, tore the page out and then handed it to Roosevelt. "They must make this enquiry of all bootblacks and cobblers in the city, commencing with those plying their trade in the vicinity of dairies. There must be no delay, time is of the essence. This must take precedence over all other police activities."

Roosevelt read Tesla's note. "What? Are you insane, man? What can be so all-fired important that my men must make these ridiculous enquires?"

"*Why,* Commissioner?" Tesla stepped back as though flummoxed by Roosevelt's stupidity. "In order to prevent the successful invasion of this planet by creatures from Mars, of course!"

I must tell you, I've never been a great admirer of New York. When the Yankees sacked the South after the War of Northern Aggression, this was where most of our wealth ended up: to my mind, this den of perfidy was the epitome of urban ugliness, an ugliness that befits the manner by which it enriched itself. The streets overflowed with wagons and carriages and a surfeit of horse manure, the pavements were crowded with a mish-mash of people bustling at too great a pace for their own sanguinity and the tenements squatted, cheek by jowl, standing as shrines to the squalor that was Yankee America.

Over it all trailed the mesh of delinquent wire which conveyed the miracle of electricity through the city and at the centre of this web of power stood the workshop of Nikola Tesla. He had the fourth floor of a six-storey building; a large, functional space crammed with electrical apparatus of all descriptions, these manned by a diligently preoccupied gang of fifteen or so workers. But far from being the portal into some utopian future I had expected, this was rather a place where too many ideas competed for too little space.

Owing to Tesla making a detour at a music store to buy – for reasons he declined to elucidate – a variable pitch pipe, our journey from Central Park took longer than anticipated, the upshot being that the meteor was waiting for us when we arrived at his workshop. Roosevelt might have been a bully and a braggart but he was an *efficient* bully and braggart.

Tesla set to work immediately. "We are fortunate," he announced, "that one of the electrical engines I used to such effect at Chicago's World Fair of 1893 is ideally suited to the examination I am about to make of the meteor."

With that he removed the meteor from the crate it had been packed in and placed it in the centre of a round steel platform itself surrounded by a large circular cage, the bars of the cage formed from cables that led to one of Tesla's patented polyphase electrical generators.

Only when Tesla had established that all the connections were to his satisfaction did he indulged me with an explanation. "Professor Ruskin's opinion that this meteor is chondritic in make-up is, of course, nonsense. This meteor is metallic and is, I believe, of Martian manufacture."

"Martian?" I enquired, determined that Tesla should explain these outrageous claims, but he remained steadfastly evasive.

"Later, Major, later. First allow me to verify my conjecture." He nodded to his assistant who worked a lever governing the level of current flowing around the cage and immediately the generator huffed and puffed into life. "There is much debate as to what are the factors which stimulate life, but to my mind the one aspect that has been sadly neglected by investigators is the importance of rotation. If our planet did not rotate life would never have emerged, without the discovery of the wheel civilisation would have eluded us and, of course, without rotation we would have been deprived of that most practical and useful form of electricity, the alternating current. But of more pertinence to our present enquiries, rotation is the key to unlocking the enigma that is the meteor."

So saying, Tesla urged more power into his contraption and, as though raised by some magical force, the meteor levitated, to hover a foot or so above the steel floor, and then slowly began to rotate. And the more current that was applied, so the meteor spun with ever greater rapidity. I will admit that I was spooked and for a moment I was inclined to high-tail it out of the workshop but, fortunately, curiosity kept my feet pinned to the floor.

"The clue to the speed of the rotation I must inculcate in the meteor was given by our musically-inclined witness. As the rotational speed increases so too, I suspect, will the amplitude and pitch of the sound created by the meteor."

It was a correct supposition. A thin, low hum became audible which gradually increased in volume and in pitch as the rotational velocity of the meteor accelerated. But there were other changes: as I watched, the colour of the meteor altered, the sphere gradually coming to emit an eerie light which suffused the whole workshop.

"Excellent," intoned Tesla. He looked over to his assistant, "I would be obliged, Alfred, if you would employ the von Stampfer stroboscope to measure the speed of the spin."

This the assistant did by causing a perforated disk to rotate in front of a lamp. "Five hundred revolutions per minute, Mr Tesla," he advised.

"If my ear does not deceive me, I think we are approaching

F Sharp," and to confirm this, Tesla took up his newly acquired pitch pipe and blew a note.

"Not quite … just a touch more power, I fancy … enough. Hold it there. What is the speed of rotation?"

"Six hundred revolutions per minute."

"Of course! It is utterly predictable that our Martian cousins should work in multiples of three, three being the most important number in the Cosmos." He looked over to me. "You have a fine pocket watch, Major – a Watham, if I am not mistaken – so I would be obliged if you would mark the time now and alert me when nine minutes have elapsed, the time it would have taken the meteor to penetrate the Earth's atmosphere."

Thus we stood, Tesla's eyes never leaving the spinning meteor as sparks began to crackle around its circumference, orbiting it a little like Saturn's rings.

"You have marked the time, Major?"

"As you instructed, Sir."

"Then I would be most obliged if you would sing out the instant that nine minutes have elapsed."

"Ten seconds… nine… eight …"

Tesla took a firm grip on the power lever.

"…seven… six… five… four… three… two… one."

Tesla threw the lever and immediately the meteor froze in mid-air, darkened, paused for a moment as though uncertain as to its status vis-à-vis gravity and then crashed down onto the steel floor.

"We have replicated the forces experienced by the meteor as it landed on Earth and I am hopeful that our mimicry will persuade the meteor…" Tesla stopped and pointed a finger. "Behold, what was hidden is now made plain. Tell me, Major, could there be any greater pleasure than discovering that which another would hold secret?"

And it was a wonderful secret: the surface of the meteor became transparent, and then peeled back to reveal what was concealed inside. There, before my wide eyes, I saw that at the heart of the meteor was a spiral, radiating out from the core, in the manner of an ammonite.

"What does this mean?"

"It means, Major, that our meteor was designed to transport the… creature that was housed in this spiral across space and to land it safely on our planet. The trail leading from the meteor was made by the creature after it had disembarked and slithered and squirmed across the snow in search of a host."

"A host?"

"It is obvious from the marks I discovered in the snow that the creature loitered, waiting for a suitable host to become available. This opportunity was presented by the dairymen who delivered the milk churns to Columbus Square, the circles made by the churns in the snow attesting to their presence. Our parasitically-inclined Martian bored through the sole of one of the workmen's boots and entered his body via his foot – the reason, one can only assume, to take command of his mind and his will. Again this was most eloquently recorded by the impressions made in the snow. You will now appreciate, Major, the urgency I assigned to the locating of a workman in possession of a size ten pair of boots, studded with hobnails, the right boot having a circular hole of three-sixteenths diameter in the centre of the sole."

"Which is why you suggested that Roosevelt directed his enquiries to cobblers and bootblacks."

"Correct."

It was then that a breathless police officer appeared at the entrance to the workshop. "Begging your pardon, Mr Tesla, but Commissioner Roosevelt requests you attend him promptly. He says we have your Martian by the heels."

"Excellent!" announced Tesla as he sprang to his feet. "Let us be away, and Major… I would be obliged if you would come heeled."

We were taken deep into the Bowery, the fetid underbelly of the city, where all of the flotsam and jetsam of the world congealed when they arrived, bemused and breathless in the New World. It stank and, as we stepped down from the cab onto the broken pavement, Tesla raised a silver vinaigrette to his nose and inhaled the perfume, but I suspected that even this was overpowered by the smell of effluent suffusing the street. And it wasn't just our sense of smell that was exercised, our ears were similarly assailed, the district being as noisy as it was pungent. It was the harmony of life reduced to cacophony with every one of the crowd of people who swirled around us shouting, singing, screaming, crying, cursing or, in the case of one lunatic, banging on a drum. I stood stunned by the febrile, desperate energy of the place and by its poverty.

The police officer who was our escort led us to a tenement, up the stoop crowded by urchins, through the battered front door and along a dark corridor where Roosevelt was waiting upon us. "The man we have taken is a ruffian named Tommy Fairbanks," said he, "betrayed by the cobbler who repaired his boots this morning. But be warned, Tesla, his wife, a strumpet named Sally, has insisted on being present when he is interviewed and she is as sharp as her husband is dull." Roosevelt made to open the door he was guarding but Tesla placed a hand on his arm.

"You must appreciate, Commissioner, that although I am able to discern some of the abilities and ambitions of these damnable Martians, the nuances are still a closed book to me. We do not know, for instance, if these creatures are able to reproduce and that necessitates we move swiftly with our interrogations. Therefore I would ask you to be generous if my inquisitorial technique becomes… robust."

"Robust away, Tesla," chortled Roosevelt, "the man we have taken is a good-for-nothing newly arrived from London and much used to hard knocks."

"And, Major," Tesla whispered to me, "if you would station yourself by the door and keep your revolver at the ready. If either of these miscreants acts in an untoward manner, you have my authority to shoot them."

The room Roosevelt ushered us into was small, cheaply furnished, with a young, brutal-looking man seated at the table and a woman, presumably his wife, loitering against the far wall. A stove was burning in the corner, the heat doing little to dispel the dampness of the room; the stove was surrounded by a mist caused by the moisture leeching out of the plaster on the walls giving the place a strange, almost fantastical, aspect.

Tesla conjured a handkerchief from his sleeve and dusted the seat of the room's second chair.

"'Oo the fuck are you?" challenged Tommy Fairbanks – a real ornery-looking brute, glowering out at the world like he was fit to be tied – as Tesla slid into the chair.

"You should be advised, young man," Tesla replied in a conversational tone, "that I have a congenital dislike for small talk and for social niceties and, when I am obliged to visit such a pestilential abode as this, such dislike borders on loathing. You will speak only when I instruct you to do so."

"Never mind all that shit, just 'oo the fuck…?"

My belief is that Fairbanks never actually saw the cane as it rotated from a position next to Tesla's side, arched through the air to land squarely – with a sickening *thwackkk* – across the fingers of the left hand that was resting on the scarred surface of the table. Fairbanks rose several inches into the air and then fell, screaming, to the ground.

"That I hope will serve as an object lesson to you. You assumed that my advice not to interrupt me is capable of challenge. This is fallacious: my instructions are not the subject of debate, negotiation or demurral. Failure to accede to these instructions will, as you have discovered, incur punishment that is swift, appropriate and painful."

Fairbanks, still groaning and casting venomous looks in Tesla's direction, pulled himself back onto his chair, holding his damaged and rapidly swelling left hand carefully in his right.

"You've broken my fuckin' 'and, you bastard."

"More precisely, young man, I have broken the middle phalange of the forefinger of your left hand. This is a painful injury, but not a debilitating one and as such I would ask you to stop whimpering," and for emphasis he flexed his cane. Fairbanks was suddenly silent.

"Excellent. And now I think it is appropriate that I introduce myself: I am Nikola Tesla…"

"The electrician?" enquired Fairbank's wife.

Tesla sniffed. "I dislike that sobriquet. If you wish to be more exact, young lady, better you refer to me as a 'Futurist'."

This drew a smile from the girl, "And what's a 'futurist' when it's at home?"

"A Futurist is a person of elevated intellect who is able to absorb prodigious quantities of seemingly unrelated information; to process, evaluate and form linkages between said unrelated and asymmetrical information; and from these cogitations to make predictions regarding how various futures might thereafter unfold."

"It sounds like another name for 'genius'," observed Sally Fairbanks.

"Genii are ten-for-a-dime, Mrs Fairbanks; if anything, I am an über-genius," Tesla turned his attention back towards the woman's husband. "And now let us begin. It is my understanding, Fairbanks, that I am not in conversation with a member of the human race but rather a representative of the Martian people."

Fairbanks' face screwed up as he tried to comprehend what Tesla was saying, this making him look as if he were sucking on pickles. "Wha? Wha' the fuck are you talkin' abart?"

Tesla frowned. "Really, there is no use in you continuing with this masquerade. You have been unmasked and the secrets of the 'meteor' you employed to journey from Mars to Earth discovered."

"You befuddled? I ain't no Martian or nuffink."

For several seconds Tesla was silent, lost in thought. "Fairbanks, I must presume that you Martians are possessed of a superior intellect and therefore you must appreciate that this mimicking of stupidity is counter-productive. If you refuse to enter into dialogue with me I must presume that your intentions are hostile…"

"You're fuckin' mad, yous is."

"This is ridiculous," pronounced Tesla. He looked across to Roosevelt. "Are you convinced that this is our man, Commissioner?"

"The very one, Tesla."

"Remarkable." Tesla pondered for a moment and then reached a conclusion. "In verification of this, I must ask you, Fairbanks, to remove your right boot. But be instructed that when doing so you are not to move closer to me than two feet, which I am advised is the maximum distance a flea of the variety *pulex irritans*, of which you are undoubtedly a most attractive host, can jump. My task today is distasteful enough without my having to leave this benighted place verminous."

"Are you saying oi've got fleas?" protested an outraged Fairbanks.

Tesla looked at Fairbanks with disgust, "Your sentence suggests that I am 'implying' you have fleas when I am stating it as a fact. And now, if you would be so kind… your boot." And he tapped the ferrule of his cane against Fairbanks' right boot for emphasis.

With a sniff and studied reluctance Fairbanks untethered the piece of string that held his right boot, hauled it off and then proffered it for Tesla's inspection. Tesla flinched back, obviously repelled by the stench emanating from the boot.

"Turn it over."

Fairbanks did as he was ordered and there, as I had expected, was a hole, 3/16ths of an inch in diameter, drilled through the sole. Once again Tesla was silent as though somewhat perplexed by what he was seeing. Then he smiled and turned to Sally Fairbanks.

"I presume it is redundant to request that you perform a similar service, young lady?"

"Indeed it is, Mr Tesla," the woman replied in a voice which was rather more commanding than the somewhat ill-educated one she had employed hither to fore.

"Does the creature with which I am conversing have a name?"

"Not one that you have any faculty to pronounce."

"What is going on?" interrupted an obviously bemused Roosevelt.

"It would seem that our visitor from Mars is somewhat selective regarding the host it inhabits and has transferred from the less salubrious accommodation offered by Tommy Fairbanks to the more intelligent hospitality of his wife. That Fairbanks has a hole in his boot despite their recent repair suggested that it is an *exit* hole. Our Martian has vacated Fairbanks and entered his wife." Tesla gave a wry smile. "But now, young lady, the game is up. You are discovered."

Sally Fairbanks gave a disdainful shake of her head. "You are a clever man, Mr Tesla. We had not expected to encounter one of your ability. But being unique, your talents are easily disposed of..."

It was now that one of the most terrifying events of my entire life took place, an event which still, with poisonous regularity, invades my dreams and upsets my spirits: Sally Fairbanks mutated into a monster! One moment she was a young and quite frail woman of twenty and two years and the next she had metamorphosed into a screaming, spitting vampyre, equipped with savage claws and long and viciously pointed incisors. She leapt at Tesla in a howling fury and would have done for the man if I hadn't drilled her through the forehead.

It was fortunate I had my dress uniform with me. Roosevelt was so grateful to Tesla for the expediency with which he had dealt with 'the Martian problem' that he insisted upon hosting a celebratory dinner at Delmonico's and, as you are no doubt aware, Delmonico's was – and remains – the most highfalutin' restaurant in the whole of New York. So, even gussied up in my best bib and tucker, Delmonico's was a test of my nerve: a poor man might despise the rich but that detestation doesn't stop him being intimidated by the varmints.

Nine of us were seated around that table in one of the restaurant's private dining rooms. Other than Tesla and myself, there was Teddy Roosevelt with his square jawed Edith in tow – who, apart from an "It is an honour to meet you, Major Arnaud," uttered not one further word to me throughout the entire evening; a bushy bearded individual named Robert Underwood Johnson – apparently an editor of some magazine or other – and his wife Katherine who had eyes only for Tesla; the multi-millionaire John Jacob Astor and his highly-strung wife, Ava, who, I reckoned, was much given to conniption fits; and finally the lovely and imperious Countess Mircalla Karnstein.

Seems it was Katherine Johnson who had taken it into her head to invite the Countess, who was visiting New York from some place in the Balkans that I couldn't pronounce without a surfeit of phlegm in my throat. My guess is that it was the combination of the Countess being both royal and a real head-turner that persuaded the Johnson dame to bring her along. Yankee nobility always has a soft spot for real royalty. Not that I was complaining: I was seated next to her at the table and, having a weakness for women with prominent bosoms and snow-white skin, I was pleased to see that the gown the Countess was wearing allowed her to flash a deal of both.

"This dinner," Roosevelt announced when we were all seated, "is being given to celebrate the triumph of one man's genius in vanquishing the most despicable enemy ever to confront humanity. But, as this is a *private* celebration, I must insist that every one of you pledges total secrecy with regard to what will be revealed this evening." He glowered at Robert

Underwood Johnston, "For news hounds like you, Robert, that means we're off-the-record."

Even as Johnson nodded his reluctant agreement, Ava Astor clapped her hands and announced that she had a great fondness for secrets and confidences, to which her husband grumped that it was unfortunate that she had not a similar fondness for maintaining them.

Hardened politico that he was, Roosevelt ignored the bickering and ploughed on. "Today, our friend and fellow patriot, Nikola Tesla, used his incomparable intellect to defeat an attack made against this planet by agents sent from Mars."

There was stunned silence around the table and then Ava Astor began to laugh. Her laughter was contagious and soon all but three of the guests had joined in the merriment. Roosevelt was not impressed. "This is not a matter for levity. I say to you flat out that Nikola Tesla, with the courageous assistance of Major Arnaud, has today tracked down and executed a Martian, whose intent was to subjugate mankind."

"Are you serious, Teddy?" asked John Astor as he poured himself another slug of champagne.

"Never more so, and as proof we have the body of our dead Martian lying in a lead-lined coffin in Tesla's laboratory waiting to be dissected tomorrow."

Astor turned to Tesla. "This is not a jape, Niko?"

"You should know me well enough by now, John, to appreciate that I am not built for jests and japes."

"Then tell all, Teddy, tell all."

And that was what Roosevelt did, after which there was a further bout of stunned silence, a silence broken by an excited Katherine Johnson. "But Niko, how did you come to the conclusion that the arrival of a meteor in Central Park was a portent of an invasion from Mars?"

"For the simple reason that I have been expecting one. We know from the work of Giovanni Schiaparelli that Mars is criss-crossed by canals, and did not Percival Lowell, just a few weeks ago, give a very persuasive speech in this very room, when he theorized that there is an advanced race of Martians inhabiting that planet. Lowell went on to say that because of the arid nature of their world these Martians find themselves doomed to extinction unless they find sanctuary on a neighbouring planet. His opinion was that the Earth with an abundance of water and orbiting in such close proximity to Mars is the ideal destination for these desperate Martians. Today's events have proven Lowell correct in every aspect of his speculation."

"But why would they come now?" enquired Astor.

"They will have recognised that mankind has now harnessed the wonder of alternating current which signals that we stand on the brink of full membership of the fraternity of intelligent life in the universe. They know that if they do not subjugate us soon we will become too powerful for them to defeat."

Astor scoffed, "You have been reading those damned stories Lathrop is running in the New York Journal where Martians are defeated by use of a disintegrating ray developed by Edison."

"I have little use for scientific romance, John, especially one where the plot turns on such a fanciful notion as Edison being able to contrive a device which functions properly." There were chuckles around the table: the enmity between Tesla and Edison was legendary.

"But tell me, Mizter Tezla, if zhese Martians ov yours are so advanced how is it zhat you vere able to best zhem?" The question was posed by Countess Karnstein in seductively mangled English.

"By the power of observation," answered Tesla a mite more churlishly than I had expected. I knew of his indifference to the weaker sex but his tone smacked not so much of indifference as antagonism. "I am able, through the diligent and detailed surveillance of all around me, to make conjectures which, to the lay man, might seem fanciful but which, upon examination, prove to be correct."

"I can vouch for that," mused Teddy Roosevelt. "On first

meeting the Major this morning, Nikola was able to discern that he hailed from New Orleans and that he had recently returned from Cuba."

"But Major Arnaud stated that I was in error regarding Cuba."

It was an awkward moment and I decided that being in such elevated company there was little risk in my telling the truth. "In fact, Mr Tesla was quite correct, I *have* just returned from service – confidential service – undertaken on behalf of the US government in Cuba and I would be fascinated to know how he reached this conclusion."

Tesla gave a gentle shake of his head. "I am loath to expound on the conclusions I draw from the use of my powers of observation: people become exercised when they find that their privacy can be breached in such a casual manner."

I bridled a little at the man's insinuation that I might be so sensitive of spirit and, having shipped half a bottle of choice claret, I gave voice to this vexation. "Tell all, Mr Tesla," I persisted. "If I am such an open book then let us all read!"

"Very well. Your recent sojourn in Cuba was attested by your announcement of your being a member of the Military Intelligence Division coupled with the knowledge of our nation's interest in Cuba, which, although unofficial, is widely known to the intelligentsia; by your complexion showing that you have recently seen service in a warmer latitude; by the macassar oil you employ to groom your hair being of a variety only manufactured on Cuba; by the inflection in your accent indicating that you were raised in a Spanish-speaking locale… these and other clues indicate that you are in New York after seeing service in Cuba."

"Bravo Niko!" exclaimed Katherine Johnson and all those gathered around the table applauded.

I was less than impressed, and now the claret began talking. "This smacks to me of little more than organised guessing, Mr Tesla. I announce myself disappointed."

Tesla's face darkened: he was not a man who took lightly to

having his talents criticised. "Then try this, Major. Your family made its fortune through the trading of slaves. Your father fought as a Colonel in the Civil War and lost everything to carpetbaggers when the Confederacy surrendered. You have never forgiven the Yankees for your impoverishment, but your penury has obliged you to take service in the US army, which has made much use of your linguistic abilities and intimate knowledge of the slave trade. You are also the US army's expert on all things relating to the Martian meteors…"

"*Meteors*," spluttered Roosevelt. "You mean there is more than one of the damned things?"

"Of course. It would be improbable if New York was the only destination of these visitations and Major Arnaud's attendance would suggest that there have been several other landings." He looked towards me. "Am I not right, Major?"

I might have been part liquored-up but I had enough of my wits about me to keep my lip buttoned. "I couldn't say, Mr Tesla."

"Couldn't or wouldn't, it is all of a piece and does not alter the fact that the Earth is now the subject of a concerted attack by malevolent Martians."

I sank back in my chair refusing to be drawn further and Tesla descended into a sulk. It was Countess Karnstein who attempted to lighten the mood around the table.

"Zo, Mizter Tezla, might I ask zhat you turn zhe glare of your ferocious intellect in my direction. Vot do your powers ov observation tell you about me?"

Tesla studied the Countess for a few moments as though reluctant to converse with her. His silence became so protracted that it persuaded Katherine Johnson to prompt him.

"Niko…"

"Your accent and your physiognomy indicates that you hail from Wallachia…"

"Vhich perhaps iz zhe cause of your obvious antipathy towards me, Mr Tezla, after all my people are the traditional enemies of you Zerbians."

"Not at all, my Lady, I carry no grudge for the several betrayals committed several centuries ago, my dislike is based on traits of a more recent vintage."

I sat up a little straighter. The tone in Tesla's voice made it sound like somebody had licked all the red off his candy. He took a sip of water and I was surprised to see that his hand shook as he did so.

"But to continue: you wear the Order of the Dragon which indicates you are a member of the House of Drăculeşti, one of the most ancient and powerful families in that part of the world. You are unmarried – the ring finger of your *right* hand is bare – which I would suggest, given your incomparable beauty, indicates a profound disdain for those of the male persuasion. You suffer from extreme photosensitivity – the pallor of your skin attests to that – and you are an extremely dangerous adversary. By the indentation your purse has made in the tablecloth I assume you have a Cloverleaf concealed therein."

This last conjecture was verified when the Countess drew the revolver from the purse, cocked it and aimed it square at Tesla. "Mizter Tezla, I vould ask you to order Major Arnaud not to attempt anything heroic; I am a first-class shot unt am unencumbered by zhe usual feminine scruples regarding killing."

Tesla nodded towards me and I had no option but to abandon my plans to disarm the woman.

"What in the devil's name is happening?" blustered Roosevelt.

"The Countess Karnstein is a Martian," said Tesla calmly, "in New York to meet with the most recent arrival from that dying planet. Am I to take it, Countess Karnstein, that you Martians prefer to occupy female hosts?"

Without the revolver wavering even for an instant from its target at the centre of Tesla's chest, Countess Karnstein rose to her feet. Looking at her in the soft gaslight, I was aware for the first time of what a powerful-looking woman she was. Her beauty

– and she was radiantly beautiful – had made it difficult for me to recognise the strength in her face but it was a strength attested by the square jaw, the flint-like sparkle in her eyes and the firm set of her perfect mouth. This was one woman – Martian – who would blow your head off and not give it a second's thought.

"You are a clever man, Mizter Tezla," she sneered, "but you have made vun fundamental mistake: ve Martians did not come to conquer Earth but merely to peaceably *co-habit* zhe planet. But vhat ve have discovered iz zhat zhe male of zhe species *Homo sapiens* is fatally flawed: men are invariably inclined to violence – even to war – in order to remedy slights, unt mit zhe weapons of war becoming increasingly powerful zhis penchant for violence can no longer be tolerated. Zoon zhey vill possess zhe power to annihilate all life on Earth, a matter of zum importance to us now zhat ve Martians find ourselves fettered to zhe fate of humankind. Zo, vot is needed is a radical alteration in zhe vay zhe vorld is governed, unt zhat zhe more civilised attitude of vomen is incorporated into political discourse. Men are too choleric unt too antagonistic to be relied upon to govern in a satisfactory manner, zherefore it is urgent in zhe extreme zhat vomen are afforded zheir full unt rightful place in zhe shaping of your species' destiny... especially as zhe survival ov zhe Martian race is now inextricably entwined mit zhe survival of *homo sapiens*. Men have failed as leaders unt zhey must be replaced by vomen!"

"You Martians are Suffragettes?" gasped Robert Johnson.

"Yes, zhat is zo. It is ve Martians who first planted zhe zeeds of political impatience in vomen."

Roosevelt slammed a fist on the table making the glasses rattle. "Damn my eyes. I always knew there was something unnatural about the demand for votes for women and now I have my proof that it is an alien philosophy."

"Alien it might be, Mr Roozevelt, but it is a correct philosophy. If ve do nut act in all probability ve vill have sumvun as bullheaded as you as President of zhe United States. Impossible! Unt to prevent zuch a catastrophe I must ensure zhere is no further intervention by zhe meddlezome Nikola Tezla. Even as I am speaking, my agents are disposing of zhe body of Zally Fairbanks, vhich leaves only one other piece of housekeeping to attend to." So saying, Countess Karnstein shot Nikola Tesla plumb centre, twice in the chest.

I stood the next morning in the smouldering remains of Tesla's workshop. It had been fired during the night and everything inside – including the remains of Sally Fairbanks – had been incinerated, this presumably the work of Karnstein's agents. Teddy Roosevelt was especially disheartened and, as he scrunched through the debris, he regaled me with his pessimistic forebodings.

"I fear the worst, Major, without Tesla I doubt whether we will be able to defeat Countess Karnstein and her Martian minions. Without Tesla I doubt we will be able to prevent the natural order of things being turned on its head and men supplanted by women in the governance of our world."

It was a dreadful thought. "The Countess escaped?"

"Indeed, she had a carriage waiting outside Delmonico's which took her straight to the docks where she boarded her steam yacht. The US Navy has been alerted but once she is in open ocean…" He trailed off into despairing silence.

"So there is no hope."

"Remarkable," came a comment from behind us. "It is remarkable, is it not, how quickly defeatism manifests itself."

I spun on my heel and there, large as life, stood Tesla.

"Tesla, by all that's Holy… how?"

"I suspected that Sally Fairbanks would be met by others of her foul kind and when I heard that Countess Karnstein had inveigled her way into the party I decided to take precautions, wearing under my waistcoat a patented bulletproof vest. I survived… but unfortunately my laboratory did not."

"Tesla, I am so sorry."

"Then you can demonstrate your sympathy, Roosevelt, by

buying me breakfast over which we three must discuss our next move in the struggle with Countess Karnstein. Make no mistake, gentlemen, the War of the Worlds is now engaged."

THE BARRICADE

Nina Allan

He would be a quiet man, Christine knew. *Gentle too, most likely. He wouldn't rush to tell you what he thought. But thought would be something he valued. A man who can paint like that would be thinking to himself all the time.*

The picture was quite small, about the size of a torn-off cover of the *Radio Times*, she supposed, no more. It was a landscape painting, not exactly uncommon in this part of Cornwall. It was different from the others though, all those nondescript pastel sketches of churches and fishing boats, even though there was a church in Jeff Turner's painting, a squat, compact building with a square tower and Norman arches. There were also two rows of white cottages, stacked one above the other like bags of sugar on a supermarket shelf. Behind the cottages lay the moor, a green and russet sprawl of brushstrokes that looked wild and disorganised but that were actually, Christine guessed, as intentional and considered as the painstaking daubs of colour that made up the harbour wall.

The harbour wall cut the picture in two. It formed a barricade against the incoming sea, and Jeff Turner's painting was called, in fact, 'The Barricade.'

The difference between 'The Barricade' and so many of the other paintings she had seen here was that it really wasn't as simple as it first appeared. If you looked at it a certain way the church and the tiny hamlet seemed not to be there at all. The buildings were just shapes and colours, a pattern of pale squarish blobs strung out across the murky moor-colours like a chain of fairy lights.

The sea was a swathe of petrel blue, the paint laid on joyously, haphazardly, not caring what it looked like.

You could stare at this mess – this joyous mess – for some minutes and see nothing but that. Then click! Your perception shifted and the church and the little houses were all in place again.

Like magic, Christine thought. As if the Norman windows and the miniature village existed only for her.

The artist's name, Jeff Turner, was stuck up beside the painting on a little white card. A short paragraph of typed text informed anyone who wanted to know that Jeff Turner had trained in Glasgow but had fallen in love with the softer, *more pearlescent* light of the North Cornish coast. He had arrived there in '87 and never left. Christine wondered if his name was a burden to him, if he was ever teased about this, then thought no, it was the right name, he was a good enough painter to carry it off. Not a genius like the real J. Turner perhaps, but the truth was that she liked Jeff Turner's painting better.

She had seen the real Turners at Tate Britain, and they were beautiful, she supposed, you wouldn't dare suggest otherwise. But they reminded her of the rooms in stately homes that were made up to look lived-in but in reality were museum exhibits. No one sat in them now, or came through in the afternoon to play the piano. They belonged to everyone and no one. They were dead.

Whereas Jeff Turner's painting was speaking to her right now. If she wanted to she could buy it and take it home.

Trevor had wandered away from the paintings to look out of the window. He was getting restless, Christine knew, because the tide was on the turn.

"I think we've seen enough here, don't you?" he said, turning towards her. "This stuff's all a bit overpriced if you ask me."

"Okay," Christine said. With Trevor it was always easiest just to agree. She wished he would leave her where she was and go down to the beach. She could explore the town by herself then, and join him later. It was a small place; they were hardly going to lose track of each other. But she knew from past experience that Trevor did not like them to be separated. If she suggested they do their own thing for a bit he would insist on staying with her *until she was ready*, growing more impatient with each passing moment but pretending nonchalance, believing he was giving her what she wanted.

Her pleasure in Turner's painting would be ruined. She moved towards the door, stumbling over the step as she cast one hurried glance backward at 'The Barricade.'

"I liked that painting of the church," she said to Trevor once they were outside. "Did you see it?" She thought about linking her arm through his, at making some small effort at intimacy. She touched his elbow instead, as a compromise. He glanced sideways at her, raising his eyebrows.

"They all seemed much of a muchness to me," he said. "Derivative."

Derivate of what? she longed to ask. Imagining his discomfiture if she had done so was almost as satisfying as voicing the question aloud. Trevor didn't care about art. He selected his opinions with care from the Sunday papers. She released his elbow and moved slightly ahead of him, trying to imagine how it might feel if they were no longer married. The heady rush of adrenalin caught her off guard.

She knew that in her way she did still love him. She loved his unworldliness, his delight in detail, the fact that he was an acknowledged world expert on the Common Dog Whelk. It was the dog whelks that brought him to life. When he was down exploring the strand line Trevor seemed almost a different person. His attention became steely-focussed, like a gold prospector's or a big game hunter's. The fussy turn of mind, the part of him that liked to store his woollens in plastic wrappers during the summer and insisted on table napkins even when they were just having bread and soup for lunch, seemed to vanish then entirely.

The first time she saw him, the Atlantic wind whipping his hair back as he gazed across the sand at Aberystwyth, she had imbued him with those qualities of the intrepid she had been looking for without even knowing it. Perhaps she had not been entirely wrong, perhaps Trevor even possessed some of those qualities. But whatever the truth of the matter it was the table napkins and the neatly bagged jumpers she noticed more now, rather than the bashful charm and sense of adventure that had initially captured her attention and then her heart.

Quite suddenly she found herself wondering what Jeff Turner looked like. A picture formed in her mind, an image of a tall man with jutting elbows and unkempt hair. She knew her idea of him was probably romanticised. The real Jeff Turner was just as likely to be old and bent and crazy, or pedantic and bespectacled, like Trevor.

It was never a good idea to get the worker muddled up with his work. If you did you ended up disappointed. If she'd learned anything in the course of her marriage it was that.

They made their way to the edge of the town, following the esplanade as far as it went then turning on to the strip of greying asphalt that eventually became the coast path. Narrow tracks ran off at right angles from the broken hardcore, dusty runnels that led directly on to the beach. The tide was out, the sea a grey-blue smudge at the horizon. Christine had an eyeliner pencil of a more or less identical shade, though it had been a long time since she had used it, or any other. Trevor didn't care for make-up; he thought it was tarty.

She watched him as he stepped off the path, his plimsolls making shallow grooved impressions in the damp sand. She knew that now he was in sight of his goal he had more or less forgotten she was there.

He's like a man on the moon, Christine thought. *One small step for man, one giant leap for Trevor Bailey.* He picked his way carefully across the seaweed-strewn rocks. He didn't like to mark his clothes, not if he could avoid it, and Christine could not help finding something ridiculous in his fastidiousness. Jeff Turner, she felt certain, would enter his studio dressed in filthy jeans and an open-necked, paint-spattered shirt.

She thought about the painting in the white-walled gallery, the way it seemed to hide itself, the church and the tiny houses sliding into invisibility even as you looked at them. She knew exactly where she would hang it: the window alcove in the small back bedroom Trevor's parents slept in when they came to stay but that was really Christine's sewing room. She had a small fold-down table in there, and the built-in wardrobe had been fitted with shelves to hold her various fabrics and embroidery silks. Trevor had paid to have the shelves put in. That was the only interest he had ever taken in her sewing.

Jeff Turner's painting would glow quietly in its alcove, like the doorway to another world. The image was so clear in her mind she could almost convince herself that 'The Barricade' was already hers.

"Trevor," she called. "I'm going to buy some postcards. I'll be back in about half an hour, okay?"

"Right," Trevor said. He was bent over a rock pool, the jagged chunks of granite jutting out of the sand like the scattered, half-buried remains of some lost civilization. Trevor moved from one to the next, turning over stones and gently moving aside clumps of seaweed like an investigating forensic scientist at the scene of a crime. *No trace of separation anxiety now*, Christine thought. She knew she could be gone for an hour, perhaps several, and that Trevor would not even notice.

If he did he could always call her. Trevor had been the one who insisted on her getting a mobile. If it had been up to her she would not have bothered. What was a mobile phone after all but an electronic tagging device under an assumed name?

For a moment she imagined a future Trevor, a man in cream-coloured chinos clambering across these same rocks a thousand years from now and uncovering the corroded body of her discarded 3G Nokia. The idea made her shudder. It brought home the fact that nothing lasted, not even the seeming endlessness of her marriage to Trevor.

She found the gallery again quite easily. She went inside, hoping it would be empty as it had been when she and Trevor first arrived there. She was disconcerted to find three or four men standing around with mugs of coffee and chatting to the woman behind the desk. *Gallerina*, Christine thought. *That's what they call them these days.* It was a ridiculous word, like WAG or newbie, words that Trevor refused to acknowledge even existed.

Perhaps she had gatecrashed the woman's lunch break. Christine started wishing she hadn't come.

"I'm sorry," she said. "If you're closed I can call back later."

"We're not closed," said the gallerina. "Weren't you here earlier?" She was Christine's age at least and a bit raddled-looking. As a gallerina you could get away with a bit of beraddlement, Christine supposed. It made you look as if you led an interesting life. If you worked on the checkout at Sainsbury's though, the same drooping eyelids and smoker's pout were more likely to make people think you were heading down the slope to death from lung cancer or liver disease.

"I was," Christine said. She could feel herself blushing. "I wanted to have another look at one of the paintings."

"A customer," said one of the coffee drinkers. "I thought you turned them all to stone, Evelyn, with your basilisk stare." He was a skinny lad, almost skeletal in fact. His black LadyBoys T-shirt was torn in several places. Evelyn, she supposed, was the gallerina. Christine's cheeks felt tight and hot, as if she were sunburned.

Two of the other coffee drinkers began to laugh.

"Shut up, Tony," said Evelyn. She turned to look at Christine, and Christine saw that beneath the drooping lids her eyes were in fact a bit peculiar: yellowish green and slightly protuberant, with the glassy quality of polished beach pebbles. "Which of the paintings were you interested in?"

"The one called 'The Barricade,'" Christine said. "The artist's name was Turner, I think."

The two men who had been laughing before started laughing again, and the skinny one, the one called Tony, slapped the third man on the back.

"Jeffrey," said Tony. "You never told me you had fans."

Evelyn ignored him. "You're in luck today then, madam," she said to Christine. "This gentleman here is Jeff Turner. I'm sure he'd be happy to talk to you about his work."

She waved a hand towards the man Tony had slapped on the back. He was not at all as he had been in Christine's imagination. A small man, shorter than Trevor definitely. His hands were wrinkled and rough-looking. In his checked cotton shirt and yellow baseball cap he looked more like a builder than a painter.

There was an awkward silence. Christine wondered why she had ever thought she could perform an act as complicated and pretentious as stepping into an art gallery to buy a painting. She should have known it would all go wrong. The only good thing was that Trevor was not here to see her make a fool of herself.

Jeff Turner took off his yellow cap. He held it between his hands and tugged at the cloth. He looked as uncomfortable with the situation as Christine felt.

She also felt sorry for him, and angry with Evelyn and LadyBoy Tony for embarrassing him in this way. She found her anger made it possible for her to finally say something.

"Hello," she said. "It's nice to meet you."

Turner took a shuffling step towards her and held out his hand. As Christine reached forward to take it, the door to the gallery swung open and four large adults wearing identical *Pirates of Penzance* T-shirts piled in off the street. They spoke loudly together in American accents.

Oh, isn't this place just darling? crooned one of the women. She was buxom as Dolly Parton, and with an identical bouncing mane of peroxide curls.

Christine smiled at Jeff Turner and Jeff Turner smiled back.

Tony and the other men had started talking amongst themselves. Evelyn was busy fussing over the Americans.

For the moment at least they were alone.

"I'm glad you liked the painting," Turner said. "Will you tell me what you liked about it?"

He had a Scottish accent, the words softly nuanced, not at all like the harsh Glaswegian she remembered from the trip to Saltcoats she had once made with Trevor.

"The colours," she said. She was afraid of sounding stupid, of saying something that might reveal her ignorance, but Jeff Turner's presence was quietly calming and she had the sense that even if she did make a mistake he would not make a thing of it. "I like the way the houses are sometimes houses and sometimes white squares. I like the title, too." She paused. "It makes you look at the painting differently. Thinking of the harbour wall as a barricade, I mean. As if it was the only thing saving the town from inundation." She clasped her hands tightly together across her stomach. "It makes me think of a war."

She wondered why she had used the word *inundation*, what had made her think of it. Not an uncommon word exactly, but you didn't often hear it in everyday speech.

She said the word silently again to herself; it rolled across the roof of her mouth like an incoming wave. They had moved to stand in front of the painting. Christine had been afraid that seeing it again would make her think less of it, but if anything the opposite was true. She felt now as if she had a stake in the painting. She knew she would not be able to leave it behind.

She wondered how she was going to be able to keep her purchase secret from Trevor. Her heart sank.

"It *is* a war," Turner said. He was looking at her strangely, as if she presented a riddle that needed unravelling. "Do you mind my asking where you come from?"

"Not far from here, actually. I was born out near Gwithian, in a room above a pub called the Harbour Arms. I don't remember it though, or only from visits. My mother moved us away to Reading when I was six months old." She raised her eyes briefly to his. "Why would you want to know that?"

"Just curious, you know. I was wondering if you might have selkie blood."

Christine laughed, not from the belly as LadyBoy Tony had done but quietly and with a hint of nervousness. "But the selkies aren't real. They're just a legend." Though when she looked into Turner's eyes there was a stillness that said he wasn't joking, a stillness that caused her to add, "Aren't they?"

The selkies were sea people, what the children's fairy tales usually referred to as mermaids. She knew of the selkies from her Cornish grandmother, and from the church at Zennor, where a carving on one of the pews told the story of the mermaid who had stolen away the fiancé of the coachman's daughter. There had been many sightings of selkies down the centuries, but everyone knew that these were cases of mistaken identity. Some of the larger sea mammals – seals, dugongs, manatees – could easily be mistaken for people swimming, especially from a distance.

None of the stories were true, though. Her grandmother said that all the old myths and legends had a reason behind them, and that most selkie tales had been invented by fishermen as a way of explaining what happened to ships that disappeared or went astray.

But just because things had a reason didn't make them so.

"Every coastal community in the world has its selkie tales," Turner said. "The names change, but the stories are mostly the same, or very similar. The Earth's surface is nearly four-fifths water, did you know that?"

"Yes," Christine said. "I did, actually."

"It makes you think. About all the parts of our planet we've never seen. If nobody's ever been there, how can we know for sure what's real and what isn't?"

"I suppose." She didn't know if Turner was being serious, or poking gentle fun at her. She found she didn't care much either way. What he said was weird, certainly, but there was an internal logic to it also, something she found oddly compelling. She liked the idea that people didn't have all the answers. She remembered a documentary she had watched with Trevor in which the ocean had been referred to as the *last great unknown*. Trevor himself was always going on about how there were probably thousands of marine gastropods still unknown to science.

If dog whelks why not sea dogs, or even selkies?

"They wouldn't like it, you know. What we're doing to the sea. All our deep-sea fishing and drilling for oil and nuclear submarines. They'd hate us for that, in the end. They'd want to get their own back. Don't tell me you haven't felt that. You understand the sea, I can tell."

Turner spoke so quietly that Christine found herself wondering if his words were really imaginings inside her own head. She felt herself jump, although she couldn't have said precisely what had startled her. She could hear one of the American women asking if Evelyn had one of the paintings in a larger size.

"I'm sorry," Christine said. "I didn't quite catch what you said."

"I said I'd like to offer you the painting at a discount if you still want it," Turner said. "I can't give it to you – that would be cheating Evelyn and Michael out of their commission – but I can name a new price." He did so, and the amount was so much lower than what was written on the white card that Christine was worried she had misheard him. Two minutes later she was watching Evelyn the gallerina wrap 'The Barricade' in several large sheets of tissue paper and bubblewrap.

"Can I pay extra and have it sent to my home?" Christine asked. Her heartbeat quickened in excitement at this sudden brainwave. Trevor always left for work at around eight-thirty, and no post was ever delivered before eleven. She could hide the painting in her sewing cupboard for a couple of weeks. For a couple of months if that felt safer. Trevor never looked in her sewing cupboard; there was no reason to.

Eventually she could hang the picture in the alcove, exactly as she had imagined. Trevor would probably think it had always been there. If he even noticed , that was.

She paid by Visa. She didn't mind that the four Americans were standing round, nodding and smiling as if the transaction had been put on for their entertainment. She said one more thank you to Evelyn then looked around for Turner to thank him also.

There was no sign of the artist, and Christine decided he had taken advantage of all the excitement to make his escape. She didn't mind, and in a way she was glad. *Artists are like that*, she thought. *They need to be alone.* She glanced down at her watch, anxious suddenly about the time. The thought of Trevor coming to look for her shot steely darts of panic into her chest.

She was surprised and relieved to see that less than an hour had passed since she left the beach. *Postcards*, she thought. *Don't whatever you do forget the postcards.*

She snatched up half a dozen at random from one of the spindle racks outside a newsagent's, paid for them then retraced her steps along the esplanade.

Trevor was in more or less the same spot she had left him. She called a bright *yoo-hoo*, which was most unlike her. He raised his hand briefly and waved then continued peering downwards into his rock pool. She wondered what he was looking at, how soon they would be able to take a break for lunch. The smell of the sea was making her feel hungry.

They drove out to a pub called The Lobster Pot just north of Hayle. Trevor said he wanted to get away from the tourists.

"You can show me your old haunts," he said. It was strange, the way he insisted on her having a past here even though he knew perfectly well that most of her memories dated from trips she had made with him.

Usually his elective amnesia annoyed her; on that afternoon it filled her with wistful affection.

It's because you want what he says to be true, she thought. *It reminds you that you might have selkie blood.*

She laughed, and thought of Jeff Turner, asking her bold as brass where she was from. She wondered what he had meant about her understanding the sea. *That might have been true once,* she thought. *But I gave up my knowledge. I gave myself up for lost, like the boy who drowned.*

A memory surfaced for a moment and then receded. *The boy on the beach that time*, she thought again. *He was a bad swimmer.* There was no way Jeff Turner could have known about the boy, and yet he seemed to know a lot of things he shouldn't have done. *Perhaps that's just what artists are like*, she thought. *The good ones, I mean.* She smiled to herself, hugging the thought of Turner in his yellow cap.

Trevor was backing the Escort into a space in the Lobster Pot's car park. He glanced at her sharply, as if she were a particularly tricky obstacle he had to navigate.

"What's got into you all of a sudden?" He kept his eyes on her a second longer before braking hard, sending the vehicle bouncing forward a couple of inches before jerking it to a standstill like a Labrador brought up short at the end of its leash. Then they got out of the car and went into the pub. It had been refurbished in sixties modern and was rather ugly but the views from its large plate windows were spectacular. The sea shimmered like a sheet of rippled glass, its jewel colours swirling together like intertwined silks.

So beautiful, she thought. *Like a foreign country.*

It had been in a foreign country that the boy had died. When she was eight years old she and her mother went on holiday to Greece. They had gone snorkelling together, just the two of them, and the revelation that her mother could swim was almost as astonishing as the glimmering, luminescent world she had discovered just a few feet below the water's surface.

Small fish, slick as knives, slipping like liquid bronze into the densely weeded crevasses in the sunken rocks. They were terribly busy, those fish. They reminded Christine of the olive-skinned, beetle-browed women hunting for bargains in the markets of Kalamata.

It was the first time she had visited a foreign country, and for Christine the holiday had become mythic in its scope and dimensions. Each day was a new page in history. Each sunset down by the harbour was like the ending of an era.

But on the ninth day of the fortnight something dreadful happened: a boy staying at the same hotel as them was killed in a swimming accident.

"He hit his head on a rock," Christine's mother told her. "He should never have dived in where he did. He should have known the sea was too shallow." She said that Christine should keep quiet about the accident as much as possible, that it wasn't fair on the boy's family to have people gossiping about it.

"It could have been me," Christine said.

Her mother told her sharply that she was wrong. "You would never have been that stupid. You swim like a fish."

And it was true, or at least it was then. The odd thing was that she had never been into the water after that summer.

How strange, Christine thought. *I haven't thought about these things in years.*

Trevor chose a corner table by one of the windows.

"Do you suppose they'll come and serve us?" he said. He glanced towards the bar. "Seeing as we want to order some food, I mean."

Trevor hated going up to the bar. That was one of the first things Christine found out about him. The discovery had disappointed her, not for what it was – the revelation that Trevor was uneasy in the presence of men more overtly masculine than he was – but because rather than admitting to his discomfiture he tried to conceal it with blustery excuses.

"I'll go," Christine said. "It'll save us waiting. Have you decided what you want?"

"I'll have the seafood pancake. And an orange juice."

Christine thought she might have the same, only with a glass of white wine instead of the fruit juice. Trevor hardly ever touched alcohol and she had grown used to doing without it. But today she had something to celebrate and she intended to do so. Her stomach knotted with excitement at this small act of defiance.

"I know you, don't I?" said the bar girl. She looked older than Christine by at least ten years. Her hands were ruined, by constant immersion in hot water most likely. Her hair though was still magnificent, coiled on top of her head like a great black snake. "Or I know your sister."

"I don't have a sister," Christine said, laughing a little. *It's the day of revelation*, she thought. She did not know if the painting was at the root of it or if the painting was just one more proof that something in her life – she did not yet know what, exactly – had begun to change. "You might know my mother though. She grew up not far from here. Ailsa Tregorrow?"

The woman shook her head. "I can't say the name rings a bell. But it's easy to tell you're one of us. We all look alike." She took Christine's order and poured the drinks, then turned away to serve her next customer, still glancing at Christine from the corner of her eye.

One of us, thought Christine. *What did she mean*? The words stuck in her mind, prickly as burdock and as tenacious. She had always thought of herself as less than nothing. Not in the way the misery memoirs went on about, all that pointless self-loathing and low self-esteem. When measured against the world and all its troubles she *was* less than nothing, her marriage to Trevor and all. Now complete strangers were asking her who she was and where she came from.

Something turned over inside her, darting up under her ribs like a small bright fish.

A neon tetra, she thought. *So colourful and brave for its size.*

The boy who drowned was called Thomas Eltham. She had seen him playing on the beach a couple of times and even smiled at him but she had been too shy to actually speak and she guessed Thomas had been too shy also.

If she had overcome her shyness, might things have been different?

The wine went straight to her head, clouding her mind. When she had finished eating she went to the toilet, wondering at the body's ability to so quickly turn one aromatic golden liquid into another. The cloakroom was at the back of the building and she could hear vehicles scrunching and backing on the gravel outside. She stared at herself in the mirror: a pale, troubled-looking woman in her mid-forties with the vague beginnings of jowls and hair streaked with grey.

What am I going to do? she thought. *I can't go on like this.*

They drove back to the hotel. Trevor sometimes liked to have a sleep after lunch, especially when they were away on one of their trips, when he invariably referred to his nap as a siesta. He took off his shoes and lay down on the bed, reaching for the book on his bedside cabinet. It was a crime thriller, something by Henning Mankell or Jo Nesbo, the kind of reading he would only indulge in while on holiday. There was a bookmark keeping his place, an embroidered strip of damask with a silk tassel. Christine had made it for Trevor as a stocking filler years ago.

She studied his feet in their jacquard socks, his obvious contentment filling her with irritation and a restless energy. She lay down on the bed beside him then took the book from his hands and began undoing his shirt buttons. It was a month, perhaps six weeks, since they'd had sex. He stiffened almost immediately beneath her touch.

The last couple of years had seen him thicken around the waist a bit but she didn't mind that. She lifted herself astride him, something she could not remember doing before even in the early days, riding him like a wave and thinking that sex with Trevor was really all right once you got him started. She imagined their bodies in close up, filmed under infrared light like dugongs or whales. Her genitals spread and glistening like the heart of a sea anemone. Trevor's penis, strangely animate, its blunt tip blindly questing as a sea cucumber.

Holothuroids, she thought. *That's the Latin name for sea cucumbers, I'm sure.* She came with a grunting gasp, as if somebody had punched her in the stomach. When she looked down at Trevor there were beads of sweat on his forehead and his eyes were closed. Wet hair straggled across his forehead, the way it had done on the promenade at Aberystwyth.

It's the sea air, that's all, she thought. *It gets to you.* Her nerve endings were still jangling. Beside her, spread on his back like a beached grouper, Trevor was already asleep.

She put on her dress, a blue cotton shift she had been meaning to wear that evening, then quietly left the room and went downstairs. The hotel felt breathlessly still, the larger reception rooms on the ground floor filled with dappled sunlight and the smell of wax polish. The reception desk stood unmanned.

The stillness seeped out through the doors, collecting in golden puddles on the pavement outside. She walked down the steep main street towards the harbour. The tide was in now. The harbour wall curved inwards, like a protecting arm. Christine stood and looked down at the water, which was so clear she could see all the way to the bottom. Large rocks rose up like castles, granite buttresses cloaked with barnacles and *Cladophora*. Christine wondered what else might be down there, further out.

She walked out on to the jetty then sat down on the concrete and took off her sandals. She hooked both arms over the guard rail and allowed her feet to dangle in the water. The sea encased her soles like silken slippers. She wished she could submerge herself completely. How strange it was, she thought, that she had not thought to pack a swimming costume. She didn't know if she even owned one any more.

"It's lovely in, you should try it."

Christine started with surprise, almost losing her grip on the metal railing. There was a girl, below her in the sea close to the jetty. She was treading water. Her wet hair clung to her head like a coat of dark paint. She was wearing a pair of black briefs, or bikini pants, but otherwise she was naked. Her breasts with their large nipples bobbed about in the green glass water like the udders of some mythical sea creature. Christine stared at them without blinking. She tried to imagine her own body in a similar state, twisting and thrusting in the water like a manatee's.

The girl's face was somehow familiar, and after a moment or so Christine realised she looked like the woman who had served her in the pub where they had eaten their lunch.

"I can't come in," she said. "I don't have a costume."

The girl laughed. "Clothes are for land lubbers," she said. She drew her arms sideways through the water and then upended herself, diving down to the bottom in a single motion. Christine saw her pick up some small object from the sand – a round pebble, a cockle shell – before swimming in rapid strokes back out to sea. Christine quickly lost sight of her. She wondered if she should alert someone. The girl would be over deep water by now. Christine didn't like to think of what might happen if she got into difficulties.

She won't though, Christine thought. *She can swim like a fish.*

She remembered seeing Thomas Eltham the moment before he dived into the water. He held himself straight as a bulrush, his arms pointing above his head.

The harsh white sunlight of Kalamata blazing off his ribby torso in diagonal rays.

Not there, Christine had screamed inwardly. *It's not safe.*

Why had she not shouted aloud? Logic told her even then that there hadn't been time. Guilt whispered that she had wanted to see what would happen, to have the scene play out before her eyes like in a horror movie.

She had seen Tom's soul part from his body then swim upwards in the clear water, shaking its little boy's head as it broke the surface then dive-leaping like a skua into the air. Diamond droplets of water streamed down, marking the place where his body had come to rest.

I didn't really see that, she thought. *I couldn't have.* And yet the memory, now that she had it, was sharp as a knife.

The boy's father let out a roar. He plunged into the sea, churning up the water like a mustang maddened by bees.

He carried Tom's body ashore. Another man, the father of a boy Tom had chummed up with, came tearing down the beach to help him. Later on, Christine saw Mark Eltham crying in the arms of this man as if they were brothers, though Christine's mother told her they had only known each other since the start of the holiday. Christine wondered if they would stay in touch when they got back to England, if Tom's death would draw them together permanently or whether they would end up wanting never to see each other again.

The other man's son was still alive, after all.

Her grandmother used to say that when a selkie died she turned into sea foam. Christine thought that as far as dying went it didn't sound too bad.

She unhooked her arms from the guard rail and stood up. Her feet left wet prints on the concrete, perfect outlines of themselves that began to dry and fade the moment she stepped away from them.

I should get back to Trevor, she thought. *He'll be awake by now.* For the first time ever she asked herself whether she intended to remain with Trevor for the rest of her life.

What's happened to you? she thought. *The only thing that's different is that you bought a painting.*

She tried to imagine what she would do in any case if she did leave Trevor, where she would go. She had ten thousand pounds in her savings account, money that she had earned before she married. It would be enough to start with, she supposed. What was harder to think about was actually telling him.

He would not yell or cry, she knew that, he would be bewildered. She thought bewildered would be worse than angry. It would be worse than anything.

Could she really face being the cause of such unhappiness?

Just as she reached the hotel she met Trevor coming out. His hair looked uncombed, flattened from where he'd been sleeping on it. He was in the middle of tucking his shirt into his chinos.

"Where on Earth were you?" he said. "I tried calling you on your mobile but you'd left it behind."

It was true, Christine realised. She'd gone out without taking anything, not even her room key.

"I went to have a look at the sea," she said. "I've only been gone five minutes."

"Someone was trying to call you," said Trevor. "That gallery. They were querying our address or something. They seemed to think you'd bought a painting. I told them they must have made a mistake."

"I did buy a painting," she said. "The Jeff Turner. I was talking to you about it this morning." Anger rose within her like the silver-bright column of mercury inside a thermometer. She realised that Trevor knew nothing about her. The person he thought of as her had not existed for years.

Later, in the darkness, she would wonder how things might have turned out if Trevor had smiled at her and said he looked forward to seeing the painting when it was delivered.

Instead he tutted.

"Where on Earth are we going to put it? It's not like you to waste money." His arms fell to his sides in a familiar gesture of irritation.

"It's my money," Christine said. "I thought I'd hang it in my sewing room." She wondered if they were having an argument, and was surprised when the idea excited her.

"The spare room? What on Earth for? Don't you at least want to put it where people will see it?"

What people? she thought. *I want to put it where* I *will see it. No one else. No people.* She looked down at her feet. There was sand between her toes.

"Well, it's your money," Trevor conceded. He shrugged, as if that was the end of the matter. Christine realised that whether it was or not was up to her.

"Let's go in," she said. "I'm getting cold."

She showered and changed. She realised she was putting on clean clothes for the third time that day. Whether this was carelessness or craziness she wasn't sure; it seemed she was now capable of either. When she came out of the bathroom Trevor was sitting at the cramped little hotel desk writing notes in his all-weather journal.

He examined her warily.

"What would you like to do this evening?" he said.

"I don't know," Christine said. "I think I'll just write my postcards."

"We could go to that fish place for dinner, if you like?"

"That would be nice."

One of the restaurants in the town had a two-star Michelin chef. Trevor cared even less about expensive food than he did about art but he always insisted on going to The Schooner because he thought Christine liked it there.

She opened her handbag and took out the postcards. There were two of the harbour, one of the lighthouse, two others of Cornish seabirds. She wrote a brief inconsequential message on the back of one of the harbour cards for her next-door neighbour Karen. The picture of the lighthouse she chose for her mother. Ailsa Tregorrow was eighty-eight now, living in a tiny one-bedroom flat in Kingston-on-Thames. Trevor seemed convinced she was in the early stages of Alzheimer's, that they should start thinking about moving her into sheltered accommodation. He had been saying the same thing for ten years. Christine knew her mother didn't have Alzheimer's any more than she did; it was just that she no longer cared what people thought of her.

I met a lady in the pub today who thought she recognised me, Christine wrote. *Isn't that strange? I think I'm going to leave Trevor when I get back.*

It felt good to try out the words. She reminded herself that she didn't have to actually post the card unless she wanted to.

She wrote two more postcards, one to her old teacher, Mike Claudel in Caversham, because she knew he enjoyed getting postcards, and one to Seven Frears who owned and ran the fabric shop and haberdasher's where Christine bought her embroidery silks. Seven was called Seven because she was the seventh child in her family. Christine thought of her as her only real friend, even though she had never seen her outside the shop. She knew that Seven owned the small apartment above the business premises. It was just the two rooms and a shower room, more a bedsit than a proper flat, but she felt certain Seven would rent it out to her if she asked.

On her last card she wrote: *Dear Tommy, I have always blamed myself for what happened to you. I don't know if I was really to blame – I probably wasn't – but I gave up swimming because of it. My mother thought it was because your accident made me afraid of the water, but it wasn't that. I thought that if I gave up what I most loved it might bring you back. It was stupid to think that, I know that now. I'm sorry you died and I wish I could have warned you in time. I wish I'd been brave enough to make friends with you properly. I'm the girl in blue shorts who smiled at you, Christine Tregorrow.*

She had to print her words very small and close together to fit them all in but she just managed it. The photograph on the postcard was of a Stormy Petrel. The Stormy Petrel was a strange bird, she knew. It spent most of its life at sea, coming in to land only to breed.

In some places they were known as Jesus Birds, for the way they had of seeming to walk on water. She put a stamp on the card and Tom's name, *Thomas Eltham*. She left the address lines blank. She hadn't known where Tom lived even when he was alive. His father would no doubt have moved away in any case.

Would her life have been so different if Tom hadn't died? It was silly to think so but it felt true nonetheless. Perhaps she really was insane now. Who could tell?

She slipped the postcards into the post box on their way to the restaurant, all five of them, the one to her mother included. As they walked down the hill towards the harbour she found herself looking at Trevor in a new way, as if he were somebody she used to know, someone who was already part of her past. That made her feel sad for a moment, and she ran to keep pace with him. He did not slow down for her. If anything he quickened his step.

"You really are in an odd mood today," he said at last. "Is there anything you want to tell me about?"

She remembered the months of their courtship, the first two years of their marriage, when any time spent apart would always have Trevor asking her that same question: *is there anything you want to tell me about?* There had been affection in his eyes then, and merriment, the sense that he really wanted to know. The phrase had been a private joke between them.

It wasn't now.

Was it me? Christine thought. *Did I kill it?*

"I don't think so," she said. "I'm all right, honestly." It occurred to her that she had never really told Trevor that much about herself. It was not that she had tried to hide things, simply that the deepest parts of herself had been inaccessible, even to her.

They walked on in silence. At the bottom of the town the sea was going out again. The exposed sand gleamed dully in the dusk, like hammered pewter. The sky dipped itself in the sea, the sun dissolving in a mist of vapours like a large pink pill. At the Schooner she ordered salt and pepper calamari and the monkfish curry. Trevor raised his eyebrows but did not comment. He didn't like spicy food, and usually she pretended she didn't either. He began to talk to her about the colony of dog whelks he had unearthed that morning, not the ordinary *Nucellas* but *Nassarius reticulatus*, which was much less common. He moved his hands as he spoke, and an excitement crept into his voice that had not been there earlier.

For those moments while he was talking Christine glimpsed again the man she had loved. The difference now had nothing to do with age. It lay in the fact that he talked, Christine knew, without ever truly caring what she thought or felt.

Trevor's parents and perhaps Trevor himself had taken for granted that she would have children. It hadn't happened, something that had once caused her grief but now filled her with gratitude.

A son or daughter would have tied her to Trevor forever; now she could disappear from his life like foam on the waves.

"Don't you sometimes wish you'd taken that job in Swansea, like we planned?" she asked him suddenly. "We could have bought that little cottage on the Gower."

"It was only a temporary contract, and the house was practically falling down. It would have turned out to be a dead end, if you ask me. We're doing all right, aren't we?" Without waiting for her to answer, he signalled to the waiter to bring the bill. "Time we were going, my little mermaid. You're looking tired."

He had not used that endearment in years. She knew he was only using it now as a means of closing off the discussion.

If only we had talked more, Trevor. I've been so lonely.

In their hotel room they watched the late news then got ready for bed. Christine lay on her side, turned away from Trevor. She felt no desire for him now, not just because they'd made love so recently but because she had already begun the process of separation.

She thought about her postcards, which would be collected with the first post the following morning. She had seen a documentary once, about the many thousands of packets and letters that for one reason or another were undeliverable. There was a warehouse in Belfast stacked full of them, a team of workers whose job it was to sort them and eventually mark them for destruction. She wondered if the postcard she had written to Tommy Eltham would one day end up there, or if by some miracle it would eventually find its way to Tom's father.

She realised it didn't matter either way. Just writing down the words had been enough. She closed her eyes, imagining an alternate past in which she and Tommy had chased each other along the beach, pelting each other with seaweed and screaming with laughter.

She had never done such things, not with anybody, but in some secret part of herself she felt that she had.

When she and her mother had returned from Kalamata they had spent a week together in Gwithian with Christine's grandmother. Christine's mother had gone off walking by herself a lot and seemed unusually impatient when Christine tried to talk to her. Years later she told Christine she had slept with Thomas Eltham's father, just the once, the night before they flew back to England and three days after Tom died.

It was just something that happened, she said. *It shouldn't have, but it did.*

Her grandmother was the same as always. She taught Christine how to make a fish pie and took her for walks along the beach and told her stories. One of the stories, Christine realised later, had been Hans Andersen's 'The Little Mermaid,' only her grandmother had changed all the names and places. In her version of the story the prince was a merchant's son from Truro and the Little Mermaid swam ashore in Lamorna Cove.

She remembered that for the Little Mermaid exchanging her fish tail for legs had been a one-time-only decision.

You will never again see your father's kingdom, the Sea Witch said. *Your new legs will hurt you like knives, and you will feel the pain of your loss with every step.*

Christine supposed the Little Mermaid had most likely regretted her decision many times. She waited until Trevor was asleep then slipped out of bed and began putting on her clothes. It was past midnight, and the centre of town stood empty and quiet, the shops, the banks, the fast food kiosks closed and shuttered like circus booths after the crowds have departed and with as little purpose.

It could all be washed away in an instant, Christine thought. Her sandals flapped against the paving stones. She thought about what Jeff Turner had said, about most of the planet's surface being covered by water. *We think of ourselves as the real world, but really we're just outposts, just colonies*, she thought. *We don't know anything.*

She imagined the main street of the town inundated, the rusted flanks of cars encrusted with barnacles, the sunlit courtyards behind the cottages a playground for wrasse and sand gobies.

Somewhere in the lower depths vast leviathans would grind through the murk, the stuff of terror and legend even for the sea people.

Here be dragons.

The moon was full and the tide was out. She had to walk a long way across the sand flats before she came to the sea. She took off her sandals and went in up to her knees, the wavelets licking her skin like the tongues of black hounds. The horizon was so wide she could not encompass it. It was a clear night. She was aware of herself, as never before, as a speck on the surface of a planet spinning in space.

She saw them coming towards her, first as flickers of movement then as dark shapes, then as the muscular bodies of swimming women. They were the woman from the Lobster Pot and the one from the jetty who resembled her so closely. Their hair was down, floating behind them in the water like black seaweed. Their shoulders flashed white in the moonlight and Christine saw that they were both naked.

She slipped off her dress. It blew away from her and landed in the water. The salt, night air flowed in under her arms, seeming to bear her upwards, although Christine supposed that was mostly the rocking movement of the waves. She leaned forward in the water, letting the sea cover her shoulders and back. For a moment she felt its chill, but only for a moment. She let her feet rise up from the sand and she was swimming.

My God, how I've missed this, she thought. She swept her arms through the water, propelling herself forward. She had never swum naked before. The sea invaded her body, persuasive and irresistible, her secret lover.

Soon she came abreast of the two women. She thought they might all go back to shore together, but they moved in to swim either side of her, urging her onward and at the same time cutting off her retreat. The younger girl had a cut beneath her right eye, as if something in the water had tried to go for her. The injury didn't seem to bother her. She kicked out playfully, sending a splash of water over Christine's head.

"You need to get under," she said. "It's not real until you go beneath." She put out a hand, squeezing Christine's upper arm and tugging it downwards slightly as if in an attempt to submerge her. Christine felt panic nibbling at her insides like the mouthing, biting motions of tiny fish. She wondered what she was doing there, if any of this was even remotely real.

"I can't," Christine said. "I won't be able to breathe."

"You will though," said the pub woman. "It's a matter of faith, that's all." There were shells in her hair, large cockles, and to Christine she seemed both kinder and more patient than her daughter.

It's because she knows what it's like, Christine thought. *She knows what it's like to have made mistakes and not have a clue how to undo them.*

"I'm scared," Christine said. "How will I know what to do?"

"Just remember who you are, and do what comes naturally. Remember how beautifully you can swim."

Like a fish, Christine thought, and dived down.

THINGS THAT ARE HERE NOW, THINGS THAT WERE THERE THEN

Andrew Hook

Fractured glass sparkles rainbow rays in the sunset, mirrored by surface oil in the puddle where a rusted bicycle is reflected at angles. Rust flakes lift and blow in the wind, thin metallic leaves; pseudo-papery fans which sooth no one. Nearby, crow picks at the ground desultorily. Neither expecting anything nor nothing.

From overhead the wingspan of a plane projects a moving cross on the rough ground, a chemtrail easing from its rear like trailing fish excrement. Once it passes, the shadow is replaced by lengthier ones of approaching evening. To the right of crow a flower, which once pushed itself out of the ground, catches the dying light of the sun, and drinks it in, stores it, anticipating the advent of yet another day. A day which never comes.

Constance always woke with the word *no* in her mouth, a password from dream into awakening. I watched her from the edge of the bed as the sunrise pulled objects from shadows like a magician's reveal. The pine wooden bedroom furniture, the black anglepoise lamp – bent like a tall old man, the hairbrush filled with cement, the television that showed only a film of dust.

If the sun was the magician, Constance was the glamorous assistant. Her natural blond hair fanned across the pillows like fibre optics, her lips a pale smudge on her mouth, her nose a tiny reminder of olfactory memories. She shifted in the bedclothes, reached for me.

I remained quiet. Perhaps she couldn't see me.

Beside her on the bed woke the shadows of the past.

I glanced around the room. Objects which were once here were no longer. Objects which had never been here now were.

Constance had moved with the times. I had moved in.

She blinked. "Did I say it?"

I nodded. "You always say it."

"I saw crow."

"You think you saw crow," I said. "But even in a dream you don't really see."

She rubbed her eyes half-heartedly, resisted awakening. "So you say."

"So I say," I agreed. Then I reached over and pulled back the bedclothes, revealed nakedness.

Later that morning we exchanged soft kisses tasting of milk. Constance photographed her breakfast both before and after she ate. I took a photograph of her spooning cornflakes into her mouth. She always took more pictures than me.

Outside, shotgun-shattered bullets of rain smashed against the windowsill. A summer storm. We had turned off all the electrical items as the skies darkened. Lightning split the clouds like a rip in a dark pillowcase, revealing white feathers. Constance froze for a moment, as if the flash of lightning preceded a photographic shot: as though she posed. To an onlooker, at least, this is what they would have seen. But I saw beyond it. I saw the feathers and the memory.

Constance was an artist, and like all artists her belief in herself was stronger than she was. But this was an integral facet of her artistry because without that belief she would be a checkout girl, an usherette, a baker. Her art came out of herself like sunlight: pure. Yet also erratic. Anything which passed in front of her cast a shadow. And it was in the shadows that the weird stuff was born. The cement-filled hairbrush, the upside-down floorboard halfway up the stairs, the childhood photographs with her own face scratched out and then drawn back in. Those elements of Constance represented her dark side, and whilst she didn't know as much I was here to cure it.

For eight months she had photographed her every waking task. Finding it insufficient, two months ago she hired me to photograph her in sleep. This proved impossible without falling in love with her, and the romantic artist inside herself realised that it was impossible without falling in love with me.

The difference between us was that her love was a falsehood based on a belief in the purity of art. Whereas mine... Well, mine was also a falsehood, a temporary aberration.

The photographs were all Polaroids. Constance disliked permanence yet craved it. One copy. This was her compromise. Some of them filled shoeboxes, others Lever Arch files. Those which depicted places within her house were pinned to the walls with interconnected photo clips. We were living inside a house inside a house. Each of the four walls of each of the rooms was wrapped as though from the inside out in photos representing what had been and what no longer was. Imagine, if you will, living inside a memory. Objects changed, but the photographs remained the same.

This was all very well. Until the arrival of crow.

"A crow, you say?"

She shrugged. "What do I know about birds? It's black, has thick wings, a beak, speckles on its feathers like oil on water. I'm not an ornithologist."

"Maybe it's a starling?"

She looked puzzled; a frown creased her brow as though drawing a line under her blond fringe.

"Or simply a blackbird," I ventured.

"No," she said. "It's a crow. And if it isn't, then I want it to be."

Artists always wanted to find significance in everything.

I was the first to tell her that she woke every morning with the word *no* in her mouth.

"Really?" Her eyes were wide, like gobstoppers painted with

blue circles.

"Really. It's a reaching out for something. Or, it looks that way."

"Does it worry you?"

I could tell that she wanted it to worry me.

"No, it doesn't worry me," I said. "Has no one told you this before?" I wasn't naïve enough to believe that she had never slept with anyone.

"No," she said. "Maybe it's you."

I thought about that. "Maybe," I said.

That morning she pulled the covers away from me. My foreskin was shrivelled around the head of my penis and she laughed.

"It looks like a walnut whip."

Then she photographed it.

One day she went shopping and I searched for a box of photographs that I knew would exist and which I eventually found under the bed, like a schoolboy's stash of pornography. They were unclear. Body parts captured too close to the skin to identify an owner or owners. I put them back carefully and decided not to think about them ever again.

But if Constance had a secret then I also had a secret. I was not who I pretended to be.

Down in the dirt, right at ground level, the twisted spokes of the bicycle spoke volumes about evolution.

Crow alighted on the upended wheel. Its weight shifted the balance. The world turned.

Flowers budded yellow and orange, forcing their way like slo-mo time lapse photography, giving the illusion of speed yet stasis simultaneously. The sun arced across the sky, gave way to night and returned again, repeatedly.

Planes flew backwards across the sky.

A day which repeatedly came, reversed, came again.

If crow could smile, it did.

"What are you studying?"

Constance slipped behind me, one hand snaking around my waist, the other holding her camera.

"Analytical chemistry."

She feigned a yawn, then yawned anyway, setting herself off. "Boring."

"To some, maybe."

She took a photo of my hand on the page. I was lying face down on the carpet in the living room. I say *carpet*, but in reality I was lying on photographs of the carpet. Constance reached past me and placed the slowly developing photograph on the floor, stapled it through the carpet and onto the floorboard as the picture of my hand and the book came into focus.

"Read to me," she said.

I shrugged. "It won't interest you."

"It doesn't have to interest me," she said. "Read to me."

So I read: *In analytical chemistry, dark current refers to the constant response produced by a spectrochemical receptor, even in the absence of radiation. Dealing with dark current is a form of blank correction.*

"That *is* boring," she said. She yawned and the flash of the camera captured the inside of her mouth. "What's *blank correction*?"

"Blank correction," I said, "like everything else in the world, is whatever you want it to be."

She moved her snaked-arm away from me. "Blank correction," she repeated. "I like the sound of that."

I closed the book. I understood none of it other than that the seed had to be planted. Dark current was an absence corrected by a blank. A nihilist would have loved it. For Constance, it would be the first step to regaining some sanity.

When I first moved into the apartment, on Constance's insistence, I was bowled over by the sheer amount of photographic evidence of her life. In the bathroom, behind her toothbrush and toothpaste, were several photographs of her toothbrush and toothpaste. The bathroom mirror was almost totally obscured by her reflected face. Within days, mine joined hers. The small cupboard under the stairs which she used as a library was like a forest of books. In reality, there were only two shelves, but a series of photographs and mirrors turned it into a literary labyrinth. I would reach for a book to find myself reaching for my own hand, in a corner where nothing was real.

"Is this natural?" I asked.

"It is if I want it to be," she said.

"Do you exhibit?"

The answer was coy, revealed nothing: "Doesn't everyone?"

Much later - weeks later - after she had told me her dream of crow - of something she had no control over and could never photograph - I asked: "Do you think he knows about you?"

"Of course!"

I turned on my side, regarded the corner of the bedroom ceiling which was but a photograph of the corner of the bedroom ceiling. "Do you think he knows about me?"

There was no response. Only another photograph. Myself caught with sleep at the corner of my eye, a gritty memory, the dirt of a dream.

I did some research. To dream of a crow might signify completion of a successful business, but to dream of one flying in cloudy weather denoted anger, loss and misery. Seeing a blackbird meant great trouble, although to hear one sing signified joy and delight. And the starling, well, that was only a small discontent. Clearly there was a hierarchy in dream birds. I needed to find out exactly the type of bird, and in doing that there was only one option: to go inside.

Nowhere to hide, nowhere to run.

Never trust a stranger.

Following the advent of crow I bided my time and waited for the right moment. We stayed up late one evening, watching Coen Brothers movies one after the other. She fell asleep, almost unforgivably, during *The Big Lebowski*. After thirty minutes I turned off the DVD, dimmed the lights, then woke her with kisses.

One to the back of her neck, one to her belly, one to her knee, one to the inside of her forearm.

She stirred, woke, the word *no* caught in her mouth and turned to a moan: I had the password. I parted her legs and moved my body across hers, finding no resistance as I eased my way inside her. She invited me in semi-sleep mode, a curling smile on her face, reflected in several of the photographs which adorned the headboard. And then, unlike the other times we had made love, I did something a little different.

I pulled myself onto her, pulled myself against her. Knee bone connected to knee bone, hip bone connected to hip bone, jaw bone connected to jaw bone. Our internal organs touched and merged. I became inside her.

And I sought out the dream.

Half-concealed in mud, half-congealed in dirt, the metallic shopping trolley stands like a reticent sculpture.

I photo it.

Picking my way across the desolate landscape I capture the images of cans, their metal lids hanging by slivers of tin like robot ballerinas in music boxes. Reddish-brown bricks stand at all angles, lying where they have fallen. Broken glass reflects the light of the flash in this dim setting, a signal to find me should anyone be looking. Crisp packets hold water like bloated frogs. A blue Frisbee, upturned, becomes a bird bath. And it is there that I wait. And sure enough, there's a sound in the air like a thousand feathers falling and after a moment the bird that is black is perched on the rim of the Frisbee, its weight tipping the water towards itself.

It drinks. And from behind the oil drum I take a photo.

Constance gasps and I push myself out of the dream and out of her body. The sheets are soaked with blood.

Only the sheets aren't soaked with blood because this is now my dream, and in that dream I wait for the photograph to develop whilst searching through my *Book of British Birds*. Soon, there is a match. I can barely look.

Elsewhere I could have read: *Dark currents within a photosensitive device are reduced through improved implantation of a species during its fabrication.*

No, I don't understand; but Constance is perfectly correct. As an artist she is completely aware that the world and its meanings can be exactly what anyone wants them to be. And through a positive negation of negative behaviour I can cure her compulsiveness and turn it around.

So I show Constance the photograph and explain that this is a starling and she takes my knowledge as read and she never sees it again.

Sometimes things are as simple as that.

Although crow won't be happy.

There are side effects. She never again says *no* when she wakes.

I know this, although I am no longer there to hear it. Yet *her* knowledge is only imparted in *my* dream.

Before she woke I removed all of the photographs from each and every surface. A blank correction. And in removing the photographs I removed the wallpaper and the bricks and the hidden electricity and the floorboards and the plaster, and each and every item that had ever had any relevance or pseudo-relevance in the life of the artist formerly known as Constance.

She wakes within a white box. A blank canvas. The things that were there then are not there now.

It's what she should have wanted.

And then – because I just cannot resist – I leave a black feather on her pillow: negating the negation.

Within the vestiges of her memory I am the trickster.

LOOSE CONNECTIONS

Finn Clarke

"Did you go to the clinic?"

"Damn." Jess dumped the groceries on the kitchen counter. "Forgot."

"I thought you were going at lunch time?"

"I was. Only Cartland wanted the marketing figures for the end of month and before I knew it – well, you know how it is."

Tom smiled; he knew how it was with Jess. He came forward to help with the shopping.

"Blimey." Jess looked at him properly. "What happened to you?"

"Uppity patient." Tom touched his bruised cheek gently. "We're doing the high-level DCs this week and one of them objected. My fault. I wasn't on the ball."

"Never a dull day for a psychiatric nurse. Do you want me to put some witch hazel on that?"

"No, I'm fine, thanks. So what are you going to do about clinic?"

"No problem." Jess began unloading the food. "I'll go next week."

"Next week's May."

"So?"

"So, you didn't go in March. That already puts you at a level two. If you miss April…"

"Fuck." Jess stopped unpacking.

"And three –"

"Three strikes and I'm off to the unit, I know. Jesus, Tom."

Jess let out a long slow breath. "How did that happen?"

"Well, it's probably something to do with the fact that you're scatty, disorganised, and have an unhealthy attitude to authority."

"You know that's eerily similar to what Cartland said when I complained about missing lunch for his bloody stats."

"Harsh, but true. Unlike Cartland, however, I have a solution."

"You do?" Jess's eyes lit up with hope. "I know I shouldn't have put it off, Tom. It's just that a level two seems so…"

"Heavy. I know. Still, better than a level three. And if you get your act together you can come with me tonight. I'm driving over to the Greater Hampton clinic then meeting Carla for a drink."

"Tom." Jess put her palms together in front of her chest and bowed. "That would be…"

"Wonderful, I know." He suppressed another smile and glanced at his watch. "We're leaving in thirty minutes."

"Thank you." Jess walked forward and kissed him on his good cheek. "You're a star, you know? Totally wasted on Carla. Too bad we don't fancy each other or I'd grab you for myself."

Tom turned away and investigated the shopping. "Too bad, indeed," he said, his back to her. "Now go and get ready while I put this away, because I'm not going to wait if you're late."

It was still daylight when they got there, an evening softness soaking in from the west, clouds rolling back for a clear night. St John's Ambulance had taken over the village church, long since converted to a community space, their black and white logo on either side of a broad black banner that stretched out above its double doors. *Dark Currents*, it said, a jagged lightning fork zapping through the large yellow letters, *Keeping Your Crime At Bay.*

Beneath it, an unkempt chubby man with a wispy beard was handing out flyers.

"Freedom for the waiver signers," he muttered, thrusting

one into Jess's hand. "Say no to the Illegal Immigrant Act. See justice done at last."

"Thanks." Jess folded the flyer, put it in her pocket and made to carry on, but Tom stopped.

"Have you got a petition?" he asked.

"Um..." The man looked uncertain.

"Or a website?"

"Website, yes." The man nodded without conviction. Tom sighed.

"Try and get a website together," he said. "And a petition. They'll really help."

The man nodded some more, staring at him until Tom turned away.

"I thought you weren't allowed to sign petitions," Jess said. "Public servant and all."

"I'm not allowed to do a lot of things," Tom said. "Doesn't mean others can't do them."

"Tom the rebel," Jess said in solemn tones, documentary-style. "The real man behind the establishment façade."

Tom rolled his eyes, pulled open one of the heavy oak doors, and entered.

Inside, a trestle table had been set up in the antechamber, its long stretch blocking the doorway into the main hall. Behind it, two clerks were manning the computers. Opposite, an ancient stone wall was lined with plastic chairs for people to wait in, nearly all full. Jess went to sit at the end of the line, picking up a leaflet the previous occupant had left behind.

"Should have brought a book," Tom said, looking at the queue.

"Here." She handed him the leaflet. "You can read us today's options."

Tom unfolded it and looked at the middle section, where different levels were set out like a menu.

"Okay," he said, starting at the top, "0.5s. This week's varied DC selection includes speeding – 42 in a 30 zone; fly-tipping;

failure to carry an ID card –"

"Always the same old options," Jess interrupted. "When are they going to get some new ones?"

"Soon, according to this," the woman on her other side answered. Large, middle-aged, with two shopping bags between her legs and the face of someone eager to talk, she unfolded her Daily Mail and pointed to the headlines: *Illegal Immigrants to Boost DC Dummy Numbers.* "Now they're cracking down on the foreigners, it says, dummy shortages will soon be a thing of the past. About time too. Not that I'd DC a foreigner, of course, but it's only fair they get their just desserts."

"Hmm." Turning back to Tom, Jess took the leaflet from him and buried her head in it, hoping the woman would take the hint. On the back was the usual spiel about DC.

Everyone has a dark side, it stated, *and since we discovered how to unleash this vicariously in a safe environment, UK crime has dropped by an amazing 92%. DCT, or Dark Current Therapy as it was originally called, grew out of developments in EST (Electric Sensory Therapy) designed to treat a range of mental health problems. Initially, this comprised electro-stimulation packages such as voices for schizophrenics, ordering them not to listen to any internal voice but that one; relaxation packages that engendered scenarios of sun and waves; phobic packages, such as the immensely popular arachNOphobia, inputting a range of basic spider confrontations whilst controlling fear levels; and so on. As technology evolved and bespoke packages became cost-efficient, however, experts began looking into how a variation of EST might be used to tackle our spiralling crime levels – and DCT was born. From the initial trials, allowing a criminal to provide dummy experiences of their crime in return for a reduced sentence, DCT has grown over the last decade to become the crime-fighting tool of the millennium. Channelling latent dark currents into vicarious action so they cannot spill over into everyday life, the –*

"Your turn." Tom gave her a nudge.

Jess looked up. Behind the trestle table, an ageing woman in an acrylic turquoise trouser suit was smiling at her.

"Next please," she repeated.

Fighting the temptation to cut and run, Jess walked over.

"Name, dear?"

"Jess Reardon."

"Thank you." She clicked the mouse and peered at her monitor, turquoise earrings dangling. "Level two, right?"

"Yes." Jess cleared her throat. "I'll take the identity theft, please."

"Identity…" The woman clicked again. "Oh." She looked up. "I'm sorry, the identity theft's not working tonight. Apparently the hall doesn't have enough power to run all the dummies. That leaves assault or… oh. The drunk driver's just been signed up." She glanced at a young man heading into the main hall. "You could wait if you want to – about 30 minutes for a level two."

Jess toyed with the idea. She could make her own way to the pub – but then there'd be no Tom for moral support. And drunk-driving scenarios weren't necessarily better, given some of the crashes. She'd be sensible, probably, to bite the bullet. With a sigh she handed over her DC card, took the assault printout and then, with a final glance at Tom, walked into the hall.

Once there, she stopped to get her bearings. Cubicles had been set up around three sides, their curtains drawn to give privacy to those inside. Above them, the evening light shone through the high stained windows, slanting different colours across the wooden floor to give the room a cheerful, friendly air. Beside her, on a table by the door, a monitor gave the booth numbers for each crime: assault was at the far end. Taking a deep breath she started down, past the gentle hum of machines and hidden people talking in murmurs, to booth number eight.

The nurse waiting for her was a skinny, middle-aged man, his white uniform hanging loose off his narrow shoulders, smudges of dirt on the knees of his trousers as though he'd been crawling on the floor. He looked preoccupied.

"Right then Ms –" and he glanced at his monitor, "Reardon. If I could just check your papers."

Jess handed them over and looked around the booth while he studied her DC card, finding herself calmed by the familiar surroundings. The dummy on its gurney next to the cot she'd use, the tangle of wires and leads around the metal box behind them, the console and split monitor with its two sets of green lines – all were just the same as for a 0.5. Perhaps, she told herself, this wouldn't be as bad as she feared.

The feeling was heightened when the nurse pulled the sheet off the dummy to reveal a young woman, early-twenties at most, looking small and vulnerable in her hospital gown.

"That's my assault?" Relief surged through her. Surely such an elfin type couldn't be too vicious.

"So they say." The nurse flicked a few switches, stared at the monitor, muttered under his breath then pressed a button. The booth light flickered, failed for a second then brightened again as a loud hum cut the air.

Jess frowned. "What was that?"

"Church hall electrics." He shook his head. "These old buildings aren't up to the energy needed. Especially not at the end of the month rush – hence the back-up generator." He nodded to leads trailing on the floor out the back of the cubicle. "Don't worry, it's completely safe. I've double-looped everything." He unconsciously brushed the knees of his trousers. Then he adjusted a few dials and pulled the first wire over to Jess. "So, if you're ready..."

Jess moved slowly over to the cot. Ready was a relative word. But the sooner she started, the sooner it'd be over and she lay still, trying not to flinch as he wired her up.

"Done," he said, all too quickly. "Okay?".

Jess took a deep breath and let it out slowly.

"Okay," she said.

The nurse nodded, went back to the console, flicked a switch, and everything went black.

She couldn't move. She couldn't breathe. Her heart was

pounding, trapped in her rib cage just as she was trapped in this… what? Where was she? What was happening? If only she could remember. But her memories were fading, drowned out by that one panoramic recollection she was forced to relive again and again.

"Help me." Who said that? Did she say that? "Help me. Please. My name is Leena Jones. I was convicted in –"

She convulsed, a spasm that forced her body from the cot, high into the air, bursting her bonds, the darkness and her tired, frightened heart, sending her flying into …

… music. Oh boy, what music. She could feel the beat inside her, pulsing through her heart, hearting through her pulse... Jesus, she was drunk. Not too drunk to dance though. Not too drunk to have a good time. The floor was crowded, bodies bumping against each other, sometimes intentional, sometimes not, angles of flesh lit up then lost again as the strobe circled. It was like being in a kaleidoscope, patterns shifting and forming, colours changing from green to red to blue, coming together and falling apart, everything merging.

She stumbled, caught her balance and turned it into a move, spinning round, spreading out her arms, jerking her hips, forcing her mouth into the wide smile she was determined to wear. When she was steady again she turned to the guy she'd bumped into, hoping for a little flirt, a little of that good time she'd come out for – but as she moved the crowed shifted, clearing her view to the bar, and she saw Mick. Correction. She saw Mick and Kelly. Together. Kissing.

The pulse that surged through her blood had nothing to do with music. Fake good time forgotten, she elbowed her way to the bar.

"Cunt," she said. The music was so loud it was unlikely Kelly heard her, but there were other ways to get her attention. Grabbing Kelly's hair, Leena jerked her head back so that Kelly's hands came up in defence, knocking over her cocktail.

Mick looked up.

"Leena?" he said, as though surprised. As though it hadn't occurred to him that she'd be here.

"Remember me?" Leena spat, a gob of saliva landing on his cheek, then jerked Kelly's hair again. Kelly started screeching, squeals of pain and fear cutting through the air as the music stopped.

"Shut up," Leena snapped with another pull. Kelly screeched some more. "I said shut up, you fucking bitch." This time she pulled so hard a tuft came out, globules of blood and skin sticking to the roots. Putting her hands to her scalp, Kelly whimpered, then slumped forward onto the bar.

In the resulting silence Leena heard a footstep behind her and glimpsed the bouncer from the corner of her eye. Darting forward, she dodged his arms and threw herself onto Mick, fingers aiming for his face while her knee sunk satisfyingly into his groin. He went white as he doubled up into her hands, making a little noise, half-sigh, half-groan.

"Bastard," she hissed, digging her nails into his cheeks. "I should hack your willy off, you two-timing *shit*."

Arms grabbed her wrists, pulled her fingers from his face, twisted one arm behind her back. Struggling, she kicked out, but the bouncer pulled her away.

"That's enough now, miss," he said.

"No it's not." She looked round the room. Everyone was staring at her. "He got me pregnant," she told them. "He knocked me up then ditched me for that –"

"Come on now, miss." The bouncer's voice was calm, but his hold was firm. He started to walk her to the exit.

"I thought he loved me," she told the room. But the room didn't answer, just shifted, uneasy and silent. Well fuck them. Twisting her head, she looked back to where Mick was still curled around his balls. "I thought you loved me," she told him, her voice breaking. "But all you wanted was a goodtime girl. Well, are you having a good time now? Are you?"

The bouncer jerked her towards the door, one arm circling

tightly around her chest until she could hardly breathe, his right leg curling round hers to hold her against his body, his other hand pulling at her hair, little stabs of pain like electric shocks zapping through her skull. Then someone turned the lights out and she was suddenly scared.

"Help me." It came out a whisper. She wet her lips and tried again. "Help, please. Help me." But the pressure got tighter and the darkness turned thick and black like the depths of a cave. "Hel-"

"Hello." It was the nurse, his face hovering upside down over hers, his forehead creased with something like worry. "All done."

"Ri-ight." Jess's voice was croaky, as if she'd been screaming. She swallowed, tried again. "Good."

"Okay?" He turned as he spoke, busy at the console.

"No," she said. "It was horrible."

He frowned, though whether in annoyance or concern she couldn't tell. On the monitor two sets of lines stabbed wildly. He turned a dial and one side settled down to a regular rhythm, while the other continued to jerk then, as he pressed another switch, faded to a steady horizontal line. He grunted, satisfied, then came over to remove the electrodes.

"A good reason for sticking to the 0.5s," he suggested.

"I'll say." Jess sat up to undo her ankle straps, but stopped only halfway. She felt as if she'd been in the fight itself, not just its currents.

"Is this normal?" she asked.

"Huh?" The nurse was already sterilising the clips, preparing for the next client.

"To feel this shitty? I never felt like this after DCing a parking ticket."

He looked over at her. "Probably just hypersensitivity," he told her, coming back to free her ankles. "Your potassium and sodium levels were fine. Stay off the booze and if you still feel bad in a day or two, come in for a check up."

"That famous DC Service," Jess muttered, easing her legs onto the floor. "Never fix today what you can put off till tomorrow."

"Pardon?"

"I said the tea and biscuits will sort me out." Never piss off the man with the electrodes. Pulling her clothes straight, Jess headed for the door and freedom. Stay off the booze be damned – the way she felt right now, a few stiff drinks were exactly what she needed.

Carla was waiting at the pub, a half-empty wine glass showing she'd been there a while.

"Sorry." Tom leant down to kiss her. "End of month rush at the clinic, you know how it is."

Carla rolled her dark eyes.

"No I don't," she said. "I never leave it so late. I am organised." Her glance slid from Tom to Jess, as though she knew precisely where the fault lay. "So," she continued, "how did it go?"

"Quite an adventure actually." Tom slid in beside her. "We had to push through a blockade of protesters."

Jess opened her mouth, but Tom glared at her and she closed it again. She remembered the flyer in her jeans.

"Protestors?" Carla perked up, scenting a story. "Tell me more."

"'Freedom for Waiver Signers,'" Jess read, pulling out the paper. "'Say no to the IIA.'" She frowned and threw it on the table. "Clear as mud. Who are the Waiver Signers anyway?"

She'd aimed the question at Tom, but Carla surprised her. "The waiver signers," she said, "are the people who signed a DC waiver – mainly the originals."

"Originals?"

"When DCs first started." Carla sat forward, enjoying knowing more than Jess. "In those days the dummies were volunteers – mostly people who had no one to go back to –

tramps, abused kids, druggies, ex-army, you know the type. They were given the option to sign a waiver – *for as long as required,* was the phrase used. I did an article on it when the Illegal Immigrant Act first came up. Either do your official time then be released to a responsible person for your probation, or stay a dummy for as long as required, with financial compensation for every year over your official sentence. Of course, in those days no one knew how successful DC would turn out to be – that decreasing crime meant increasingly fewer dummies, so that 'for as long as required' would turn out to be much longer than anyone had ever intended."

"You mean they're still dummies? All these years on?"

Carla looked uncertain. Tom took over.

"Those who are still operational." He made a face. "The problem from the government's point of view is that they're starting to burn out – you could see that in the guy handing out the flyers."

"Jesus." Jess shook her head. From anyone else she'd have dismissed this as exaggeration, but Tom was well placed to know.

"I don't understand the neuroscience," he continued, "but at the hospital we call it loose connections. Their scenarios start to leak into the system – along with some of their cognitive functions. Overuse, I suppose, like with the old standard EST packages. They end up the equivalent of those movie videos that went all crackly over time." He took a sip of his beer. "In a small controlled environment like ours, there's no real danger. Any hint of electrical contamination and we do a mild wipe – hell – I've had two myself this year – but imagine if that started happening in the general population?"

"Hence the rush to get through the new Illegal Immigrant Act?"

Tom nodded. "They're phasing the dummies out as they corrupt, but if the government released them all now they'd owe them a fortune in compensation. Far better, from their perspective, to let them quietly fade away until they're too brain damaged to cause any trouble. Especially if they can start using foreign criminals to replace the originals."

"But that – that's…" For once Jess was lost for words. "How can they get away with it?"

"No one cares," Carla said simply. "Why would they? I mean, these people were friendless even before they became criminals. Who'd give a toss about them now?"

Jess thought about it. "So they're fucked," she said.

Carla frowned; she didn't like bad language. She turned to Tom. "And that's your protest? A few burnt-out anti-waver signers?" She sighed. "I suppose it might make page eight."

Jess felt a wave of distaste rise in her throat, an urge to shake Carla's complacency out of her. She should try being a clinic dummy, see what it felt like to be zapped and zapped then left to rot… The thought surprised her – she wasn't normally vengeful – and lifting her glass to break the mood, she discovered it was empty. She waved it in front of the others.

"My round. Same again?"

Tom shook his head and lifted a nearly full pint. "I'm driving."

"Please." Carla smiled perfunctorily and turned to Tom. "Now, wait until you hear my news. A maisonette's just come up on the market…"

Jess escaped. If Carla was in her 'let's move in together' mood, the conversation would go downhill from here on in. She knew what Tom saw in her of course – the woman was stunning. And she guessed he liked her controlling manner and the clear, precise structure she gave him after a chaotic day at the madhouse – but personally it got right up her nose.

"I've bumped into some old mates," she invented when she brought Carla's wine over. "If you don't mind, I'll just go and sit outside with them for a bit."

"No problem," Carla said.

"Do they want to join us?" Tom asked at the same time. The couple looked at each other. Tom smiled and shrugged.

"See you later then," he said. "Have fun."

Jess took her bottle of Leffe out to the beer garden and sat next to the stream that separated it from the rest of the village. Taking a long swig of beer she felt herself relax for the first time that day. This was more like it. She gazed at the stream unseeing, absorbing its gentle gurgling, and told herself that after this drink she would go back inside, be sociable. She didn't feel like it though. She felt wiped out, physically exhausted, as though she'd literally been dancing and fighting the night away. What she actually wanted to do, she decided, draining half her bottle, was stay out here in the evening calm and get pissed out of her mind.

When the cold drove her in an hour later her head was thick with the combination of alcohol and residual DCs, the floor unsteady beneath her feet. She stopped at the entrance to the public bar, holding tight to the door frame in case it tried to move away from her, and looked around. The place was packed now, a popular country pub on a balmy Friday night, the area around the bar heaving with people, colourful and vibrant in their spring clothes. It was like being in a kaleidoscope, Jess thought, patterns shifting and forming, colours changing from green to red to blue, coming together and falling apart, everything merging…

"Have they gone?"

"Huh?" She looked around. Tom was squeezing through the crowd to her side.

"Your friends. I don't want to spoil your fun, but I'm on early shift tomorrow. Five am start."

"Sure. Right." She stood a little straighter and let go of the door jamb. The world lurched. Tom grabbed her.

"You're drunk," he said. "Jesus, Jess, you know you shouldn't drink after clinic. You're such an idiot." He said it kindly though and took her arm. "Come on, let's get you to the car."

They were in the car park when it happened, Jess sandwiched between Carla and Tom at the far end as a car turned on its headlights. The beam shone into Jess's face, dazzling her like the glinting of a strobe, and for a second everything went dark except for the jagged light in her eyes. A pulse started beating in her ears, rage coursing through her body, and when Carla stumbled in her high heels, knocking against Jess, Jess pushed back as hard as she could.

"Cunt," she hissed. "Fucking bitch."

For an instant Carla's face was caught in the headlight, her mouth a wide O of surprise, then darkness flowed in as Tom got between them.

"Hey, cool it. It was an accident, Jess."

"An accident," Jess spat. "An accident." She pushed Tom in the chest, making him stagger backwards. "You two-timing shit. I'm *pregnant* with *your baby*, and you call it a fucking *accident*. Well, I'll show you an accident."

Turning back to Carla, she pushed her into the wall, wrapped her fingers in Carla's long black hair, and smashed her head against the bricks. Carla gave a little grunt, sagging as her legs gave under her, and Jess tensed to do it again – then stopped, her hands rising into the air, her body jerking uncontrollably before she fell unconscious to the ground.

Everything was dark and still and hard. She hurt, but when she tried to see what was wrong, she couldn't move. Then she heard a faint sizzling noise, a hissing with louder crackles accompanied by a blue-white light, far away, but closing quickly, spreading out like a wave hurtling towards her. She tensed for the hit, felt energy surge through her, light yet powerful, then relaxed. Bright colours flashed behind her eyes and in the distance she heard voices.

"…calling the police."

"No. She was drunk as a skunk. Disinhibited after a level two. You know what that can do."

"That was her choice –"

"Jess," a new voice said. Jess started: it was so close as to be almost in her ear. She tried to open her eyes, but couldn't see beyond the whirling colours.

"Jess," the voice said again. "Listen. We don't have much time."

Jess frowned in concentration, her head bleary with drink and pain. The voice was familiar.

"*Jess.* Concentrate, will you."

"OK," she said, though she wasn't sure her lips moved. "Who...?"

"It's Leena. Listen, you have to help us."

"Leena? But…" She was confused. That made no sense. "Where are you?"

"Inside you," Leena said. "I left some of my currents in your body. Only –"

"You *what*?"

"It's amazing." Leena's voice was rich with joy. "I couldn't get a lot through – just a quick leak into the wires during the outage – but then you got this surge of electricity, knocking out your system and magnifying mine so that…"

Jess stopped listening, trying to remember what had happened. She had a sense of rage coursing through her, of Carla cowering, of intense pain then – nothing…

"Tom must have used his Taser," she said.

"Well that's worth knowing." And Jess could feel Leena take the knowledge and flow it through her system, the electricity sparking and jumping. "Now, what you must do is –"

There was a flash behind her eyes, a sizzling sound and a smell of burning.

"Shit." Leena's voice turned faint and crackly, like a badly tuned radio. "No," she said.

Jess felt sick. She spasmed, limbs tensing against rough tarmac, and fought to breathe.

"Help me," Leena said. "Please. You have to DC a higher level. Get up to Danny Monroe. DC Danny Monroe. He'll tell you what to do next."

The static was worse now, almost drowning her out, and when Leena's voice came again it was small and desperate.

"Help us," she said. "Please. Help us with Danny Monroe." Then there was another spark, like the zap of an insect killer, and everything went dark. Slowly other voices, normal, distant and angry, phased in.

"She committed a crime," Carla said. "A full-on level two assault. And I'm the victim. So why the hell shouldn't I report her?"

"She wasn't herself," Tom replied. "Jess hasn't got a violent bone in her body. I don't know what's going on, but –"

"Well I do," Carla cut in. "I know exactly what's going on." She paused and when she spoke again her voice shook. "You prefer her to me, that's what's going on. You'd rather see her get away with a crime than see justice for your *girlfriend*."

"Carla –"

"I've always suspected it," she continued. "All those reasons why you couldn't come out at night, tired after a hard day's work –"

"I *was* tired. I work five am shifts, goddam it –"

"But now I've got the proof. Well, if she's what you want then you can have her. You can have each other – two DC dummies together – level two assault and illegal use of a Taser, that should help boost the numbers, eh? Maybe if you're lucky, you can even get booths side by side."

There was a silence then, a dark falling hole of no return, broken by the distant sound of laughter from the pub.

"I'm sorry, Tom," Carla said quickly. "I didn't mean –"

"Goodbye," Tom said.

"What?"

"I'll take my house key before you go. You won't be needing it again."

"No Tom, please…" Carla trailed off. When she spoke again, her voice was cold and vicious. "You'd do anything for her, wouldn't you? That manipulative, scheming bitch has got you in the palm of her hands –"

"I said goodbye." Tom's voice was resolute.

After Carla's footsteps had faded into the distance, Jess tried to move. Nausea flooded through her and she groaned.

"Jess?" She felt Tom crouch down beside her, his hands round her shoulders, supporting her as she tried to sit up. "Jesus, Jess, I'm sorry – but what the hell were you doing?"

Jess sat up, breathed deeply a few times, then opened her eyes. Tom was in front of her, his face worried and searching.

"Are you okay?"

She tried to laugh it off, gagged instead, then shuddered, suddenly very cold.

"I don't know" she said.

"We need to take you to a hospital."

"No." Panic rolled through her, though she wasn't sure why. "I can't," she said. "I mustn't. It's not me who needs help Tom, it's her."

Tom frowned. "Carla doesn't need your help, you can be sure of that. More like the other way round. She's got every right to press charges, you know – and the way she's feeling right now…"

"Not Carla." Jess shook her head impatiently, then regretted doing so as the world spun. "Leena. The waiver signers. They're – " She stopped. The frown on Tom's face was increasing, shaded with concern.

"Leena?" he asked.

"My dummy." Warning feelings told Jess to stop right there. "I mean, what you said in the pub," she continued. "It's awful. We have to try and help them."

"We do." Tom didn't move though, didn't stop looking at her with an expression she didn't quite like. "It's true a hospital will give Carla ammunition though," he said after a moment. "If we go to Daventon Central this whole thing will come out."

"Agreed." Jess nodded gingerly. "No hospital then."

"No public hospital," Tom amended. He grinned. "I could

take you to work though – give you a mild wipe there. If we get your currents back on an even keel you're away – all evidence erased. You'll be back to your normal self and Carla won't be able to prove a thing."

Another blast of panic surged through Jess so powerfully it was physical and she bent over as her stomach spasmed.

"It'll clear the effects of the Taser too," Tom told her. "You'll still have the entry marks for a few days, but a wipe will get rid of the stiffness and nausea, I promise." He glanced at his watch, then reached out to help her to her feet. "Come on. If we go now we'll hit the graveyard shift. I'll sign you in as a student helping sort the broken ESTs – we can pretend you got contaminated."

Jess accepted his hand and got up carefully. Her mind was all over the place, as though trying to go in two different directions at once: the mental equivalent of patting her head and circling her stomach at the same time. Part of her agreed whole-heartedly with the plan, was grateful for it, and was trying to remember how she'd got into this mess in the first place. But another part felt desperate, scared to the point of a cold courage that had nothing to lose, its intensity spilling over into everything else.

"Tom?" that part said, as he helped her into the car. "You have some pretty heavy-duty dummies in the secure unit, don't you?"

Since Tom's inmates weren't legally responsible for their crimes, they couldn't become dummies. Instead they used the high-level ones as part of their treatment, visiting them in the secure DC unit that had been purpose-built next door.

"Certainly do." Tom plugged his Taser in to recharge and slipped it into the cup-holder between their two seats. "Murderers, rapists, kidnappers, paedophiles – they're all levels five and six." He glanced at her before starting up. "But you don't need to worry. The wipe clinic's completely safe. Besides, we're not doing a dummy run until 7am – you'll be long gone by then."

Jess nodded then leant her head against the window as Tom began to drive through the country lanes back into town. Savouring the cold glass against her forehead, she watched the shades of darkness go by with unseeing eyes.

Help me, Leena had said. *DC a higher level.*

She turned back to Tom. "And those high-level DC dummies are moved around the country?" she asked. "So the inmates get variety? Just like us, only more gruesome?"

"They do." Tom glanced away from the road to look at her. "But there's nothing to worry about, honestly. It's just like a prison – people can get in easily enough, but it's a completely different ballgame getting out."

"Right." Half of Jess's head began to get its bearings. "What do you know," she asked, "about Danny Monroe?"

"Old Danny?" Tom's voice grew fond. "Best of a bad bunch, he is. He only ever kidnapped for money, you know – never hurt them. Once, even, when the ransom wasn't paid, he gave the kiddie back." He laughed. "Which was his downfall, of course. But compared to most of them, Danny's all right."

"He's there?" Jess was surprised at the excitement in her voice, the sudden surge of hope. "He's in your unit?"

"Oh Danny's a regular. We all want Danny, poor bugger. His 'as long as required' won't ever run out. And since Dr Parsons has more strings to pull than most in this business, our inmates get to DC him pretty often."

"How did he do it?" she asked. "The kidnaps?"

"No one knows." Tom took the turning into town, his face lit up by streetlamps as he drove through the suburbs. "Well, the police do, of course – they gave him a total EST – but they're not telling. Apart from that, only those who DC him will ever know."

"But he was good? Before he was caught? At getting people out?" Jess thought about it. "I mean, he made a career out of taking children from rich, paranoid people in ultra-secure buildings."

Tom shrugged. "Must have been. I mean, Jesus, he got Lord

Eston's son out of the Parliament crèche, and they don't come much more secure than that."

Jess nodded, her head clear now, her thoughts steady. It was all coming together.

"Here we are."

The hospital was an old Victorian job, red brick and high archways looking almost elegant behind the razor wire and cement outbuildings that had been added over the years. To its right was the secure DC unit, all modern reinforced concrete and smoked glass gleaming in the security lights. Tom drew to a halt outside the gates, put in his card and keyed in the code as Jess watched. Once he'd parked up though, after turning off the engine and headlights, he sat still, saying nothing. Then he turned to look at Jess.

"When you were unconscious," he said, "that is, when people are unconscious, hearing is the last thing to go. And Carla said some things… That is, I wonder if you heard what Carla said – implied – about me, and…"

He couldn't quite look her in the eye, and with another surge of clarity the other part of Jess's brain realised that what Carla had said was true. That Tom had always cared about her more than he'd let on, that what he was risking for her now was based on far more than his good nature. Her heart twisted as she realised what that meant and she opened her mouth to say something, to acknowledge it – then the desperation kicked back in, cold and steady.

"I didn't hear a thing," she said. "Apart from some buzzing." She shrugged, the same old oblivious Jess. "I must have been well and truly out of it."

"Right." Tom nodded slowly, his expression half-relieved, half-sorry, then he shook himself and reached for the door handle. "So. Ready to do this?"

"Ready as I'll ever be." Jess smiled, a weird, lopsided grin, then picked up the Taser from the cup-holder and zapped him just above the heart, holding it there until Tom slumped back into his seat, unconscious. Leaning over him, Jess smoothed the beads of sweat from his forehead, looked at him for a long moment, then kissed him gently on the lips.

"Sorry," she said.

She pocketed his security card and Taser, took a deep breath, and walked over to the secure unit.

SLEEPLESS IN R'LYEH

Lavie Tidhar

INT. TOM'S HOUSE – SEATTLE – DAY

In his house in dread Seattle Tom lies dreaming. The dreaming occurs nearly every night. Tom tries booze, then pills, but nothing seems to help. The dreams come despite all his best efforts at oblivion.

Tom was married once. His wife had blonde hair cut in a bob, and a cute nose, and a beautiful smile. Tom wishes he could say she had kept smiling but the truth is she stopped smiling around about the time she began losing her hair. It fell out in clumps and along with the hair and the smile she began to lose weight. Tom tries to remember the way her hair smelled, the shampoo she used; it had coconut oil in it, but all he can remember is the septic smell of the hospital room. He never really talks about this. He hates that it's such a common story. That everyone has someone who dies this way, in a hospital room very much like that one – maybe even that precise one, since his wife wasn't the first or the last person to be wheeled out of that particular room. Everyone has a fucking sob story.

It rains in Seattle, that's one thing he's pretty confident about. It rains a lot and the rain is soothing at first, at night, in bed, but soon it becomes not the sound of rain but the sound of waves, lashing against a ship, the sound of the restless dark currents of the sea, and he sways on the deck, and lightning strikes, illuminating a sky as black as coffee, and something monstrous rises out of the sea, and thunder spreads out to the horizon with the sound of war.

There had been a kid, too. Jonah. Tom never talks about Jonah.

In his king-sized bed which feels too large, and empty, Tom lies dreaming. As the sound of the rain becomes the sound of the waves, so the call of cars becomes the call of cars outside becomes the call of something else, something primeval. Tom stands on board the ship, an old steamer that belongs in a museum. Something rises from the black waves.

INT. THE DAILY FOG EDITORIAL OFFICE – DUSK
MEG stands in JASON'S office. Jason is the editor of the *Daily Fog*. Jason is seated. He is short and bald and wears glasses. MEG is short and pretty and wears glasses. Her blonde hair is cut in a bob. MEG is pacing. JASON sits with his hands folded in his lap.

MEG: Conceivably such beings or great powers may have survived.

MEG waves her hands to punctuate her point. JASON looks at her placidly, and she sighs.

MEG: The path of this story leads through the manuscripts of crazed men... it follows trails of oozing slime, the dark currents of desire, through swamps where idol-worshippers enact forbidden rituals... it is the tale of maddened professors and haunted sailors... the manuscript could change everything, it could –

JASON: Think of the film option.

MEG: What?

JASON: Never mind. What do you need, Meg?
MEG: I need more time.

JASON sighs.

MEG: And... I need more money.

JASON: What is it now? Another flight to *Australia*? Another visit to *Norway*? We're not *Newsweek*, Meg!

MEG: This story is the most important story of your life.

JASON: Of *your* life, Meg.

JASON: The answer's no, Meg.

MEG glares at him. JASON looks back placidly.

MEG: Then I quit.

JASON rubs his stomach, as if it hurts. He shuts his eyes. There is the sound of a door slamming shut. When he opens his eyes again, MEG is gone.

INT. A MONASTERY IN FRANCE – NIGHT

The siren call rises out of the black waves. It is a keening, awful sound, crossing the darkness of night, traversing the Earth's atmosphere, from one side of the planet to the other, vibrating like a cosmic string, speaking in a language ancient beyond sound itself.

In France, in a monastery high above the snowline in the Alps, an ancient monk wakes up with a wordless cry. His ears are bleeding. He claws at his face, his nails are long and dirty, he claws at his face as though trying to remove the mask of its humanity to reveal something primordial and eldritch underneath. He isn't found until Prime the next morning. Four of his fellow brothers are needed to hold him down. The afflicted brother has clawed his own eyes out. He has bitten his tongue and blood comes frothing out of his mouth. He tries to speak, though he cannot. The sounds he makes are nonsensical. *Ph'nglui mglw'nafh*? the brothers think uneasily. They carry the brother to the infirmary, but by Vespers he passes away.

EXT. OUTSIDE THE DAILY FOG OFFICES – DAY

The most merciful thing in the world, I think, is the inability of the human mind to correlate all its contents. We live on a placid island of ignorance in the midst of black seas of infinity, and it was not meant that we should voyage far.

...and so on and so forth, Meg thinks as she storms out of the office. She knows she's got a story. She's been hunting it for months, following a trail of mouldy documents and old accounts: the papers of Francis Wayland Thurston of Boston; Inspector Legrasse's *Memoirs*; Gustaf Johansen's Journal; and Abdul Alhazred's curious tale of antiquity, *Al-Maghrib al Aqṣá*, or *The Farthest West.*

There is something in the South Pacific ocean, Meg knows. It is something like New Caledonia, the island that is the only remaining tip of the sunken continent of Zealandia. But this is not *Nouvelle Caledonie.* No French or British colonial power has ever set foot in *that* place. For countless aeons it has lain below the sea.

She is determined to find it.

INT. TOM'S BEDROOM – NIGHT

VOICE: Tom. Tom.

TOM: Go away. Please, leave me be!

VOICE: But what of your son, Tom? What of your wife?

TOM: They are dead.

VOICE: That is not dead which can eternal lie, Tom.

TOM: I don't... leave me be!

VOICE: With strange aeons even death may die.

TOM tosses and turns; the sheets and the bed are soaked through with his sweat. The voice continues, seductive, awful. It is coming from everywhere and nowhere.

VOICE: The city lies below the sea, but it can rise again. Let me tell you of its beauty. Let me tell you of the corpse-city, its eldritch non-Euclidean geometry, its streets of awesome beauty and despair. Most prominent of the city's features is the citadel, Tom, crowned by a solitary monolith. Remember the citadel, remember the monolith. You could see her again, Tom. It is in my power to give this much to you. To hold her in your arms again, to smell her hair again. Find us, Tom.

TOM: Jonah? Jonah?

The voice changes, become childish and sweet like poison.

VOICE: It's me, daddy!

TOM: Jonah!

TOM wakes up. His heart is beating wildly in his ribcage. His hair is plastered to his brow with sweat. He blinks into the darkness then, slowly, sinks back into bed, burying his face in a pillow. His shoulders shake, but he makes no sound as he cries.

EXT. R'LYEH – ETERNAL NIGHT

The city lies below the sea, but it can rise again. Let me tell you of its beauty. Let me tell you of the corpse-city of R'lyeh, its eldritch non-Euclidean geometry, its streets of awesome beauty and despair. Most prominent of the city's features is the citadel, crowned by a solitary monolith. That old Norwegian, Johansen, is said to have seen it, but that was a long time ago, and the stars are different, now.

EXT. PORT VILA, VANUATU – DAY

Meg flies to Sydney. In budget class they show *Dagon* and *Reanimator* and *Finding Nemo.* It's a long flight to Australia. In Sydney Airport Meg buys two donuts and a coffee from Krispy Kreme and waits for her connecting flight to Vanuatu. It is three hours from Sydney to Port Vila, and when she lands at last it is very humid and a gibbous moon shines down on the small airfield. She can smell mangrove swamps.

In Vila she hires a boat with the last of her money. Captain Gregor, a Russian or German previously convicted of smuggling heroin to Papua New Guinea, has an old schooner that he swears will take them anywhere. She gives him the co-ordinates and he looks at her strangely. The co-ordinates are for a region within the Pacific's Pole of Inaccessibility, the deepest and farthest point from any landmass.

But Meg's got American dollars, and American dollars buy anything, even loyalty.

EXT. ISLAND OF VANUA LAVA, VANUATU – NIGHT

The siren call rises out of the black waves. It is a keening, awful sound, crossing the darkness of night and travesrsing the Earth's atmosphere, from one side of the planet to the other, vibrating like a cosmic string, speaking in a language ancient beyond sound itself.

The old *kleva*, or *majik man*, sits under the banyan tree alone. He has sat up all night, drinking *kava*, that dank, brown liquid that makes the muscles loose and the mind sharp. He has seen much, beyond the islands to the depths of the sea, and heard the murmur of the waves and of the sea's deep dark currents, and he is afraid.

The *olfala bigwan* is rising, he thinks – the great old one, in the pidgin of the islands. He remembers the anient stories, and in the secret caves deep in the forested mountains there still remain ancient paintings in the colour of copper or blood, and the terrible hieroglyphs in a language none can read that seem to shift and leer as you see them. There is a place deep in the mountains, by the volcano, where an ancient stone statue still squats, a hideous thing with wings and tentacles and teeth, carved, perhaps, by ancestors, perhaps by... something else. There is a pool of sulphur water around the carving, and everything that lives dies when it comes too close, and the statue is surrounded by the preserved corpses of sparrows and giant freshwater prawns.

The kleva is worried, for the song coming from the depths is both terrible and beautiful, as seductive as it is repulsive. He has heard such a call once before, when he was a young boy, but that was then, he thinks uneasily. And the stars are different now.

INT. TOM'S BEDROOM – NIGHT

In the dream he walks through the nameless streets of the nameless city. Sharp angles lead nowhere. Streets shift and change as he walks. Movement is sluggish, as though he's pushing slowly through water. Hieroglyphs depict hideous creatures on the walls; they shine in a phosphorous haze.

A voice calls out, far away: 'Daddy? Daddy?'

He tries to hurry. Ahead of him rises the dark citadel. He thinks he sees a woman standing there; her hair is blonde, illuminated like phosphorous deep underwater, the only sign of light in this dark place. The city whispers around him. It seems to rise; when he looks up he sometimes thinks he can see cold and terrible stars, like ancient watching eyes.

EXT. THE SOUTH PACIFIC – DUSK

MEG and CAPTAIN GREGOR stand on the deck of the *Sonia Greene*. Beyond the ship a strange landmass rises. The sky is red and black and eldritch lightning forms an intricate spider web across it. The rising landmass is black and slimy green, and the first thing to pierce the water is a strange monolith.

MEG: Johansen was right! It rises!

CAPTAIN GREGOR takes a bottle, pulls the cork out with his teeth, spits it over the rail and takes a swig. Something strange seems to happen; all sound ceases as the citadel and its monolith rise from the waves.

CAPTAIN GREGOR points. The bottle falls to the deck and smashes without sound. CAPTAIN GREGOR'S mouth opens in a silent scream.

The picture blurs. There seems to be something in the water, a dark shape, possibly tentacled.

When the picture returns there is no sign of CAPTAIN GREGOR.

INT. BOAT IN NORWAY WATERS – NIGHT

The siren call rises out of the black waves. It is a keening, awful sound, vibrating like a cosmic string, speaking in a language ancient beyond sound itself.

In Norway an old man, the son of an old man, lies awake in

his boat, dreaming, nevertheless; dreaming with eyes open, dreaming of an ocean and the dark currents that move in the depths below, dreaming of a man and a woman converging on this single point, dreaming of a citadel rising from the depths, of an old schooner with a hull covered in barnacles, of tentacles reaching out like a whisper from the depths, of a man and a woman and a gibbous moon. he lies shivering on his bunk and the cold wind howls outside, and the sea screams, in a language too old for any human to understand.

EXT. GREEN LAKE, SEATTLE – DAY

All lakes are the sea in miniature. In a flashback scene TOM is on a boat on the lake, with JONAH, who is played by a young curly-haired actor. The sky darkens. Each is wrapped in his own thoughts. It is not a happy scene. In a flashback-within-flashback TOM recalls the last days at the hospital. He was there to hold his wife's hand when the heart monitor flatlined.

Waves rise on the lake. Clouds gather above. There is a storm. TOM and JONAH try to row back to shore but the wind picks up and waves hit their little boat. We have the vague impression of some vast dark shape under the water, dark currents forming into tentacles that rise out of the water, but this could just be the light.

The boat capsizes.

TOM: NO!

They are both flailing in the water.

TOM: Jonah!

JONAH's head bobs in the water. For just a moment his hurt, confused eyes look directly at the camera. Then a wave passes over him and he goes under.

TOM: Jonah! No!

TOM dives. We follow him, into the dark water. The currents push at him; he tries to find Jonah; the lake is dark and murky; he is losing his breath; his face twists in pain and we CUT to:

EXT. THE SUNKEN CITY OF R'LYEH – ETERNAL NIGHT

The sunken city of R'lyeh is arisen from the depths, a corpse-city of non-Euclidean geometry overshadowed by the dark citadel. A boat hovers in the shallows of the sea beside the black, slime-covered rock before the citadel. The *Sonia Greene* is abandoned, though a solitary human figure stands before the great entrance to the citadel: MEG, wet and bedraggled and alive. She waits.

EXT. THE CITY OF R'LYEH – ETERNAL NIGHT

TOM is walking the streets of R'lyeh, the citadel keeps escaping his grasp; he takes turns that lead into other, alien dimensions, following the laughter of his boy. Then he sees her. She is standing by the black rock, at the entrance to the citadel. He runs to her.

EXT. THE CITY OF R'LYEH – ETERNAL NIGHT

'Tom?'

'Meg. Meg, it's you. It's really you.'

'I didn't think you'd come. I... I waited. I've been waiting for a long time, Tom.'

'I lost my way, Meg. In the dreams. I lost my way. It was hard to find the right path. The stars all lied.'

'The stars are different now.'

'What's behind the door, Meg? What's behind the door of

the citadel?'

'Silly Tom.' Affection colours her voice. 'You know what's behind the door. You've always known.'

'Death,' he says, at the same time that she says, 'Love.'

EXT. SOMEWHERE IN THE SOUTH PACIFIC – NIGHT
A man, a woman, the ghostly outline of a child between them holding both their hands. A citadel rises into the sky. The immense black door, as black as night, begins, ever so slowly, to open. Above their heads the stars shine bright and terrible and true.

INT. TOM'S HOUSE – SEATTLE – DAY
In his house in dread Seattle Tom lies dreaming.

TOM: Jonah?

TOM: Shares at three point eight.

TOM: What? No.

TOM: I love you too.

TOM turns in his bed. He cries out in nameless dread. The sheets are soaked with sweat. Outside, it rains. The sound, like waves crashing against the hulk of a ship, like the sound of love, slowly grows gentle. TOM sighs and turns over in his sleep.

Damnation Seize My Soul

Jan Edwards

Mercedeys Benks stepped out of the main airlock, keeping her back to the wall whilst she surveyed the concourse. After 'crowded', the first word that came to mind was 'dirty'. Though dirt hardly described the layer of engine grease and soot, acquired over many decades, that gave T'uga its distinctive hue and odour. Filth, she thought, is a more embracing term. But if she called any landmass in this universe home then it was this one: T'uga,the sole construct on a barren clod of craters and rifts. Surrounded by a handful of makeshift airlock tunnels, it resembled nothing more than a bloated tic, as did many of the creatures that scurried within it. Few returned there without great need.

Queen Victoria's Admiralty had known it as *HMS Resistance*, once-along-awhile; for a ship it had been, and the largest Dreadnaught ever launched. So large that, away from the witches and mediums of Earth, those who had stolen her could never hope to produce enough ectoplasm to sideslip the mighty steam engines. Running her aground would have been their only viable option.

The concourse was more crowded than she would expect so early in the day. Mercy had often seen T'uga's denizens in turmoil, yet seldom so determinedly space-bound as today. They toted duffel-bags and banded trunks – and an obvious urgency to be somewhere else. Plainly something big and bad had stirred the anthill.

T'uga had become a port of refuge, and a highly profitable one now that Mercy and her ship, *The Grace,* had found both the becalmed *Resistance* and her thief, John Hicks, and towed them to this safe haven. The recollection had her rubbing her scarred right hand against her waistband. The old sword wounds had begun itching at the memory of their inception: when Hicks had not accepted her terms as easily as he might. Mercy had far too much invested in T'uga to endanger its existence.

"Something's wrong." She said. "I can smell it."

"You wish our brother to atone for the wrongs he did you? That is your right. Llyr may not help you in this, though he will not stand in your way."

"Should I not try? Evnissyen served us all a great wrong."

"Would changing his fate make such a difference to the past wrongs? I doubt it."

"I must do this, Bran ap Llyr."

"What is done cannot be mended, Branwen. You of all here know that right is not always held by the mighty. But honour at least is on your side. You have my blessing to try. Yet to avenge your blood, Branwen, then you must spill his. If that is the course you have chosen I will provide you with a second chance. But he is not one to be bested easily."

"I will fight him again," she replied. "As often as needed, Bran ap Llyr. I do not fear what is to come. It is in the remembering that I find pain."

"It pains you to recall?"

"No, brother. When I feel pain it is already too late."

"Ships astern." The *Annika*'s steersman sang out, gesturing eastward..

Captain Awilda Synardus stared – and swore. Pushing back the wisps of red hair escaping their tight braids, she shielded her eyes against the sun and read the clouds feathering westward in white-mackerel shafts. That at least was in her favour. "If this bunch of slugs can shift us out beyond the headland we should make good time."

The four ships under Awilda's command slid rapidly forward with each crew bending willingly to the oars. None questioned Awilda's choices of target or enemy. Woman or no, Awilda was her father's daughter. The sword that hung across her back, and the vivid white scars across her right hand, were testament to her fighting and survival skills. Awilda could hack and stab with the best of them.

"Captain." Steinn glanced at her, an odd expression on his broad features. "'Tis himself."

Awilda nodded. She needed no telling. Eivan's red and yellow wolf's head blazed across each closing sail like spilled blood and molten ore. She balanced lightly on the gunwale; one arm hooked around the carved prow, and stared toward the distant ships. "Eivan Brans-son, by Odin." The man she would destroy for daring to approach her father with offers of marriage and drudgery to be forced upon her. That was no match for a daughter of kings. She bowed to no man, nor ran from him. Instead she had vowed to destroy him. Just as he had destroyed her home and family in return for her refusal.

Her ships were swift with the tide in their favour as they swung about to meet the enemy, and their silence was broken only by the *whap* of sail and sluice of oars across the dark, deep waters of the fiord. Then a chant was whispered somewhere in the flotilla. *Aa-wil-da*; each syllable drawn out in distinct separation. Sword hilts and javelins were thrummed against shields, softly at first, growing harder as the voices gained force. "*Aa-wil-da, Aa-wil-da, Aa-wil-da.*"

Across open water came a steady reply, "*Eiv-an, Eiv-an, Eiv-an.*"

Awilda stood in the prow, one hand aloft, and smiled at stray enemy arrows falling far short of them. Eivan did not have proper control of his crew and that could be to her advantage. She waited until arrows fell a bare arms-stretch from them. Only then did her fist drop, signalling the first stabbing volley into their enemy. She slipped from her vantage point to avoid the returning fire, leaving her proud Dragon-prows to snarl defiance at the opposing Wolves. Awilda barked the order to swing to port to avoid locking prows and becoming trapped. As starboard sides came broadside to each other, lines were thrown to snag the opposition's gunwales and draw them together into one huge battle arena.

Chants from each side roared out their defiance vying to overpower the other in sheer volume. Swords, javelins and shields clashed as the warriors from either side launched into hand to hand combat; chants now forgotten in the full-throated roar of a battle charge.

Awilda searched among the gore and armour for Eivan.

A sword thunked against her shield; she staggered back, parrying the blow with a sweeping stroke of her own. Her attacker landed another shattering blow and her shield cracked top to bottom. She threw it aside and hacked at him with a double-handed slash, severing both his sword arm and a goodly chunk of neck. Blood clouded her vision as arteries sprayed death across her face, but Awilda only wiped with the back of her hand and scooped up the fallen warrior's shield. Leapt across from one shallow hull to the next, blood rushing through her brain like a waterfall in the full-blown flood of spring thaw; singing in her head with the wailing howl of a Valkyrie calling her warriors to victory or glorious Valhalla. She stabbed and slashed a path across two more hulls: to the prow of the central ship and the man she had vowed to kill. She raised her sword high, staring Eivan in the eyes; pausing to savour the recognition she expected.

Too late she parried the double-handed slash which connected with her midriff and swept her over the gunwale into the churning, red-stained brine.

"The sands will not run out just yet," said Bran ap Llyr.

"Sands shift with the tides, and mainly on your whim," Branwen replied. "I did your bidding and claimed my reward. Yet you deny it me."

'Not my bidding but yours, though I gave you my word. The time was wrong, sister. Chance comes to you again and he shall not walk away unchallenged."

Mercy pushed past Sheyn and concentrated on regaining her bearings. T'uga's inner workings morphed with the waxing and waning of dominant businesses that plied their dubious trade in the concourse. A different mix each time she returned, but always a thriving community. T'uga was a lucrative venture; even the few hundred guineas which Hicks bilked her for during her long absences was nothing against the security that this place gave her.

She could not recall exactly when the Dreadnaught's hulk had mutated into T'uga, nor whether it was the ship or the tiny planetoid on which it sat that was T'uga in truth. Confusion and lies were a habit with anything attached to John Hicks. Mercy hardly cared. The ship had been sufficiently disguised from the Admiralty – still seeking their missing leviathan – for many years now. T'uga it was now, with a mythology of its very own, populated by pirates and brigands and assorted low-lives from across the known and unknown universe. None cared what T'uga had been as long as it stayed free of Victoria's dominion; or that of Napoleon, or Lincoln, or any other of Homeworld's leaders.

That population, or at least those who bothered to notice her in their panic to leave, were regarding her now. Most with curiosity, a few with open hostility. She eased the sword that hung at her left hip, fingered the pearl-handled pistol that hung at her right; she also checked the knife on her belt and the small derringer in her sleeve before moving off. This being her home port she had not disembarked from *The Grace* fully armed. Checking the weapons that she did sport, however, was a subconscious act.

Nodding at Sheyn to follow, she moved across the concourse with that measured lilt of one more used to steel-framed grav-boots than the fancy thigh-high leather variety she sported today. Her eyes flickered toward the ceiling lenses just once and she resisted the temptation to flipthem a finger; turning the move into a preening of the tangled red curls twisting from beneath her wide-brimmed hat. Real hair in a life-long spacer was a mere luxury; red hair was a rarity. For Mercy its rarity proved her lineage back to the Chieftain Eoghan Ó Máille and beyond. Mercedeys Benks was a living legend – and she loved it.

The deck had begun to vibrate beneath her feet, as if flexing atrophied muscles. A distant hiss and chatter of engines rattled through the passages. That part of T'uga which was the *Resistance* had awoken. Mercy paused, frowning. Her scarred hand rubbed absent-mindedly at an itch under her belt. Yes, it was commercial sense to keep the power house of T'uga in running order, but this did not feel like a routine turning over of its vast engines. She placed a hand on the bulwark and felt the steady throb of a well-oiled engine shivering through her palm. She glanced back at the surveillance camera, openly this time, her head canted in query. Hicksey should know she was on guard.

Sheyn laid a warning finger to his lips. "Gather what wits you have, lass. There's a storm a' brewing," he whispered.

"Here?" She laughed. "This is T'uga. And I'm not afeared of a little roughhousing."

"Lass, there's a little blow and there's a solar wind. And if'n you trust that Cap'n's gut of yours you'll never be far enough adrift to roast alive."

"This should have ended Bran ap Llyr. It should have ended then."

"The Wheel turns. Courage, Sister. Evnissyen will be punished for his deeds and your son avenged."

"It must end now."

"Patience, Branwen. Your balance shall be gained. When the Wheel of Fate runs deep enough to find better purchase."

Grainne toyed with her braided hair, its legendary red now streaked with grey. She looked around the deck, content despite a need for rubbing comfrey into the white scar on her right wrist that ached so damnably these past few years. Wind snapped extra canvas above her, and deck-boards creaked beneath her feet as the masts took up the strain, and her fast brigantine, *The Grace*, flew toward her prey.

Finding Eivan's small sloop was a surprise. She had followed his pirating trail for weeks now, and although she admired both his panache and appetite for spoils, she didn't like the cut of his jib on any other score.

"Load up the chain-shot," she roared. "Fire when ready, Master Gunner."

"Aye, sir."

Salvos of shot, chained in pairs, swirled toward the sloop's rigging. Whilst most fell wide, one coupled-missile swung its way into the mizzen, cracking the mast mid-length.

"Catch every breath, boys. She shan't gain port ahead of us. Earn your crust you slack-jawed vermin! Work your useless backsides or feel yer boson's lash!"

The gunners found their range: chain-shot smashed around the main mast and swept into the crowded mid-deck, cutting a swathe through the crew. The main-mast wavered, slowly arching downwards, its inexorable fall slowed by ropes and ladders and the damaged mizzen's wind-filled canvas. The sloop listed to port, trailing its broken mast in the ocean: a huge sculling oar, slicing water which was turning red with the blood of the fallen.

The Grace moved in for the kill, her slim hull skimming nimbly toward the crippled sloop, ploughing through smashed wood and human flotsam alike. The gunners had abandoned the cannons, not wanting to damage their prize more than necessary, and took to the deck guns, sending deadly blasts of metal fragments toward their wounded prey. Smoke wafted across the deck and stung Grainne's nose and she snuffled at it gleefully, allowing that distinctive and oh-so-familiar odour to taint her vision and sting her blood.

The sloop could not even limp for safety and was jerked around in a lazy spiral by the trailing masts. Shot peppered *The*

Graces's decks now as Eivan returned fire in the only manner left to him.

Gunpowder haze hung too thick for the light wind to disperse quickly. Gunshots merged into a contiguous chorus with the curdling, agonised cries of the wounded together.

"Prepare to repel boarders," Eivan bellowed as the ships slid alongside. Boarding ropes and hooks snaked from *The Grace's* rail.

Grainne checked her belt for her precious pistols and then hefted her sword and dirk in respective hands. *The Grace*'s crew were already swarming toward the sloop's deck and she was eager to join them.

"For, not to the age do I strive, nor for ever am I wroth, for the spirit from before me is feeble..." she quoted grimly. "And the souls I have made…? For all the souls I have made … are about to be joined by their brother!"

She dashed forward, clambering onto *The Grace*'s rail. She teetered there, looking toward the sloop… and down the barrel of a well-oiled pistol.

Eivan mouthed a last farewell as he pulled the trigger.

Grainne had no time to wonder. She was down between the hulls; sucking in blood-tainted brine with her final breath.

"The tides are turning, Branwen. He has found a current that can sweep him back."

"As he has done so often before. He seems always to find a way, and I am tired, Bran ap Llyr."

"The quest is yours to pursue, sister. Or not."

"A blood oath I made, Brother. I must succeed. Given time."

'Time is all you have, Branwen. Now at least he is out of his element."

'If that be the case, then so am I, and we will both stand at risk."

"Enough." Mercy held a hand up for silence and listened intently for signs of life along the next corridor. It was oddly still beyond the engine rumble. Even the hubbub from the concourse had died away. She did not believe in coincidences; to her suspicious mind engines firing up the moment she stepped aboard smacked of arrogance and challenge.

The engine thrum slackened and she nodded satisfaction. "With me," she snapped, initially taking the companion way toward the cabin berth she retained on T'uga. Once clear of the concourse, however, she doubled back through the maze of corridors toward the bridge, with Sheyn close at her expensive boot heels.

They halted just one turn short of the bridge ladder. The engines were still idling, the soft *shush* and *kashomp* of the turning pistons slow and steady and, at this proximity, also very loud. The smell of soot was heavy in the air, and over that the dank, musty, unmistakable odour of ectoplasm. T'uga was preparing to fly.

At the sound of footsteps on the ladder, they hid in the nearest cabin. Mercy kept the door open a crack, pistol at the ready, watching as two sailors passed by. Both were trim and lithe, shaven-headed, clean-jawed and all-round well-washed. They could only be Navy; and her blood curdled.

"Trouble," she grunted. "Brace of Jack Tars."

Sheyn crowded her shoulder for a glimpse. "Just the brace?" he said.

"So far. Where the hell have they sprung from?"

Sheyn spread his hands. "We've had no sightings of Admiralty ships for weeks."

"We should've known that was odd just on its own." Mercy opened the door a little further and checked the corridor. The crewmen had rounded the corner. They would be setting up sentry duty on the bridge ladder. "So Hicksey is expecting us," she said. "I am going to skewer that little rodent."

"Unless I get to him first," Sheyn replied.

"We need another way up to the bridge." She grinned at her companion. "Through the Captain's Sea Cabin. Hicksey's own state rooms. Follow me." She slipped away from the bridge ladders toward the officer's quarters.

The further they crept along strangely deserted corridors the more Mercy's instincts were rattled. If the Admiralty truly had taken the bridge then T'uga was no longer a safe haven. The question she asked herself was: had they come in with or without Hicksey's help? He would do almost anything to rid himself of Mercy and her hold both on him and T'uga. But handing over his biggest asset and risking arrest? Whatever the whys and wherefores of her ex-partner's involvement, it was certain she would not be allowed off the ship voluntarily. Which brought her to the next question: how many were there? Doubtless a naval vessel somewhere hidden nearby, but they had to have arrived in a small ship. Which meant a small task force. Her most obvious option was to cripple the command and then make a run for open space.

Near the end of the final ladder leading into Hicks's rooms stood a sentry in naval slops and bellbottoms. So Hicks's own domain was under guard. Did that mean the Navy weren't here by invitation?

The engines' hum changed once more: turning faster, approaching running speed. Whatever her business partner's situation, the Navy seemed set to reinstate T'uga as Victoria's Dreadnaught.

"With or without you, Hicksey my old shipmate." Mercy drew her small knife and inched forward, signalling Sheyn to cover the far side of the corridor. She needed the ensign to look away, however briefly; a raised voice from the deck above gave her the chance she looked for. He looked up, his well-shaven throat exposed, and Mercy lived up to repute by showing none of her name's sake. Sheyn helped her drag the twitching corpse into the nearest doorway, propping it there. The blood trail could not be hidden, but she hoped this would not matter very soon.

Tweaking out the dead sailor's pistol and knife, Mercy tucked them into her belt and ran to the ladder. Climbing silently, she reached to the top and peered across the bridge to assess her opponents. There were three naval ratings on deck, and two officers. And Hicksey – standing close to the helm. That answered her first question.

Mercy slipped up the last few steps and dodged into the deserted Coms recess, followed swiftly by Sheyn.

One rating rested his hands on the wheel while the others stood ready at the engine controls. The officers were gathered together, their attention fixed on the small bank of screens to the helm's left, and away from Mercy.

"I see nothing of her, Hicks." The Commander was young. His pips and braid achingly new on jacket and hat. So young that she wondered how he was ever worthy of rank at all.

"Eivan Bransson," she muttered. "Viscount Bransson's youngest brat. Damn his blood."

"The Honourable Eivan," Sheyn added. "A sneakier rat never walked any deck! Honourable –"

Mercy motioned him to silence, intent now on the room's occupants.

"…then worry," Hicks was saying. "When it comes to survival, Mercy Benks has the instincts of a cockroach. Once we're all stardust, there she'll be, plying the stars."

"One woman against Her Majesty's Navy." Eivan's tone left Mercy in no doubt what he thought of that idea. "No matter. *The Resistance* is our goal, Mr Hicks. Mercedeys Benks can wait."

Hicks made no further comment but grinned and shook his head slowly.

Eivan signalled the ensign. "Are we ready to cast off, Mr Lane?"

"Yes, sir. Warlocks are powering up the engines and awaiting your orders. *The Reliant* has left cover and is moving into position as escort."

"Excellent. Then lift off; and slow ahead, if you please."

The young officer turned, his face pale. "But sir, the exiles are still leaving. You gave your word on their safety..."

Eivan stared back – a cold glance. "I said we would leave when it was safe for us to do so. We needn't concern ourselves with a little scum floating above decks. Most would be bound for the gallows in any event." He stepped back to get a full view of the screens forward. "Mr Lane?" he prompted.

"Casting off, sir. Engines slow ahead."

As he spoke the engine note changed, deepening, guttural and laboured. The decks juddered, rocking wildly for a moment; lurching to port.

From outside Mercy could hear faint noises of tearing and grinding and shouted warnings. She could imagine the pandemonium in the concourse as those attempting to flee T'uga hurled themselves clear; many to certain death as *The Resistance* rose quickly, ripping free of its camouflage of silt, debris and squalor – built up over its many years aground.

The view on screen changed from crags and rifts to clear, dark, sky.

"Full ahead," Eivan snapped.

"Full ahead, sir."

Engines vibrated as the reborn *HMS Resistance* leaped upward and forward. The screen darkened to the eternal night of space.

Mercy signed to Sheyn: which of the Navy men should be the first to die – which of them she wanted. They needed no words after so many battles, so many brawls; so many ships.

Now it was time. She could feel it.

The Resistance was heading into ectopic-slippage. In a few minutes it would slither through the universe in a pale wave of ectoplasmic shimmer. If she did not act, *The Grace* would be left far behind, and regardless how much affection Mercy had for T'uga she loved *The Grace* – and loved her freedom even more.

With a howl she bounded forward, despatching the steersman in one move. Whirling around, she brought her cutlass slashing across the Number One's throat before both of her booted feet had returned to deck.

She saw Sheyn plunge a knife in another crewman's kidneys before leaping toward the second. She had time to think how efficient he was for his age, when a shot rang out at close range.

Lead ripped through her; she felt it tearing her gut out through her back. The controls would be covered...

A second shot struck her. .

Eivan was gaping, wild-eyed and terrified; still pointing a pistol at her belly. She eyed the space between them, wondering if she was still capable of making a lunge at him before he got off another shot. She could see Sheyn across the room, holding Hicks at bay, just waiting for her to give the word to finish him.

"Hold!" Eivan shouted. "Or your captain dies."

Mercy raised her hands slowly to shoulder height, palms out in the traditional gesture of surrender. "You fire again young pup, and we may all die." She smiled grimly, wincing at the pain her raised arms gave to her shattered gut.

"I take no orders from a pirate."

He was shaking; she could see the tip of the barrel waver, almost smell his fear. She lowered her hands as slowly as she had raised them. "Don't be a fool, Eivan."

"From your lips, Benks, it's Lord Bransson," he replied.

"Oh, Eivan, such formality. After our last meeting I hoped we could be friends."

"I am no friend to a thief and a pirate."

"Then I am sorry for you, lad." She let her hand slide toward her belt and the dagger concealed there. "You might want to put the gun down."

"You are not in a position to dictate."

"Perhaps not, but I can try to even the odds a little." Mercy flipped the dagger from her belt, sending it stabbing through the space between them, piercing Eivan's chest and heart.

Maybe it was muscle contraction; perhaps instinct. Eivan's finger jerked the pistol's trigger, returning a sphere of lead toward his killer.

She felt the control panel behind her warming with the sudden leaking of ectoplasm, and she had time enough to wonder how so much valuable fuel came to be amassed so far from Earth before the bridge erupted into quivering and insubstantial shadow. The ship wavered between the solidity of present existence and its far-distant destination, before becoming a mass of swirling debris ringed by dissipating ectoplasmic shock waves, eddying out toward the void.

Cold; the intense chill of nothingness all around her. Adrift amid the flotsam that had been *The Resistance,* she turned slowly and watched the hulk drift away from her, spewing chunks of metal and wood into the universe, like breadcrumbs strewn across a pond. Her hat had drifted away, and her red hair floated free in a blood-red halo that wrapped around her pale face; her last – her final – vision.

HOME

Emma Coleman

I was standing on a bridge looking out across open fields and blue sky. I was at peace. The stream below was busy; the water tumbling and hurrying over rocks; the insects buzzed and two tiny birds chased each other back and forth over the stream.

"Pretty as a picture, in't it?"

The man appeared out of nowhere. He was at my side, pressing softly against my arm, before I was even aware of another person nearby.

"I could look at this view all day," he said, sighing.

I edged away as discreetly as I could but the man sidled up to me; his bony shoulder nestling by my own.

"The only problem is finding someone to share this with, someone who appreciates what I mean." He sighed again.

I tried to forget his presence and concentrated on the tranquillity before me; the sunlight soaking into the fields and the vivid green was inviting.

"Yep, I could happily have this view forever. That grass looks so vibrant doesn't it? Fair makes me want to roll about on it, naked."

I slid across once more. The man did the same. Silence followed but my concentration had gone; I couldn't enjoy the scenery anymore and so began to inspect the stranger instead.

He was younger than I expected; his skin was smooth and his hair was a thick, mahogany mane. He wore a dark brown coat and a skinny tweed scarf hung from his neck. He didn't look at me while I blatantly stared at him; he simply smiled at what was in front of us. I was beginning to wonder if the man was blind; his mind's eye painting the beauty he described, when I noticed something poking out of his pocket. It was a bag of mint humbugs.

"Would you care for a sweet?" The man asked, fumbling for the bag, "They're crunchy."

He offered the humbugs and I put my hand in; I felt about in the packet, enjoying the texture and sound, then pulled out one shining sweet. I was puzzled.

"This is no mint humbug." I whispered.

"I never said they were mint humbugs." The man said, popping one of the sweets into his mouth. He sucked on it hard; swallowing and grunting quietly.

I peered at the thing held between my thumb and finger; it was struggling to get free, the little thorny legs wriggling about and the antennae straining.

The stranger started crunching loudly and I dropped the June bug out of fright. It fell like a pebble and clattered on the wooden planks. The man stamped on it, grinding the beetle into the bridge.

"Past its best that one, try another." He shook the bag; he still hadn't looked my way and he was smiling broadly.

I looked back to the view of fields and sky; clouds were gathering to cast dark blue shadows on the bright green pastures. I ignored the stranger's attempts to entice me with his bag of hideous treats; he shoved it towards my face and scrunched the bag as if the action would make me take another one.

"Suit yourself," he said, and launched the packet into the stream. I watched it sweep back towards me on the current, bobbing along, and a couple of June bugs clambered out. I was saddened to see the bag get overwhelmed with water and sink slowly down.

"What did you do that for?" I asked quietly.

"They weren't as good as I remember them and I don't handle disappointment very well."

I looked to the fields again; the clouds had gathered together menacingly, dark grey and blue with tinges of violet, and I felt a cool breeze. My teeth chattered.

"Oh dear, that doesn't look too promising, we might be getting a spot of rain. Shouldn't be out here when a storm's raging, we'd better get going."

He grabbed my hand and pulled me along the bridge. His grip was rigid and cold – as if his hand had been left in a refrigerator all night – and I tried to wrench myself free but the stranger simply tugged sharply.

"Don't be silly, I told you, you don't want to be out here when there's a storm. Too dangerous." And he led me on.

My arm went limp and I lost all sense of direction; the cold had suddenly given way to humidity; the thick air clouded my head and I felt dizzy but the stranger dragged me on. I was conscious of the hedges; tall, dark and spiky, and I was caught on the cheek, the deep scratch causing me to cry out.

"Where are we going?" I asked.

"Home," was the simple reply.

"Home?"

"Can't be out here, not now. Home's the best place to be." He tugged sharply again and I tripped on the uneven earth; the ground was hard and embedded with large stones; the sickness in my head was making me faint.

"Come on, no lagging behind." The strange man spoke softly, his thumb stroking my hand.

"But I don't want to go home."

"I've told you, home's the best place for you now."

And then the rain started. The brooding sky had completely smothered us and huge, cold drops fell tentatively. Seconds later the heavens opened and the rain fell harder and with urgency; my head was dripping wet and the sickness vanished.

"I said I don't want to go home!" I shouted at the stranger's back. We were under trees now; the flapping leaves were sodden and struck me in the face. My eyes scrunched up and I struggled to see the blackened overcoat ahead or, for that matter, the cold hand that was wrapped around my own. I was alone; the stranger had disappeared but somehow I was still being pulled along and couldn't free myself. The bones in my wrist hurt; I could feel his fingers almost gouging into them and I struggled to twist my arm loose.

"I'm taking you home," the wind seemed to say through the branches.

"Let me go! You're hurting! Let go!" I screamed, wrenching my arm this way and that. I gave up. I was scared; the fear was bewitching and my wrist throbbed.

The trees began to thin out and the gloom of early evening rain clouds was metallic. But I still hadn't heard a rumble of thunder or seen a lightning strike.

"You're a liar! There is no storm! Liar!" I screamed out again, but I was pulled onwards.

Once out of the trees I saw, thirty feet ahead, a fence with a stile. Sitting on the stile was a beautiful girl; her legs were long and naked, her hair was long and black and she was staring up at the sky, letting the rain pour down upon her. She was dressed in a cotton smock and red shorts, her feet were bare and she held a bottle of wine. As I approached, I watched her drink; a dribble of red juice dripped onto her white top.

I forgot my agony and didn't even notice the invisible grip; I felt as if I were floating, drawn to the girl on a hovering carpet.

She didn't look at me when I reached her. I gazed at her face, still offered up to the bursting clouds, and saw such beauty – creamy skin, cornflower-blue eyes and long dark lashes that twinkled with rain drops.

"She's magical," I whispered.

The girl lowered her face and looked at me dreamily.

"Hello," she said, with a voice like a summer breeze.

"Hello," I said, mesmerised by the mouth that smiled shyly.

She returned her gaze upwards; taking another drink of wine. The rain was easing; the clouds lighter and a creeping coolness enveloped me.

"Oh no," the girl said sadly, "it's stopping."

"I'm happy about that," I said, "I don't like rain."

The girl's face was melancholy.

"I'm sorry, I have to go."

She got up; her muddy feet slapped onto the wooden stile and she turned, fixing me with frightened eyes.

"You're going home too, aren't you?"

"Yes but I don't want to," I stammered.

"Neither do I." She spoke quietly, looking away.

Suddenly she exclaimed, "Let's run away. Let's walk and walk and never go home."

My heart nearly burst with excitement and I nodded.

"Come on then, give me your hand."

I held her delicate fingers as she climbed over the stile; I followed in a daze of ecstasy. On the other side, she slipped her hand round mine and we hurried across the field. It seemed to go on forever as though it were the only thing on Earth. But I didn't mind; I was with the loveliest girl I'd ever seen and would happily have run with her for all time.

"We're going the wrong way, we must go back," she said, slowing down and pulling me to a standstill.

"No," I said, "we can't go back."

"We have to."

"No, we're not! We're not!"

I was screaming at the girl; the most beautiful girl ever born, and I panicked. I watched her eyes darken like the clouds – cornflower to steel – and she gripped my hand hard.

"Yes we are." Her mouth tightened like her fingers; what I once thought were delicate had become thin and pointy, the tips arrowheads piercing my flesh. My heart pumped quickly but my mind was motionless and, before I knew what had happened, I was back at the fence with the stile.

"He'll find me; we shouldn't be here," I said, fearfully.

I looked at the hand clutching my own; blood trickled from

the wounds.

"Let go of me, you're hurting."

"Have some of this and the pain will go away."

The girl offered me the bottle and I took hold of it; I looked at her but the face was hidden; her hair was swirling like tendrils under water and obscured the beauty I wanted to see.

A gloom was creeping over me and I felt darkness inside. I stared at the wine, the pain was getting stronger, so I put the bottle to my mouth and drank and drank until the liquid spilled over my lips. Warmth seeped from my throat to my belly and I was delirious.

"How are you feeling?" I heard the girl say, as if in a dream.

"I want more."

"There is no more; that was the blood of Jesus and you've drunk him dry!" She laughed; a high-pitched jangling of bells and I saw her throw her head back in slow motion, the tendrils of hair snaking about her face hypnotically.

"That's not true," I said, trying to fend off the sickness that jabbed at my stomach.

The girl's hair wrapped around my head and pulled me in. Through hot eyes I saw her beautiful face; tears like claret slid down her cheeks and she said sickly, "Maybe it wasn't Jesus' blood."

I dropped the bottle to the ground and clutched my head.

"Oh, are you tired?" Her voice was distant and she'd let go of my hand. "Home's the best place for you now, time to go, it's time to go home."

Something flapped against my knuckles and I peered through my fingers. It was the tweed scarf, dangling from the young man's neck and blowing softly in the wind. He leaned in close.

"Ready?"

I was shaking uncontrollably; I closed my eyes tight, begging silently for the man to vanish. The wind blew harder and the scent of damp earth was sweet to me.

'Go away! Go away! Go away!' I said over and over again in my mind. 'Go away!'

The wind died and there was complete quiet; I dared not open my eyes.

'Has he gone?' Has it worked?'

When I gained courage to look, I saw night. The dark had descended in seconds and I was all alone. My breath came in bursts; my heart hurt with terror of everything. Where was I to go? I didn't know where to turn for safety but running was all I could think of doing; just run and get away from this place. I started to lope across the inky grass as quickly as I could.

The small wood I'd been dragged through was barely visible but the black of the dense trees was my focal point and I ran towards that. I stumbled and fell. I ran on again, my legs shaking. I tripped on a mound of earth and sprawled on the cold grass; I whimpered pathetically as I picked myself up once more. My eyes strained to see the wood but I could only see darkness; the ground, the sky and everything between had merged into one shade.

"Where am I?!" I screamed. My voice seemed stunted and to me sounded like a whisper. I tried to run again but couldn't; tears seeped down my face and I wanted to collapse; my body ravaged and unable to stay upright. I crashed to the ground.

In an instant, I woke from my unconsciousness. There was a huge full moon lighting up the countryside. I could see the boundaries and the sky and the small wood. And someone, a man perhaps, standing in the middle of the field. He was stock-still; like a scarecrow. I blinked and looked again; the scarecrow was moving. I clambered to my feet, preparing to flee, when a voice said, "He'll get you."

Pressing against my thigh was a big fox; he was warm and musky.

"Who is he? What does he want?"

"You. Quick, run!"

The fox bristled and made a dart for the wood; I grabbed

hold of his brush and was pulled along, bent down and unstable. The fox was strong and I held on for dear life; he made me feel protected.

"Not far now!" The fox panted.

The wood was bearing down on us. My hand was damp with sweat and the brush was slipping from my grasp. If I tried to get a better grip, I'd have to let go and the fox was too quick; I'd lose him and I didn't want to.

"Nearly there." He barked, but his tail slithered from my hand. I saw him sprint low, onwards, and I couldn't keep up. My heart wanted to burst; the pain stabbed and I stopped running.

I was at the edge of the trees, the black trunks like guards, and I didn't know what to do.

Something made me turn around; a prickling on my neck and, to my horror, I saw the scarecrow, stock-still, not far behind me.

Indeed he was a scarecrow, sprouting with straw and covered in sackcloth. He had no face except for a slash in the cloth; straw poked out like teeth and I thought I saw him smile.

"Between the devil and the deep, dark trees," the scarecrow whispered.

He stepped forward, his limbs jerking as though an electric current had passed through him, and his teeth lengthened.

"Come here." He spoke soothingly.

He stretched out both arms spasmodically and took another step.

"Keep away!" I shouted, backing up to the trees.

"But I like you; I want you to know how much I like you."

He jerked forward again.

"I don't want to know! Leave me alone!"

He stretched the slash wider and let his arms fall to his side.

"I can't."

I turned quickly and ran off into the wood. I crashed through the undergrowth blindly, not daring to look back. Soon I was deep in the trees and all I could think was, 'keep going, keep going 'til you get to the other side.' But the branches started to stretch and close around me; they were blocking my path, forming gnarled fences and I had no choice but to twist and turn.

"Why don't you want to go home? What are you so afraid of?"

I was spinning, mentally and physically; all I could see were the swaying trees, bending and making a cage around me.

"I'm not afraid, I just don't want to go home yet, I whispered.

"You are afraid. And you should've gone home hours ago."

The voice was coming from below; I looked to my feet and there was a box. I was compelled to touch it; smooth, cool and solid, the box was wooden. I tried to prise open the lid but there wasn't one; it was seamless. A strange blankness overcame me and I stroked the silky object. Then the box began to grow. I tried to back away and remove my palm but couldn't; my hand was stuck. I yanked hard but the skin of my palm was glued to it, as if the box was a block of ice.

"Let me go!" I screamed, still trying to free my hand, but the skin was ripping. "Let go!"

I struck the casket with my free hand; I hit it again and again. My fist was damp and I knew it was blood but I continued to punch and punch.

"Let go! Let go!" I shouted with every smash of my fist. The wood was splintering.

"You'll never be forgiven, you should've gone home."

My fist was punching something soft and wet and the blood wasn't mine. I pulled my hand away and with it, hair. I recoiled in fright; the hair was long, and it kept coming. I staggered backwards, gagging.

"And I thought you liked her."

"Who?" I asked.

The man with the tweed neck scarf crouched down at the head of the pummelled girl.

"Still beautiful, I heard him say.

Transfixed, I could just make out the man piece together her face and then he began to reel in the hair.

"Why didn't you come with me? This would never have happened if you'd come home."

He was pulling me in and sighing.

"Poor girl, poor, little stray girl…well, at least she's home now."

The hair knotted around my fingers and he continued to reel it in. Frantically, I tore at the strands, stumbling backwards and panicking when the hair seemed to get tighter. I was getting closer to him; I could smell the rotting vegetation of his breath and I whimpered.

"Oh dear, you seem agitated," he said, heaving me to his chest, "Why?"

His cold body pressed against my own; I felt sick and couldn't answer.

"Is it this? Her hair?" The man delicately picked at the strands around my fingers until I was free. "There, it's gone."

"Why did you do that?" I asked.

"Because I know what's going to happen," he replied, twisting the length of hair into a rope. "You're going to run and I'm going to let you go."

"What?"

"Run away."

"You're letting me go?" I couldn't believe it.

"I said, run away. Run, run, run; run away as fast as your legs can carry you."

I was static; was it a trick?

"You're still here. I told you to run." He twitched. "Well, it's time I went."

And the man with the tweed neck scarf turned and walked further into the trees. I watched him disappear and only then did I move.

How long I ran for I didn't know but eventually I could see the trees thinning out and the world seemed lighter.

Dragging my tired body on, I was out of the wood; the sky was turning grey and mist hung softly over the field. I saw the hedgerow and knew the stream wasn't far away; I urged my limbs to make one final effort to reach familiarity.

I could hear the gurgling of water as I walked hurriedly alongside the hedge.

The grey sky was becoming yellow as the sun crept up from the horizon.

I stopped when I saw the bridge and smiled; it was as perfect as I knew it should be; the happy stream, the chorus of birdsong and the green fields that stretched on beyond.

"Thank God," I sighed, and walked to the bridge. I enjoyed the sound of my footsteps on the wood; the solitary sound of one person, and I gave myself a minute of solitude before moving on.

I leaned on the handrail and stared at the water tumbling over rocks. Moths flitted to and fro and a Kingfisher darted out of the low hanging trees, vanishing on the other side. I smiled again and then felt myself frowning.

'Why did he do that? Why did he let me go?' I was puzzled and couldn't figure out what I'd done to ensure my freedom. 'And I wonder where 'home' is.'

I shook my head and tried to dislodge those thoughts; it was time to go.

Taking one more look at the scenery, I turned and went back across the bridge.

"Pretty as a picture in't it?" The man looped his arm through mine, threading the length of rope and tying it round my wrist, "We can look at this view all day."

A CHANGE IN THE WEATHER

Rebecca J Payne

We live beneath a veil. From the south-western horizon of the sea, where mists rise up from heavy churning waves, the overhanging shroud stretches taut into flat grey skies above, smothering the town. From the shingle beach I gaze up and try to imagine the morning sun. I can no longer remember the last time it shined here, only a burnt and rusted carmine glow behind the chimney stacks in the east where it slowly rises behind winter's curtain.

Portland. South-west veering west, six to gale eight, increasing severe gale nine for a time. Rough or very rough, becoming high. Rain then squally showers. Moderate or poor.

Wet stones shift and grate beneath my feet as I walk the length of the old sea wall. Someone has vandalised the seafront map again, thick marker pen drowning the streets in a deep black, turning them to dark rivers that snake their way inland, consuming houses, parks, hotels. I reach up and touch the peeling surface of the board. A smudge of ink comes away on my fingertip, still half-damp in the early morning.

Fastnet. Westerly or north-westerly five or six, occasionally seven for a time. Moderate or rough. Showers. Moderate.

From somewhere I hear the calling of gulls, but there is nothing in the heavens, nothing but the grey dome above, and the roar of the waves below. I raise the pocket radio to my ear, better to hear over the sound of the ocean, and the speaker spits and crackles to me.

Low Fitzroy. One thousand and four, slow moving, filling one thousand and seven by midday tomorrow.

A green-grey tide makes its way to land, inch by inch across the shingle. Scraps of garbage tumble in the water as it churns over empty lager cans and polystyrene trays. Half a mile out from the shore I see water breaking roughly over a string of warning buoys that bob like orange sweets tossed into the current. Above the beach a red flag flies. I wonder who would commit themselves to these waters on a day like this, to the darkness blossoming beneath the chopping waves.

Finisterre, intermittent rain, visibility one mile, and rising slowly.

The long-wave signal fades and dies. I slip the radio into my coat pocket.

It will not be today. But it will come.

After each new rain, dirty water pools in the sunken parts of the pavements. I walk through them in old shoes that never really dry, but this doesn't bother me too much. The whole town is damp. Hundreds of little terraced houses huddled together in winding, narrow streets, their sea-facing walls battered and corroded by salt winds.

I walk up the steps that lead away from the harbour, the cobbles sloping north-east to the seventeenth century stone church. Once built to welcome fishermen back to the safety of land, its thick wooden doors are closed now, and the few boats that sit behind the harbour wall are old. Nobody will come here until the sun returns. Behind the church spire the town rises further, to the old factories, their brick towers reaching up to pierce the dome of mists, channelling all that work and heat and labour into empty space. Once birds hovered there. Now I hear them screeching, calling for scraps of food, but cannot see them, as though they have been shot out of the sky with arrows and brought to earth to pick the streets clean.

Falling water drums against the darkening bay window. I sit sideways on the window seat below, nestled in a blanket on old leather cushions, the radio in my hands.

Wight. South-west three or four, backing south-east five or six later. Slight or moderate. Showers, rain later. Good, becoming moderate or poor later.

Across the room, half-in half-out of the doorway, he eats thin rice noodles from a bowl.

"You should turn that off, Cassie."

Plymouth. South four or five, backing southeast five to seven, perhaps gale eight later. Moderate or rough, occasionally very rough. Showers, rain later. Good, becoming moderate or poor later.

"Please turn that off."

The rain keeps falling.

No ships can be seen from the sea wall. When the sun returns, ships will come, I tell myself. Ships stocked with goods, with food, with people. But for now the horizon is a shield of vapours, a lonely place, and the seas beneath churn and mix. Below grey waves I see them blossoming; black flowers on ancient vines, coming up from some unimaginable depth to feed on our light. Rising slowly, rising, always rising, like negatives of snowdrops in the time before the spring, shooting up as portents of what is to come. From a pocket I draw out my radio, turning the long wave dial until I find the signal, nervously listening for the news, knowing it must be coming soon.

Lundy. Westerly veering north-westerly four or five. Moderate. Showers. Moderate.

The flowers beneath the waves turn to me like sunflowers with their faces to the sun. The radio hisses. I watch the tide move ever inwards, bringing dark vines towards the shingle of the beach.

Fisher. In north, easterly five, increasing six to eight, in south, variable, becoming north-easterly four or five, occasionally six later.

Encroaching flowers of midnight bloom below the surface, their petals spreading wide in a riot of deep black as they fill the oceans before turning inwards, shrinking, dying from sight.

In north, moderate, in south, moderate or rough. In north, rain, in south, rain, fog patches. In north, poor, in south, moderate, occasionally very poor.

If it be not now, yet it will come.

The ink has stained my skin in a fingerprint.

Against the cliffs by the sea wall, one door stands unlocked; a solitary café that opens its doors to the people who remain through the winter. I stand at the doorway for a moment wondering why I want to go inside. I can feel electric fires running but they don't warm me, just dry my skin. From behind the counter a woman in a charcoal apron looks up and half-smiles.

Inside the café there is a strange silence. I hear the sound of metal teaspoons hitting porcelain, the whine of metal chair legs shifting on the vynil floor.

"Tea?"

The woman at the counter hovers by a large metal water heater. I can't remember what I'm supposed to say. She pulls down on the heater tab and steaming hot water begins to flow. I watch the ritual unfold as she pours milk, stirs, taps the spoon against the mug. She walks around from the counter and puts the offering down on a table next to me, and I remember now that I'm supposed to sit down here, sit down and drink it.

I sink into the wooden chair and wrap my hands around the mug. There are people in here, but I try not to look at them. They sit in pairs, wrapped in coats and scarves, and they look the opposite of me in my damp shoes.

In the mug a teabag floats forlornly in a sea of brown liquid. It's hot to drink but tastes of nothing.

Down by the churchyard an old man sits on a damp bench, a tray of food on his lap. I stand by the railings and watch as a group of boys in hooded sweatshirts and baseball caps descend, chirping and cawing, grabbing chips from his grasp and spilling them, eating them from the ground before flocking away down the street, looking for new victims. He waves his cap after them in anger and yells, but they are already gone.

The church bell tolls noon. I fumble with numb hands for my radio.

There are warnings of gales in Viking, Forties, Cromarty, and Rockall.

I walk beneath the railway bridge, feeling its rusting girders creaking under the weight. A section of road has been fenced away, tarmac and stone ripped up to dig a hole deep into the earth, but there is no one here, just abandoned tools lying still by the crater. This place smells like burning.

I walk on to the other side where steps lead up to the platform, and there, perched on the edge of the bridge, I see the hooded boys leaning over, staring down at the town in the failing light, looking for pickings. As the sound of a train approaches they break and run flying from the wall, down the steps and past me, away; I don't look back to see where they go, just listen as the train pulls in, its wheels screaming against the tracks, feeling the rumble overhead as it slows.

Doors slam as people step away from their carriages. I wait at the bottom of the stairs for them to come, and one by one they filter down, no more than half a dozen, all shrouded in winter coats and scarves and hats. I wait as each person passes me by, but there is no one here for me, nobody returning.

I wait while the train pulls away again, the noise moving slowly above me, darkness falling quickly all around. It is almost evening. Panic rises within and I reach for my pocket.

High south-west Norway, one thousand and thirty-four, moving slowly south-eastwards, expected Skagerrak one thousand and thirty by same time.

I clasp the radio in my hand as though holding it tight will make good news come.

Irish Sea. Westerly veering north-westerly five to seven. Rough or very rough, showers, moderate.

There is a roaring sound, but there are no more trains. I stand between the burning brick walls that curve up and over me and I try to remember who I waited for.

Stornoway. Wind north west, seven miles, one thousand and four, rising slowly.

I have more hours before it comes. I turn for home.

"I can't take you doing this anymore, Cassandra."

He is emptying the batteries out of my radio. I watch him walk into the bare light of the kitchen, and I hear them strike the bottom of the bin like tiny bullets.

Outside, the storm rages. Winds blow in from the surface of the sea, choirs of invisible birds straining at the telephone wires, plucking and sounding them in an cacophony of fear.

He comes back, turning over the sketchbooks and canvasses that lie piled up like bodies throughout the room. He pulls out a half-drawn still life of a bowl of violets and pushes it into my lap.

"This one. Just finish this one."

I reach out and trace my finger over grey lines that tell of where bright purple flowers should blossom on the page.

"You have to finish something. You can't go on this way."

My eyes dart to the radio on the bookshelf, silent. It would be so nice to see the sun again.

He only calls me Cassandra when he's angry.

My eyes move to a table in the corner of the café, tucked away by a tall curtained window; an old picture of a green landscape hangs on the wall. No one sits there, just two empty rattan chairs and a faded table cloth. In my mind I see a man sitting with a newspaper unfolded, but I look again and there is nothing, just table, chairs, tablecloth.

On the table next to me, two lovers in flashes of red are

sitting close together, oblivious to anything but each other. I want to warn them, to tell them to run for higher ground.

"How are you doing, Cassie?"

The woman in the charcoal apron is standing over me. I open my mouth but nothing comes, and she puts her hand on my shoulder.

"I'll get you another cup, pet. Don't you worry, alright?"

She takes my half-empty cup away. The lovers put on their hats and coats and leave, arms intertwined.

Table, chairs, tablecloth. Always the same yet different, and always the grey sea beyond the window, grey and squirming.

The living room smell damp. Yellowed plaster crumbles on the walls, and I walk through the house, tracing every crack with my fingers, feeling them widen beneath by touch. One by one I count them. The same as yesterday.

In the kitchen the stove gives out a feeble warmth, and nothing is left to stoke it, so I wrap myself in a pale blue blanket and fill the kettle with water. After an age, steam rises and clings to the cold walls, and I make tea. Across the room sits the kitchen table, two chairs, tablecloth, and I try to remember the missing figure, newspaper, plate, something filling the void.

Sole. Westerly veering north-westerly five to seven. Rough or very rough. Showers. Moderate, occasionally poor.

In the living room the blue fairy lights strung across the bay window are reflected back, blurred and distorted by the raindrops against the background of the midnight street. The clothes airer by the radiator sags to one side, and I run my hand over a shirt that hangs from it, still wet. Nothing will dry in this house.

Rockall. Westerly veering north-westerly five to seven, occasionally gale eight for a time. Rough or very rough. Squally showers. Moderate.

A blank canvas is propped against the bookshelf. I imagine how it would feel to paint ships gliding beneath the sun with sails in full bloom, great vessels of raw sienna with sheets of white, presiding over bright waves of cobalt teal.

Malin, Hebrides.

Tumbling waves, all blues and greens and teeming with life, white foam on the surface sparkling, iridescent.

West or north-west six to eight. Very rough or high.

I want to live to see those ships in the sun.

Squally wintry showers. Poor, light icing.

Gale force eight veering westerly imminent.

It is coming.

The mug has gone cold in my cupped hands. Light is fading outside, dropping down to meet the squalling sea. The woman in the charcoal apron is cleaning the counter, looking at me with sad, impatient eyes.

"Don't you have somewhere to go?"

The pier is silent but for the lapping of the tide against rusting pillars. The faded colours of the amusement rides look tawdry now, and all is battered by the winds that blow in without mercy, ice cold and vatic. There was a time when these wooden planks stood warm and dry and children ran up and down them in the sun. Now this skeleton in soaked to its very bones.

At the end of the pier I see the hooded boys sitting on the railings. They don't know what is to come. As I draw near they spread their arms out wide and take off into the air, screaming.

There are warnings of gales in Rockall, Malin, Hebrides, Baily, and Fair Isle.

By the railings I look out to the dark seas and I see them clearly now, in bloom, filling the whole ocean with their dark vines, moving with unstoppable currents to reach every inch of every shoreline. Their roots are deeper than the fissures of the ocean floor and older than the sun whose light they have sucked from the world.

Low Faeroes nine-hundred and seventy-eight losing its identity by oh-six-hundred tomorrow.

No one else can see, nobody understands what it means,

what it has been warning of. Like trails of ink dropped into water they spread, stirring, coalescing until the seas themselves are stained black.

Low one-hundred miles north of North Utsire nine-hundred and seventy-three expected three-hundred and seventy-five miles north...

I stand upon the railings and drop the radio into the waves. Ancient tendrils reach up and clasp it, bearing it away on tides of thorns. There are no more warnings. The great dome above the Earth has thundered shut forever.

Dark waters rush in to me from every side.

It is here.

BELLS RINGING UNDER THE SEA

Sophia McDougall

"Why won't you talk about her," you said. "Was she such a terrible person?"

"She really kind of was," I said. "Wish I'd never met the woman."

Awful thing to say, of course – worked that one out even before your face crumpled and you curled in on yourself and wouldn't say a thing to me the rest of the evening. But saying anything that would make you leave the subject alone for five seconds was almost worth it.

It was sort of true. She was terrible. She contained terrors. She was all shine and motion and rip currents and undertows and sharks.

Mostly, she was terrible to herself.

Not only, though.

God, ten years gone and the fights I still have with her. Sweating on the interstate, loading the van, queuing for takeout – takes someone asking why I'm running around with a face like a slapped arse (not that they put it that way, out here) before I even notice I'm doing it.

Mel, I'll be thinking, that's *another reason* why you fucked up. Will you just admit how fucking unfair this all is? Why did you ever even marry me in the first place?

Not that it's just me bullying her, though -- in my head she gives as good as she gets.

And I don't beg her to come back. Always choked the impulse off before it could draw breath, though there was a time I used to walk around the house a lot just hearing myself saying, "please".

And now I can't find a nice word to say about the poor cow, can I; it all sticks in my craw along with the "Mel come back" stuff. So this is why I'd rather just go on fighting with the woman in my head and not actually say anything.

But I guess that isn't going to wash. Hasn't for a while, in fact. So I ought to think about what I am going to say.

I could tell you a bit about the wedding, I guess.

It was kind of a cliché, honestly, but that only makes it easier to get the basics across: a list of fairly standard things for the kind of people we were then. Barefoot on the beach. Candles on the white sand and beads around Mel's neck and the full moon and the stars out and all of that. Sticks of incense burning, though all you could really smell was that lemony mosquito repellent, but I kind of loved that smell back then and even now, some summer nights when I catch a whiff of it drifting from a neighbour's back yard… it gets under my lungs and yanks at something so hard I want to scream or smash things or cry or drive into the ocean, and once in a very, very great while I do those things.

Except never that last one.

Anyway, the wedding: pretty much the second the rings were on our fingers Mel grabbed my hand and ran straight into the sea in her wedding dress (which was only a patterned sundress she'd picked up from a market stall that morning, after all, but still). And we whoop and kiss and float in each other's arms. We're so incredibly pleased with ourselves. We are amazing. Marriage is amazing.

Then she tips herself over and slips down deep, glossy black water closing over pointed toes, and doesn't pop back up. So there am I, the new Mr Melanie, left bobbing alone on the dark surface with the floating petals from her wreath of moon daisies, for minute upon minute, saying, "Okay Melanie, it's not *funny,*" like she could even hear me.

So eventually of course a small hand yanked hard on my foot and then slithered up my leg to pinch my arse. Then I'm all enveloped in giggling wet Melanie who's kissing and nipping at the back of my neck and I never feel like coming out of the water.

Jesus Christ, Melanie.

She'd been practising holding her breath since she was tiny, she told me. Long before she ever thought of being a diver. Sitting in the windowsill at the old place in Cornwall, staring out at the sky and not breathing just for the sake of not breathing. Pushing herself farther and farther away from the world. Then worming her way down to the bottom of the local pool and clinging onto the lowest rung of the ladder in the deep end, for seconds and later minutes, there in the chlorine blue, until stars hovered in front of her eyes. Dreaming of Lyonesse.

Maybe that was actually a big part of her problem; I mean that shit cannot be good for the developing brain. Maybe half of all the bollocks that happened on that awful trip, out in the mist and under the waves, was straightforward *brain damage.* On her part. I guess on mine, it would have had to be some kind of hysteria.

Except that doesn't make a damn thing any better.

… afar off as it were in the element, huge and mighty hills of water, tumbling one over another in such sort as if the greatest mountain in the world had overwhelmed the low valleys or marshy grounds. Sometimes it so dazzled the eyes of many of the spectators that they imagined it had been some fog or mist coming with great swiftness towards them, and with such smoke as if the mountains had been all on fire; and to the view of some it seemed as if millions of thousands of arrows had been shot forth all at one time, which came in such swiftness, as it was verily thought that the fowls of the air could

scarcely fly so fast: such was the threatening fury thereof.

I offered Mel a toke a day or two after I met her, on the beach at Noosa. She shook her head. She didn't touch weed, she said, because it made her hallucinations worse. Hallucinations which, incidentally, she suffered from all the time.

"But not *now,*" I protested.

"Oh yeah," she said, breezily. "They look as real as you do,"

"How do you know they're *not,*" I said. I didn't mean to be a dick about it, I just had no idea how you'd navigate so much as a trip to the supermarket let alone go skipping from ocean to ocean, when there's flayed-skull type things glaring at you out of the air all the time.

"Context," she said.

"Wow."

We didn't say anything for a bit.

"Planning your escape from the axe-murderer?" she asked, brightly, though I wasn't thick or stoned enough not to see how shallow the brightness was.

"Nah," I said. "I'm fairly fucked in the head and all." Then I got a bit worried I'd been offensive. I just wanted her to know I did have some idea of what it meant to have your mind get away from you. I'd taken a little too much of this and that over the years; had a lot of family I didn't talk to; had scars all up my arms that weren't all as old as I'd have liked. Still have those, obviously, though now they're old enough. First time we went to bed, Melanie kissed them. Girlfriends had done that before and I'd never liked it – felt like it was all about how *tender* and *accepting* they were and I'd have liked to just get laid occasionally without the reminder of what a fucking mess I used to be. But when Mel ran her tongue over them and murmured "they look like gills" it felt different.

Seeing as we ended up shagging, Melanie couldn't have been that offended with me, though she did raise her eyebrows and smile at me in a kind of aren't-you-just-*adorable* way, which I guess

I could have been offended at in turn, but I wasn't.

I *liked* it.

The remains of the dead were washed from their repositories, and several skeletons appeared scattered upon the beach. A stone coffin, containing human bones covered with tiles, was also seen, but before it could be removed, the violence of the surge broke it in two pieces.

My diving buddies from Australia had all said that there would be no decent sites in England, which is wrong, and that English sea freezes your balls off ten months of the year if you so much as look at it, which is right. Still, even before Melanie I'd got some vaguely patriotic feelings about the old grey Atlantic booming under the English chalk – which, being as much British as anything else, I'd a right to. Something austere and uncompromising about that flexing armour of steel and that made it the more beguiling when it would soften in the sun into blue or rose. And though it's also true that often the visibility down there tends towards the fairly crap, that used to feel kind of fitting to me: all those wrecks and reefs were properly hidden and secret in the greenish dark, so not just anybody could get to see them.

Also, you'd never forget you were in an alien place that wasn't really meant for you. Which is a big part of why anyone with any sense wants to go there.

We've already dived the wrecks of Spanish galleons and German bombers. Now Mel's dug up an actual drowned town not far from our cramped Sussex cottage, which is not that surprising given both Mel's interests and the fact that in England, nothing's ever all that far away.

(Though sometimes, I've wondered, did she know about it before? Is that why she wanted us to live there? I'd expected her to want to go back to Cornwall, though after everything that she'd been through with her mother I'd bought it readily enough when she said it was too painful. Probably it just *was* and I'm being paranoid but this is another fucking thing, Melanie – another thing that I'll never fucking *know* and if I'm not being reasonable that would be because of *you*.)

"When a storm's coming," said Mel, "You can still hear the church bells ringing under the sea."

She loved her drowned city stories. Lyonesse, which got her started, Kitezh, Cantre'r Gwaelod, Atlantis, Saeftinghe, Ys; the wicked towns sunk by angry gods, cursed by kidnapped mermaids, dragged down by watery devils. She loved all the monsters swept under by Noah's flood, the queens who turned into sea-nymphs, the unrotted sailors still lying peacefully on their bunks in sunken ships.

And she loved it when it any bit of a story came true, and so I hadn't known her very long before I was well-acquainted with the fact that little old Britain is not, in fact, immune to tsunamis and other aggressions of the sea, and so there are around a billion underwater towns looped all around the island. And practically every fucking one of those fucking stories has that detail about the bells, that you can still hear them – on nights without a moon, or when there's a storm, or when something horrendous is going to happen to the people left on land.

"So is there actually anything to *see*," I asked, feeling I'd probably have heard about it before if there was. "Or are we talking some really exciting sand?"

"It's not all about the pretty fishes, Lloyd," she droned. Melanie took the usual freediver thing of laughing at bubblers a stage further: as far as she was concerned, you weren't serious if you went down there just to *look* at anything. It was about inhabiting the planet's depths, about distance and remoteness. It was about just plain *being underwater*.

If you'd seen her dive you'd understand. The first time I laid eyes on her, I was standing on the roof of the deckhouse of the HMAS Brisbane, watching the lionfish and the noon wrasse stream past in flashes of neon, and this creature just *flies* past my head – *soaring* like a lark through air. Short yellow-white hair flaring and rippling around her head like a burning halo. A plain black cossie leaving almost all her skin bare to the water, while the rest of us are covered head to foot in our wetsuits, tanks on our backs and masks over our faces, practically indistinguishable from each other. While she could only have been herself. I could barely believe how far and deep a single breath could take her, how long she could make it last. I couldn't take my eyes off her either. How long since I'd first seen her, now? Two, three minutes, and she's still gliding around the hull like she's never even heard of air. When she swooped down the wreck's funnel into the boiler room my chest ached in sympathy she clearly didn't need. Then no sign of her for what seemed like forever; then she burst out the other side of the wreck like an opening anemone, and startled a shriek of bubbles out of poor Barry who was minding his own business hovering over the gun turrets. And then she took off, skimming away into the blue, and I sort of assumed that was the last any of us would see of her, that she was just this fucking… *spirit* or something, flickering through.

"Anyway, yes there's stuff to see," said Mel, sitting on our kitchen table amid the debris of watercolours and paper and grinning. "Skeletons still wash up out of the old churchyard there all the time."

"See, for me that's *not* an incentive," I said.

"Wimp," she said happily, and didn't elaborate that her entire life was spent in the company of way worse stuff than that.

She *was* happy. She'd been out of the hospital six months; the new meds were working great, no side effects that particularly bothered her. She still *saw* all the usual crap, but she was used to that and at least the burning faces in the wallpaper didn't *talk* any more. She was selling a bit of art to a greetings card company – sad-eyed mermaids and black-winged angels for gothy teenage girls. ("You leave gothy teenage girls alone," said Mel, sternly).

I felt prouder of her happiness than maybe I should have, like it was a certificate of how very much *my* shit was together. I wasn't just *married,* with a *job*, and a *mortgage,* I was also demonstrably capable of seeing my wife through an extremely grim episode without caving in or going in any way loopy myself. And though in principle I knew she'd have more bad times, I think I still felt like we'd given her mental problems a kicking they'd never forget. And I didn't even have any of my own any more.

Mel was training hard, and maybe-possibly had some sponsorship lined up for a contest in the Andamans in August, and even if that fell through we were going to Boracay in November, and already had money enough to pay for it even if we wouldn't be able to do much in the way of eating.

In the meantime, the English sea was as close to warm and welcoming as it's ever going to get.

Mel'd nag me sometimes to ditch the tank and the mask, all that clumsy stuff between me and the water, and even though I loved to watch her swim unhampered, I'd argue that she was the one who was missing out. "But you're tied to the surface. I mean, it's amazing how long you can go on your own air but, still, it's *minutes*. You can't *stay* down there. I can."

"That's true," she'd say sadly. And she would scuba from time to time, when there was no other way to get where she wanted. And I would join in with her training to lengthen the time I could hold my breath, and sometimes I'd try leaving the gear in the boat.

But I couldn't really get past the feeling that I was drowning. Couldn't stop missing the ready oxygen at my lips.

So usually we each did it our own way. Beside's it's just safer, if you're freediving, to have someone there who isn't. Sometimes they black out, freedivers, bodies still clutching the one breath locked in their lungs, and even if you get them to the surface they won't let it out to claim another. It's not even technically drowning.

So this time I'm piling all the usual stuff into the little hired boat, and Mel's got her goggles and the monofin that makes her move through the water like a mermaid and out we go.

Another thing I loved about the English sea was that slight shock when you got into it, the way you had to fight the reluctance in your flesh no matter how many times you'd done it before. It never, ever makes it too easy. Used to give me a little thrill of some kind of conquest even before I was fully under.

Melanie straps her dive light to the shoulder of her suit, though I know she hates having to bother with even that much baggage. Mine's already clipped to my belt. She slips in first, as usual, and I tip myself over after. Don't take in anything very specific about the surroundings at first as I'm still enjoying how the water changes the light, makes it something with a texture and a weight, how it changes the rhythm of my heart. Also, Mel always thinks that if we're alone and occasionally if we're not, the first minute of a dive is an excellent time for a bit of feeling up.

When we're done with that she sinks away from me, and fades almost at once, first to a dim green silhouette, then to nothing but the hazy electric glow of her light. The visibility is awful, for all the sea's been quiet for days. The water's thick and smoky with silt and, a few meters further down, with waving strands of kelp.

It's clear to me at once that, at least from my point of view, this is going to be a pretty boring dive. Well, not exactly boring: I still *like* to see starfish plastered to rock and blennies moseying around the sand. But there's nothing new, and there's nothing interesting about the terrain, and, as for the town, well – I'm increasingly getting the feeling I was right and it's only still there in the most minimal possible way.

I could watch Mel, of course, when she comes close enough: the sunlight glowing dimly through the white polypropylene of the blade fixed to her feet, rippling criss-cross over her skin.

After zigzagging around for a bit we find the hummocks of tumbled brick. They get a bit more organised as we go along – you can just about recognise the layouts of buildings and I think Mel, ahead of me, might be swimming down what was once a street. But still, it's basically all rubble -- it's really not like we were ever going to run into Stonehenge or a castle down here. No bell tower and no bells left, whatever the stories say. I do find a long ridge of larger, squarer blocks of tawny stone, chiselled hundreds of years ago and I'm sure this is fascinating if you're really into mediaeval architecture. Or if you're Mel, but I'm neither of those things.

I swim closer to the half lit shadow that's Mel and find her drifting upside down, trailing her fingers through the sand. We exchange okay signals, then she heads up for gulp of air and while she's gone I try and see things her way. I get a vague shudder thinking of people walking these streets, talking, eating, doing their jobs – how I'm swimming through their sky. Even more of one when I imagine the sea trampling in like an army and claiming a few hundred of them as tribute. But I don't think that's exactly what she's after here; I mean it's not really the *people* she's into, she can get enough of *people* anywhere. No, I think it's that here the thing she spends so much time chasing as deep and as far as her body will take her, edges close, lines up to the world she has to live in.

She's back, an undulating shadow streaming on into the dark, and I seem to have got myself to a weird place in my head and for a moment I feel this is a private thing of hers that I shouldn't be here for and that I kind of don't *want* to be.

I decide I'll just focus on the wildlife, thanks, even if there isn't anything here I haven't seen a million times before. I meet a hermit crab bumbling around over the remains of a long flint wall. He isn't bothered by the beam of my torch, so me and the hermit crab hang out together for a while.

The crab scuttles across a fallen block of stone that's shaped differently from the others – a wedge shape with a gentle curve to it. The keystone of an arch.

And I get a bit more interested because I think maybe there's something carved on it – though it might just be the work of the water – and I reach out to brush the silt away.

And that was about the last second of my life that I thought I understood. And so it follows that trying to explain anything that followed is hard enough even in my own head.

So, let's start with this: I've known conditions to change very fast at sea, especially in these waters. But never that fast.

The closest thing to a warning is that for an instant the visibility gets a little better. The particulate in the water's all dragging away and down, and I see Mel is closer than I thought. We look at each other. Mel's eyes wide with something I've tried and tried to decode all these years, though at the time I thought it was simple alarm.

The sea snatches hold of her, whisks her off faster than my instinctive cry can bubble out of my mouth. Her light blinks out. And mine goes dark the second after that, so by the time I'm yanked to the bottom it's pitch black.

It's like a huge storm wave's come out of nowhere and piled itself down on us. I have this detached, sarky moment to think 'he died doing what he loved' and then just nothing but *fuck fuck please no fuck Mel Mel Mel* as I bounce over rock and brick and silt, churned arse over tit, helpless in the grip of what's dragging me further and further out.

My lungs burn. The regulator's been jolted from my mouth. I can't get enough control, enough *time* to get hold of it before I'm hurled over again. I can't do anything. Certainly can't equalise the pressure in my ears.

My ears. It must just be my own pulse, chiming huge and muffled in my skull, but I start to hear the ringing then.

Dragged up, turned over, bashed down again. It stretches out, somehow; I stop feeling the impacts, spend longer floating dreamily in the water's dark hold.

And something runs over me, light and sure, like a slow stream of bubbles, like an appraising hand, and I don't feel like I'm alone. I think again, *Melanie.* But it isn't her.

Bash into the sea bed again. Softer landing again. Away into blue-green-black.

I'm in our bedroom at home; the windows are open and moon wrasse dart in and out. The bells are louder, clearer, more joyous, like there's a wedding going on. Melanie's sitting on the windowsill, swinging her legs. She's in the sundress she got married in, with a wreath of daisies on her hair, which is blazing and swaying around her face with the rock of the water. She looks back at me, gives me the OK signal and pushes herself out. I'm not scared for her though we're on the top floor and there's concrete underneath, because of course she floats. She hangs there outside the window, and I go over and she reaches through and puts her arms around my neck, lays her cheek against mine. She might be talking but I can't hear because she hasn't any breath, and doesn't need any now. Beyond her there's – well, there's nothing.

Nothing but the mountains higher than Everest, the chasms spilling out magma, the valleys too deep for sunlight to touch. And all the monsters swept off with Noah's flood, the queens who turned into water-nymphs, the sailors fast asleep in their bunks.

Then I think: this is bollocks. The fact is that I'm hallucinating at the bottom of the sea where I'm in the process of getting the shit kicked out of me.

I thud hard on the and then nothing's holding me any more. Can't orient myself for a moment but eventually I work out that the bottom is down *here* and the surface is *up there*. I get hold of my regulator. Heaven of oxygen in my mouth and maybe I am going to survive this after all. I thrash upwards faster than I should; I try to slow myself but at this point I really can't make myself worry all that much about the bends, not set against getting out of this *now*.

Light and air on my face. I let the reg drop out of my mouth again and breathe and scream Mel's name.

Where the hell are all those waves? I thought I was coming up into the middle of a crazy freak storm. But the surface is just as placid as when we left it. But what there is though is thick, thready white mist the water. I can't see much further than I could down below.

And I can still hear the ringing. Sad, blurred swells of sound, pulsing heavily off the water. But I shout for Mel until I almost stop noticing.

I had oxygen at least part of the time. The girl can hold her breath a long time, but no one can hold it that long.

I start swimming inelegantly, becoming aware as I do it that I'm pretty beaten up and remain very much in need of a significant dose of luck. All I can do is hope blindly I'm going in the direction of the shore or Melanie or no, *both, both, both* for godsakes.

Then, amazingly, there's the boat – barely thirty yards away from where I came up. I was sure I'd have been dragged twenty times that and more.

I think maybe Mel's already found it and is just lying in the bottom too exhausted to answer me, and though I know really this has to be bull it helps get me there. I flounder over and drag myself up, and the boat's empty of course, but for the bottled water and a packet of fucking sandwiches.

There's the dry-bag with both our phones.

I really don't *want* to ring for the Coastguard because I don't want to think of Mel as being *lost at sea* rather than fleetingly out of sight, but I'm not a total idiot so of course I grab the bag and I sit there, stabbing at buttons, shivering a little, blood dripping from elbows and knees, in the middle of all the white.

And the ringing. I don't listen to it, exactly. It's all around me; a solemn, deep, endless tolling from all around me. It's getting hard to imagine it ever stopping, but I still don't actually listen. By now I've got a very strong feeling I don't want to listen to it, just like I don't want to think about the storm surge that tore us up under the water but hasn't left a trace on the surface.

But I can't exactly help but think about the fact that now neither of our fully charged phones will turn on.

She'll have come up somewhere and just can't find the boat in the fog; it's amazing enough that I did.

I yell her name some more.

What if she's blacked out down there and I'm not there to grab her?

At that I'm out of the boat and under the waves again before I can even think. The water's calm enough now and I spray streams of bubbles around as a signal. Plough my way deeper and I guess it's shock and all, but God the water feels freezing now. My torch comes back on and every shadow and rock the beam catches looks like her.

I really can't swim properly – feel like a donkey's kicking me in the chest every time I move my arms, and my left leg's fucked somehow too. I flail my way to the surface again and shout some more except by now I'm kind of on the edge of hyperventilating or sobbing and I hate the way my voice comes out, almost as much as I hate those bloody bells, because it sounds just as hopeless.

Then there's a quiet, flat voice saying, "Lloyd."

Mel is sitting in the boat. She's just there. Not gasping for breath or anything. Her knees are drawn to her chest and her skin's covered in goosepimples and she's looking straight ahead. Her hair is beginning to crinkle as it dries. There's not a scratch on her.

The bells aren't ringing any more.

I lumber up into the boat and stare at her. "Jesus Christ, Mel," I gasp, when I can speak. "Where were you?"

She doesn't say anything.

"Are you okay?" And at this I either start shaking badly, or notice that I was shaking already. "Oh, fuck, Mel," I stammer, reaching for her. "I thought –" I get her into my arms, and then I'm crying helplessly into her damp hair.

It's the relief, I think, the relief.

Mel lay against me quietly, patiently. Then after a while she detached herself, started up the motor, and she took me home.

I chattered like a moron all the way, trying to talk enough for both of us, also trying to get a handle on what exactly had happened. "That was fucked up," I gabbled. "I kind of... saw stuff, under the water. It was like there was… someone, who –? And when I couldn't find you, I kept hearing –? Did you hear the –?" No answer. "Did you – I mean, it's just that – Mel, did you see anything?"

"Nothing, Lloyd," she said, sounding so tired. "Just water."

I was in bad enough shape that we clearly had to go to the hospital. Melanie drove me there and sat silently beside me, and her hand in mine was cold.

"So what *is* that accent?" asked the doctor who was slapping my x-rays up on a lightbox.

"Just Australian," I said blankly, the way I'd say 'Just English' back in Oz, because who can be bothered with all the ins and outs of *that.*

"Oh, I can hear it now!" she said. "You know, I was halfway to guessing Canadian, because when I think someone sounds American only not quite –"

"I *don't* sound American," I said, ridiculously, like I'm back in high school. Look, no offence and all, but the two years in Seattle which comprised Mum's shitty second marriage were not a good part of my life, and I didn't yet know how grateful I'd end up being for them.

Anyway, I'd got some excuse for being a bit shirty: two cracked ribs and a broken left fibula, besides an ample collection of gashes and scrapes. No diving for me for a while.

I had no idea how long 'for a while' was going to turn out to be, but even at the time I felt I wasn't as upset as I should have been.

They checked Mel over too, because when they asked how long she'd been under, whether she'd lost consciousness or swallowed any water, she couldn't give a clear answer. And I think even someone who didn't know her could see there was something off. They shone lights in her eyes, listened to her lungs. They didn't find anything wrong. They told me to keep an eye on her, like I wouldn't have done anyway.

Freedivers almost never get the bends. They can come and go as they like, no toll to pay for crossing so many times between water and air.

Mel hadn't got the bends, but she wasn't ever the same.

If I'd said, *my wife never came out of the water,* and the old Mel was here, she would have rolled her eyes and said "Oh the *drama.*"

But frankly I can say whatever I want about the situation now.

She couldn't train. She had to pull out of the contest and she didn't give a toss. "Who cares who can stay down longest," she said dully. "It's *minutes* anyway. Like you said."

"Mel," I said to her, "I think we ought to get you back to the doctor's." She exhaled wearily and did that sort of fake-looking at me I was getting to hate: she'd turn her face towards me, but not quite meet my eyes, like I wasn't supposed to notice she was gazing hopelessly at a point somewhere to one side and far beyond me. "I think you're depressed."

"Wow," drawled Mel, "I married a genius."

"Well, then, if you know you're sick, you know you need help."

Melanie slumped deeper, letting her head down on the kitchen table like it was too heavy to keep up, and mumbled, "Fine."

"The hallucinations, Mel," I said patiently. "Are they worse? Are they talking again?"

"I *said* I'll go," she growled into the tabletop. "Isn't that enough to get me out of this conversation?"

"I just want to know what we're dealing with."

"*We,*" said Melanie, "are not dealing with anything. And no, for your information, they're exactly the same as fucking normal." A spasm of ugly, bitter energy jolted through her, enough to get her head off the table but not more. "And why are you so interested in trying to *fix* me anyway. Just sit back and enjoy the crazy. This is what you signed up for in the first place."

This got me just as hurt and angry as, for whatever reason, she wanted it to, and maybe it would have been better to actually show it. But she looked so hollowed out and weary and frail, and I knew she was sick, so I just said very carefully, "That's not true."

"You married a headcase to make yourself feel sane. You keep being so nauseatingly *patient* with me because you like a *challenge*. Well, you've bitten off more than you can chew with this one."

(There's one argument that's gone the rounds in my head ever since, believe you me.)

"I want you to be okay," I said at the time.

"You have no idea what it would take to make me okay," said Mel.

Maybe I'm making it sound like it was all snapping and swearing at me. It wasn't. That was the awful thing of it. Mostly, whatever I suggested, she'd listlessly do. Eat something, Mel. Take your pills. Why don't you do some art. (Compliance on that one far slower and more laborious than everything else). She'd been back to the doctor's, and she was on a waiting list to see a new shrink, and I was waiting for the meds to *work,* like they always had in the past, even if it took a lot of time and worry and fiddling about.

A month or two later I decided her hormones were probably snarling things up and when they got back to normal things would settle down.

I thought about going along to the doctor's myself. Saying, "I might be having auditory hallucinations, doctor. I keep thinking I can hear bells ringing in the distance, especially when I'm close to my wife." And I knew I was a hypocrite because I couldn't ever bring myself to do it. I just looked up "tinnitus" on the internet over and over again and left it at that. Which meant that I couldn't talk to Mel about it, even though sometimes my mouth felt stuffed with *Melanie can you hear that,* or *Melanie something happened down there, didn't it, tell me what you saw, tell me, tell me…*

Because if I ever *did* say that, then, well...

When I wasn't watching, or coaxing, or ordering her about, Melanie did less and less. As far as I can tell, when relieved of an audience to perform for she just sat by the window and stared at the Downs between our tiny house and the sea. She also spent a lot of time in the bath. I didn't quite pick up what was weird about that for a while until I realised that when I went in after her there was never any steam in the air. She didn't use the hot water.

We couldn't go to Boracay in November, in the end. Too much else going on. My leg healed and I thought about getting back in the water, but I didn't feel right leaving Melanie behind and I really didn't want to suggest she came along.

I remember lying curled against her motionless back. It was maybe three in the morning. "Melanie," I whispered, like she could even hear me. "Come back, please."

But she did. After a long, long time, she whispered, "I can't."

She'd come back for me once. At least, she'd tried to. And it was getting pretty obvious by now that she thought it had been the wrong decision.

In one of those stories, the flood doesn't come to punish the town but to save it. Beautiful, virtuous citizens rejoicing as the water rises to take them home, and the invading hordes roar in and are entirely flummoxed to see their prey swept out of their reach forever.

And yes, that one has the fucking bells still ringing under

the fucking water and all.

Okay, so here's what I know happened.

It's not like I could stick to her all the time. I did have the old day job to worry about.

I'm busy trying to figure out what the fuck these people have done to their SQL server. And then it I realise that the *tinnitus* that's been ebbing and flowing through my skull for all these months has stopped, completely. The inside of my skull feels suddenly wide and bare and clean.

Melanie had hired the same boat as before, which later washed up, empty, a few miles along the shore.

She took her hated scuba gear, and no, I don't think that was to make it look more like an accident. I think she wanted to be sure of getting out as deep and as far as she could.

She didn't leave a note. And she didn't take a light.

So no one was there and no one knows for sure, but here's what I think.

First of all, I think when she'd told me she'd seen *just water,* down there beyond the sunken town, I think that was true. I think she saw the wild expanse of secret space she'd always wanted, offered to her, empty of all the horrible traffic through her brain.

I think, when she thought she'd gone far enough – or as far as she could, more likely – she pulled off her mask. Yanked the regulator from her mouth. Shrugged off the harness with the tank and peeled away her suit. And then waited, hoped, asked for another chance.

After that I don't know what happened.

I know there shouldn't be any doubt about what happens when a person vanishes into the sea. It's self-explanatory. She was ill. She was ill, and it wasn't her fault, and I couldn't help her enough, and so she died. And anger is a normal part of grief and all of that, but after ten years I shouldn't still be stuck on it.

It would have helped, maybe, if we could ever have found

her, but the human bones that wash up from time to time on that beach have never been hers, always turned out to be centuries old. Though the first time that happened it shook me up a fair bit.

And there was this other thing.

I was a wreck for a long time, of course. I had to go and see Mel's mum in the nursing home, and ended up not even telling her what had happened, because she could only vaguely remember Mel anyway and didn't know who I was at all and what was the point.

Slashed myself up a bit on more than one occasion, even though I tried very hard not to, because I was extremely worried about getting to the point where I'd have to check myself in somewhere and, well, I had responsibilities.

My own mother was pretty great about clearing the old place out and finding room in her little flat in Forest Hill, while I looked for somewhere new. I couldn't stand living so close to the sea.

But I'd lived half my life in the water. I'd loved it far longer than Melanie. I dreamed of the sea constantly (I still do) and they weren't all bad dreams. Eventually I got to a point where though I didn't want to dive anywhere Mel and I'd been together ever again, I started to think a big group dive somewhere nice and sunny with a lot of coral and colourful fish wouldn't be so bad. Maybe back home (I was starting to think of Oz that way). Maybe the Yongala, maybe Heron Island.

I wasn't quite ready for that. But then one of my old mates got engaged and a lot of the guys, many of whose names I can no longer remember, accumulated for a stag weekend in Dorset, and after a bit of coaxing I went too. And they all did a great job of not being weirded out by the presence of The Widower. And on the hungover second day there's a plan to head down to the beach and go surfing. It's summer again, and actually legitimately boiling, not just "hot for England", and I think: I can manage this. I'm no great shakes as a surfer, but you can't grow up near an Australian beach without some idea of how it works, and the swell here wouldn't challenge a baby. And it'd be a nice compromise, to be on the sea but not in it.

And it was beautiful for a while, flying over the water, in a glittering veil of spray, and tumbling off once or twice and coming up laughing among the rest.

And then I'm a little further out, just sitting on the board, legs dangling in the water, feeling the sun on my skin.

Then a small hand yanked hard on my foot.

More from the shock than anything, I went straight under.

I wasn't wearing goggles and my eyes shut against the salt on instinct. I didn't open them. But I could *feel* her, the water quivering and sighing with her, and her hand making a mischievous grab at my arse, her arms sliding over me, her lips on the back of my neck, and if I could just open my eyes and see her…

But I couldn't. I couldn't, I couldn't.

So then, because I had to, I shook myself free, swam back to the beach, walked straight up it without once looking back, got in the car and drove away. I didn't say a thing to anyone. And the only time I've even seen the sea since then was when I flew over the Atlantic on my way here, and I didn't more than glace at it then.

On the way home I had to drive through a village which was humming and shimmering with ecstatic church bells and I had a panic attack and nearly crashed the car.

It turns out ditching your whole life is a lot easier than it's made out to be, provided you've really made up your mind. I didn't do it as thoroughly as Melanie had, but I quit my job, and got on a plane, and figured out most of it at the other end, and I never came back. I have various ready-made answers to the "Oh and what brings you to Kansas" question, but have more sense than to come out with the truth, i.e: "it's the furthest possible place from an ocean where the locals still speak English." And so thank god for Mum's crappy second husband, and the hitherto useless technicality of my American citizenship. It made it all so much more convenient. But I'd have found a way to transplant us to the middle of China if I'd had to.

By now at least some of the reasons why I don't want to talk to you about this, and why I'm still so pissed off with your mother, should be obvious. Bailing out on me's one thing, but what about you? And God knows it's not fair, but how can I help but wonder if she ever really tried, if she was just waiting out the months until November, one hand listlessly draped over her swelling belly as she stared out at the crest of the Downs. Serving time until she could swim away and leave us both to it.

And if I'm not insane, if I'm the tiniest bit right about what happened in Dorset, then how dare she? How could she think I'd leave you?

Forget that. There's just the fact that even putting the best possible spin on the whole sorry business, it's not exactly *cheerful*, and I don't want to upset you or scare you.

But there's the other thing, and the worst thing. What if it didn't scare you? What if you'd understand more of it than I do?

You were there too, that day, swimming deep in the dark inside Melanie, though we didn't know it yet. Whatever happened to us, whatever I thought I felt look at me, what if it saw you too?

I knew I should never have caved on that above-ground pool you begged so hard for, no matter that it's a glorified paddling pool. I found you there a week ago, sitting cross-legged at the bottom, open-eyed, looking up through the water at the sky.

And yesterday morning you were standing staring out of the bathroom window, eyes full of dreamy haze. You said, "Look, Daddy, it looks like waves," and I followed your gaze at the billows rolling across a silken green ocean of unripe Kansas wheat. And you smiled and tilted your head, as if across all these thousands of landlocked miles, you could hear the summoning bells ringing under the sea.

In Tauris

Una McCormack

We saw them before they saw us. They came from the south, along the coast road. There were two of them. The day was hot and they struggled to make progress. They each carried packs and bronze pistols. We watched their approach through steel spyglasses. (We have many machined tools, which we use at need.)

As they came closer to us, they acquired individual characteristics. This can make matters harder, and so it should. One of them was shocked; wandering the dark valleys that lie beyond despair. On a bright sunny day, this, more than the weapons, signalled danger. On the other hand, he was near the end.

We noticed that his comrade carried him.

We moved back behind the perimeter and waited for them to arrive.

When the waiting was over, we opened the gate and came out to meet them. We greeted them in their language, which we had all used once upon a time but which was now not ours. When we spoke, they did not believe what they were hearing. They did not hear what we were saying.

We said: welcome. We said: you are safe here. We said: you may come inside.

We did not say, indefinitely.

The one who was carrying his comrade said, "Who are you? Whose side are you on?"

We laughed.

The other (by various signs marked as 'superior') stepped forwards. He put his arms around the nearest of us. Selene did not prevent him and he wept into her breast. We heard his whispered supplications. He said: "Mother of Mercy, Queen of Heaven, Star of the Sea, Mother of Patriarchs, hear your son your servant in this his hour of need..."

He said this again and again.

We took them inside. We were not at any point afraid of them.

We put the shocked one to bed. We gave the other food. He told us their names, which we heard grudgingly. He told us their story, which we have heard many times before.

He said: "We were amongst the last onto the arks. Half-a-day out, we looked back and saw the last of the bombs fall on the city. Mother of Heaven..."

His words failed him. Abigail filled his cup. We noticed that before he drank he thanked her in an automatic fashion.

He said: "Sailed three days. Made good speed. Tried to think of what was ahead, not behind us. Then the ark was targeted. Went down. Lost the lot – good people! Devout! They were our charge and we lost the lot. Michael," (this, he said, was the other's name), "this is what's eating him. 'Our charge, Paul,' he said to me, 'and we lost them'."

He stopped. We did not ask him to continue but we waited and we gave him our attention.

"Four of us on a raft. Still huge waves from what happened. Hector dead before we reached the shore. Buried him at sea. Michael said the words. A week at sea, maybe more. When we landed, we went north. We knew the eighth and twelfth chapters were to rendezvous in the north, so we went north. Simon died. Two of us left. We walked a while. Saw settlements. Got food. The locals pointed us this way, so we came this way. And here you are. Here you are."

Here we are.

He looked round slowly, as if noticing our number for the first time. "Wonder where you came from. How you got here."

The view beyond the window showed him long-standing houses, well-established fields and gardens and orchards. In twos and threes we rose from our chairs. We guided him to bed. Ofure said later that before he slept he knelt and said his prayers. Mother of Mercy, Queen of Heaven. Mother of Patriarchs. Star of the Sea.

We put the pistols away.

When they woke, Michael sat looking at his hands. We offered him small tasks to keep his mind busy. Paul devoted himself to fixing their talker. Some time passed this way, both profitably and unprofitably. Some of us noticed how they exerted a fascination upon others of us, mostly the children and several of the younger adults. One of these, anxious to stand out, produced a screwdriver and offered this to Paul. Michael took it. Some of us noticed that, after this, he noticed us more.

Then matters came to a head. In the night, we were woken by a great disturbance. Rising, we discovered Michael searching the house, the cabinets, drawers, common spaces, chests, and other containers. When he found tools, devices, and machines, he added them to the pile. He noticed that we were there. He said: "What else is there? What else do you have?"

We did not respond.

He said: "Do you have materials? Do you have the ability to *make* any of this?"

We did not respond.

He said, in a clear voice: "Do you understand what has been happening away from here? Do you understand? All of this," and he swept his hand across the pile, "could prevent a great deal of suffering."

We did not reply. Ingrid reached for one of the pistols.

He was there first.

Even then we would have let them go. But he said: "You do not need to be afraid. Not any longer. You are under our protection now."

We were a confusion. Many single voices struggled to be heard and hold sway.

For example:

Amina said that we should have expected this.

Athene said that we had a duty to help those in need.

Ekaterina said that we must not make any rash decisions.

Chloi said that we should not have allowed them to stay in the first place.

Bridget said that we had a duty to protect ourselves.

In the midst of this, they left. Some of us remarked that they took tools with them to mend their talker.

Athene went with them.

We continued to dispute. Later in the day, we came to our conclusion.

We drew lots. One of the younger adults, Iphigene, was selected. Because of her youth, I went with her, although in any technical matters she no longer needed my guidance.

We packed only what we needed for the task. We ran swiftly and silently along high ground and made good time. We came to their camp late and watched through the night, under a thin moon. In the uncertain dawn, as they rose, she got them in her sights. After, she wept a while.

She is young and she is strong.

We returned to our settlement. We returned to our work. We returned home.

We are here. We have always been here. We have not gone away. We shall never go away.

We listen. We measure every word. We measure even the

ones you think are uttered in private, amongst yourselves, in your own language. We hear and we translate. This makes us aware of our contingency. This makes us aware of the conditionality of our existence. This makes us aware that we have only been granted permission. It is not enough. It will never be enough. We will be ready, when permission is withdrawn.

We are still here. We have never gone away. We have tools that we teach others to use. We will seize the means, tear down the master's house, smash the world machine. We are Fury. We are Kali. We are the new moon. We are the dark inexorable undertow and the great obliterating wave. Our rage is rational and righteous. We will not fall silent. We will not fall, silent.

LOST SHEEP

Neil Williamson

Hope To Die fizzed into coherence. The cabin-bubble, frantic with the ghostlight of tactical displays, reverberated with noise: the scream of a klaxon, the imperative twitter of warning systems, the groan of superstructure under stress and the laughter of the man who occupied the gimballed chair suspended in the centre of the sphere. Daniel Gibbs, youngest child and official black sheep of the Gibbs Galactic Cultures dynasty was scarlet, shaking and sweat-soaked with excitement.

The scrawling displays slowed and, one by one, the warning noises diminished until only the blaring klaxon remained. "We'll be havin' the siren off now, Danny, yeah?" Hope sounded a little annoyed. "You complete cock."

Gibbs relaxed, spun lazily in the chair. His laughter dwindled to a sigh.

The klaxon cut out. "All that noise, mate." Hope's vocal pattern was still the abrasive baritone she'd picked up from her most recent scrap of Earthwave. It made everything she said sound peeved, but in this instance there was even more than the usual amount of – what had she called it? – *nark*. "It is really not fucking necessary."

"All right." Danny pouted. What wasn't *necessary* was his ship, however human it might pretend to be, complaining about noise. He'd been warned about her attitude when he bought her. For the price he'd paid for her, though, he could put up with it most of the time. If nothing else, her abrasiveness kept things from getting boring. "You have to admit it adds to the drama, though," he said.

The ship approximated the sound of breath drawn in through teeth. "Don't you start with me about fucking drama, you nonce. I fried my quantum racks to a crisp there finding a safe spot of space for us to pop into. You just had to sit back and enjoy the ride."

Now she was really killing the buzz. "Aw, come on, Hope. We're safe, aren't we?"

"Of course we're safe. No thanks to you. They're getting closer, you know. Your family the Hegemony, the representatives of who knows how many law enforcement and security agencies... and let's not even mention the bounty hunters? Bunch of fuckers. Do you know how many fucking spins that took us?"

Danny shrugged. As far as he was concerned the occasional need for a speedy exit was an occupational hazard. It went hand in hand with the notoriety and the rewards; at least, when there *were* rewards. Their riotous escape had been a distraction from the plunging disappointment experienced on arriving at the planet whose cultural rights he'd been planning to claim-jump. A newly discovered planetary system was rare, and a virgin culture an order of magnitude more so. He'd had the rights deals secured and the money spent long before Hope slipped them into the system, but as soon as they arrived he knew they were too late. The cultural claim notice broadcast across the system's media spectra had made it all too clear that the Hegemony had got there first by some margin. The euonymists had already begun their naming work on the inhabited planet, and the Hegemony-wide broadcast and trade rights too were neatly parcelled up among various divisions of the Gibbs Corporation.

Disappointment, in fact, was barely sufficient to describe how he had felt. He had been raging. The whisper from the Grüber Brothers was supposed to have been exclusive. In the tantrum that followed the realization that it was anything but, Danny had vowed expressively and in several languages to make sure that they were repaid for their mistake. It might still have been possible to sneak close enough to the new world to grab some footage that he could flog quickly before the sanctioned cultural tsunami rolled across the Hegemony worlds, but in his prolonged incandescence he'd lost the opportunity for even that consolation.

When the sudden swarm of antagonistic ships bore down on them, Hope took over and their escape became a rush of coherence and decoherence that Danny had no chance of following. The displays had swum with snapshot ghosts, lingering images of threats that were already a subspace spin away: everything from Hegemony hulks to diamond-glitter drone arrays, all of them hunting for him with the same cut-throat avidity with which he sought unsanctioned cultural novelty to titillate the jaded palates of the populated galaxy. All attempting to outmanoeuvre Hope's tactical strategies. Pieces moved, bets spread; a game of risk and reaction. Even as they cohered, Hope had sent them spinning off again to some other point in space, the ship juddering with imposed seizure imperatives, jerking under weapons fire, but every time they'd managed to slip away, try again. It had been a wild ride.

"Over *seventeen fousand* spins" Hope said. "This malarky is getting too risky by half. Remind me why I do this again?"

"Because we're a team?" Hope usually went along with that *shtick*, but on this occasion her only response was a snort of derision, so he followed it up with: "And because I own you."

After a beat, Hope said: "Well, you'll be hearing from my brief on that score, wontcha?"

Danny didn't know what a *brief* was. Hope picked up the most unlikely phrases from the old Earth broadcasts, the strung-out signals that had leaked across the light years during that short period of the planet's history when high-powered, modulated EM had been the primary method of media broadcast. Commercially speaking, Earthwave material never went out of fashion, and dedicated collectors could make a modest living. Danny's sister, Imelda, headed Gibbs Old World. It was a minor division but it provided a steady contribution to the family fortunes. That was Mel all over, though. No ambition. She'd always been perfectly content with her allotted role, seeking out those vanishingly faint signals, collating humanity's old stories.

Old stories, though. Who cared? Next to the corporate soaps and the melo-historicals, where the ratings were really at was discovering how weird other people – on other planets, in other systems – could be.

The galaxy was immense, and in a couple of thousand years of human colonization still only a fraction of its treasures had been uncovered. The thought of what else might be out there waiting to be found, and exploited, constantly thrilled him. Planets, civilizations, hilarious sexual practices: when it came to entertaining the masses, novelty was everything.

He'd never understood how or why his ship had become a stodgy old Earthwave nut.

"Where are we, anyway?" Danny said.

"Don't know, do I?" He heard the sulk in her sigh.

"Yes you do."

"All right, keep them on," she muttered. One, two, three displays blossomed on the curve of the bubble. A galactic limb. The details of the nearest star clusters. Proximity estimates to the nearest Hegemony worlds, to the nearest habitable world, to anything. All, literally, astronomical.

Hope didn't need to say it, but she did anyway. "We're way out there, mister."

"Take us somewhere else then."

"No can do, buster. Seventeen thousand jumps takes it out of a girl. I'm going to put my feet up and take it easy."

"What?"

"Didn't ya hear me? Ya got cloth in your ears? We need to recharge, and there ain't a whole amount of energy out here. It's gonna take a while."

Danny groaned. "How long?"

"One hundred and sixty three hours. Give or take a

smidgen."

"A *smidgen...?*" It was then that he cottoned on that Hope's voice had changed. The blunt baritone had been replaced by a brassy, rapid-fire patter. At least this time it was female. "So let me get this straight," he said. "There's no energy out here, but you've managed to find Earthwave?"

"Give the boy a doughnut!" The cheerfulness was already grating. "But that's just about all there is. So for the forseeable, you'll find me tucked up with a new, old movie. Want to watch?"

"No." *Movie* was one of her favourite Earthwave words. A movie was like a melo-historical, but not as good.

"Your funeral, mac. See ya in the funny papers."

Privately, Hope agreed that the escape had *been exhilarating. She relished the excitement of her role in Danny's story. Just like in a movie: she was the loyal companion, the wisecracking sidekick, the grumpy getaway driver. She even put on voices so she could play the parts properly.*

Dramatic thrills like this were why she had agreed to Danny's ownership. She loved her Earthwave movies but there just weren't enough of them, so she'd sought out her own adventure. It had been a proper rollercoaster right from the start, full of intrigue and escapes and brushes with the law. Lately, though, the excitement had worn thin. If this had been an Earthwave drama it would have come to its conclusion by now, but Danny was never quite clever enough or daring enough to pull off the great coup that he dreamed of and Hope always managed to extract them from the inevitable pursuit. All in all, it was becoming tiresome. On balance, she was coming to the conclusion that she preferred her movies after all.

To be truthful, she was only sticking around with Danny now to see what happened at the end.

It took only a fraction of the estimated downtime for Danny to go crazy with boredom. While Hope drifted in space, scooping up atoms, he ate, slept, played his interactives. When he grew tired of those, he scoured the most recent feeds for leads, recatalogued his finds, even attempted to reconcile his financial affairs.

"All right," he shouted. "Show me a movie."

Without comment, Hope displayed the moving image on the bubble: a grainy office scene with a man and a woman talking over each other so rapidly as to be incomprehensible. From what little he could follow he gleaned that they worked for a media organization, but they were using methods of securing their stories that seemed, bizarrely, to be considered illegal at the time and their endless arguments on the subject formed the bulk of the story. They might have been in love too, but that seemed coincidental. Beyond that, the experience was a mystery. He kept watching in hope that something might explode; it often did when things got tedious in Earthwave dramas. On this occasion, however, he was disappointed.

"Why did the police arrest that man?" Danny moaned, more to have something to say than because he cared.

"Just follow the story, bozo. It ain't *War And Peace*."

"It'd help if there *was* a story. Although I still fail to see why that's always so important to you."

"Buster, if you can't watch a movie without complaining, so help me I'll..." She broke off.

"You'll?"

Shh.

The imperative was not uttered aloud, but directly via his C-link. Danny's blood cooled. If they had been tracked down already, they'd be unable to spin their way out of trouble.

What is it? he replied.

There's another ship out here.

There was a pause while she assembled whatever data she was receiving from the grey market multiband sensor arrays that he'd installed specifically for the purposes of knowing what was out there before anyone else did. In the business of cultural claims you needed every advantage you could get.

"What kind of ship?" Danny said aloud.

"An old one. I *think* it's an original Sol system generation rock."

"Don't be stupid. It can't be."

"If you're calling me a liar, Mac, you can take it up with my sweet old grey-haired mother."

"All right, all right." Anything to keep the peace. She was still wrong though. It really couldn't be an original gen-ship from the time of the first diaspora. Not all the way out here. Although, now he thought about it… it wasn't *inconceivable* for a ship to drift this far out into the darkness. If the guidance systems had been damaged or if its crew had succumbed to attack or contagion, transforming their vessel into a drifting tomb, awaiting discovery. It wasn't *impossible.*

"What else?" he said.

"Hold your horses. There's only so much you can tell from external scans."

If this ship was what Hope claimed... it'd be a *goldmine.* Danny was already thinking of the deals he could make. Legitimate ones for a change. He might even be able to *sell* something to GOW instead of sneaking footage from under their noses all the time. He pondered over whether it would be better to sell off the contents individually or hold out for passing them off as a single lot—a living museum. Mel would piss her pants over that.

"Well?" His voice quavered with impatience. "How do we get aboard?"

Hope laughed. "We ask the occupants, obviously."

The rock was occupied? "You're seriously telling me that some fluky tomb-raiding bastard stumbled on this before us?"

"Not exactly, bub. This ain't no mausoleum. Someone on it just hailed us, and they're *very* friendly." She effected a low whistle. "And you're not going to believe this. They claim to be the descendants of the original crew. Ship's called the *Saint Rachel Of The Further Fields*, a privately funded resettlement venture that left the Sol system on June 18th 2189 OEC. The original heading was one of the Vela worlds, but they never completed their journey."

Danny juggled some figures. "2189 by the Old Earth calendar—that was before subspace spin was discovered. They can't have been travelling linear all that time. That's hundreds of years."

"*Thousands.*"

When Danny had absorbed this information, his spirits soared again: not only was the ship a relic but, if it had been travelling the dark reaches between systems all that time, whoever inhabited it was a living link to Old Earth.

"What are you waiting for?" he yelled. "Get us over there!"

"No need," Hope said. "They're coming to us."

This was how it always was. Just when Hope thought Danny Gibbs's story had run its course and was lumbering towards the inevitable buffers of ignominy and incarceration, something new cropped up. A glimmer of hope. She had been with Danny long enough that she needed no persuasion that her owner was an incorrigible and unrepentant bastard. He sought out novelty not for its own intrinsic value, but for financial gain and for how much it would add to his own notoriety. Just by following his orders she was legally complicit in most of his less savoury activities. But, if there was anything she had learned from her Earthwave dramas, it was that no one was beyond redemption. And if there was one thing she couldn't resist, it was the possibility, no matter how slim, of a happy ending.

Danny was examining the unrefined exterior of the asteroid and marvelling that it had once been easier to build a deep-space worthy vessel by modifying a lump of rock rather than simply fabbing it. Wherever the vessel's travels had taken it, they had not been without incident. The lumpy surface sported craters of various ages as well as black scorch marks, glittering silicate growths, and a field of weird conical structures that scans indicated had once been quasi-organic. This ship had been about. He stared hard, as if the ancient object might vanish the second he took his eyes off it. He hardly dared blink.

"The *Saint Rachel* has agreed to provide us with an energy feed," said Hope. "But they want something in exchange."

Aha, there it was. He'd known this was falling too easily into his lap. "Go on, tell me."

"They want to meet you."

"They *want* me to come aboard? Straight off, without coercion or anything? What's the catch?"

Hope's reply was pensive. "Why does there always have to be a catch? Apparently you're the first human they've had direct contact with for several generations. Naturally they're interested in meeting you and hearing your story. Everyone's got one, ya know. And there are precious few of them out here in dead space." Her sigh was pitched somewhere between exasperation and disappointment. "Of course, you can always make up a lie. That's what you're good at, right? They'll never know the difference anyway."

Danny brayed. He could certainly lie.

The welcoming committee wasn't up to much.

During docking, Danny had spent time concocting a tall tale to impress his hosts with; hopefully enough that they'd be open to the idea of negotiations. He'd even gone to the trouble of getting the look right, dragging out his old uniform and cleaning the boots for the first time since his disastrous visit to that colossal ball of sucking mud known as Banou. That affair had been the last in the string of shitty down-the-pecking-order assignments that had persuaded to leave the family service and go freelance. He'd got himself a ship, some decent clothes and sworn never to don the familial straitjacket again. Ah, well. Screw principles. His story wouldn't be mentioning any of that. As far as his audience knew, this uniform was that of a military officer, not a corporate lackey. The ribbons spanning the serge told of a much-lauded career in service; the crumples and stains betraying the hard times that had befallen him after being heroically injured and honourably discharged. As far as his story went, he would be making exactly the right impression.

His hosts could at least have made a similar effort. When he exited the docking chamber he was met by a cluster of crones, peering from behind each other like timid children. On second glance, though, they were not perhaps as old as they seemed. Certainly, they wore unflattering woollen robes, their curly, greasy hair came in various shades of grey or white, and the teeth revealed in their off-putting smiles of welcome were yellowing pegs, but many of their faces were incongruously youthful. If they had been citizens of the Hegemony he would have been surprised only at their aesthetic choice, but he had been expecting people as isolated as this lot to be much more primitive.

The woman at the front of the cluster stepped forward. "Master Daniel Gibbs. You are welcome aboard the *Saint Rachel Of The Further Fields*." Her voice had a soft vibrato to it. "We are simple travellers across God's far country, but the sisterhood would be honoured if, while we attend to your needs, you would share a meal with us, and perhaps tell us a little of yourself."

Sisterhood: collective name for a female-only religious order, Hope supplied over the C-link, helpfully, filling in the gaps in Danny's knowledge. *Saint Rachel: character from prime Christian text known as The Bible. A keeper of sheep who became the wife of someone called Jacob. God: character from The Bible around whom Christianity was—*

I'm aware of who God was, thank you.

Danny grinned. This was going to be a piece of cake. He stepped forwards but was halted by a polite shake of the spokeswoman's head.

"It is our custom to remove our footwear while aboard the *Saint Rachel*."

He looked at his boots. It had taken hours to get anything approaching a shine out of them.

Just do it, Hope whispered.

Grumbling, Danny complied. He paired his boots neatly before joining the women in the corridor beyond.

"Oh..." He looked down, wriggled his toes in the sudden,

soft warmth.

"Carpet making is one of the textile crafts to which our order has dedicated itself." The leader flexed her own toes. The nails were exceptionally thick. "You may address me as Bell," she said, walking on.

Danny lingered, mesmerised by the carpet's pattern, a race of mathematical and organic geometries that intermingled in beguiling fashion. The other women had to crowd him to drive him on in the wake of their spokeswoman.

"Bell?" He trotted reluctantly after her. "Captain Bell?"

The woman's chocolate eyes regarded him with something like humour. "Simply Bell."

The carpeted corridor led to a huge internal space. It was ringed and criss-crossed by gantries, stairs and walkways on many levels both above and below the one on which they entered. Peering over the rail, Danny had a dizzying view of the floors below him falling away towards a flat, green expanse. Looking upwards, he was almost blinded. The interior lighting in here was brighter than the suns on many worlds he had visited. There was warmth too, though not quite enough to take the edge off the circulating air.

"We will be delighted to conduct a tour later." Bell had noticed that he was staring. "But the dinner hour is upon us. This way please."

The group filtered along the carpeted gantry and down a nearby stair. On the balcony below was an expansive commons. Here the design on the carpet spread out, complexifying to an impressive scale. Danny's eyes, constantly drawn to the pattern, felt on the verge of making sense out the abstract designs, but there was too much in the way. The floor was obscured by tables, a serving counter, and a sizeable complement of rough-robed crew, ready for their meal. Danny's group descended the stair and a murmur of expectation rose to greet them.

When they approached the servery, he realized that one of the women was trying to get his attention. "I'm sorry? What's happening?"

The woman's grey hair stuck out in long tufts. Her close-lipped smile bordered on obsequious, her voice tremulous. "The Bell is selecting what she wishes for her evening meal."

Danny watched as the spokeswoman lifted lids on each of a selection of tureens and platters, nodding and conversing with the servers. He couldn't quite make out what was in the dishes, although there was a worrying amount of greenery on display and the steam that drifted over was only vaguely aromatic. He preferred his food meaty, spicy and mildly hallucinogenic, but he was well practised at gritting his teeth and smiling in the name of a business opportunity.

Bell finally pointed at a deep pot, and was briskly served from it with a bowlful of stewed vegetable matter. Immediately, the other women lined up and selected the same choice. Danny must have allowed his confusion to show. The sister who had spoken to him before gave him an understanding smile. "We follow the Bell's lead," she said. "She's never wrong."

Danny, reminding himself that religious communities could be prone to strangely slavish behaviour, nodded as if he understood, accepted his own bowl of steaming roots and sat with his hosts.

"All of our food on board the *Saint Rachel* is grown naturally." Bell speared a chunk of something fibrous. The fingers that manipulated the fork were tipped by horny nails and when she bit into her forkful Danny got a good look at those teeth. He had thought they were badly kept, but in fact what he saw were strong yellow pegs. They mashed efficiently on the vegetable.

Danny took a mouthful of his own meal. The taste was actually not too bad, but the vegetables were barely cooked. On his first attempt to crunch into them he feared he might actually have broken his own teeth.

"Delicious." He choked, sluiced the mouthful down with a sip of water. When he had recovered he said: "If you don't mind, me asking, What happened?"

Took your time, Sherlock.

Danny ignored Hope. His focus was on Bell. It wasn't just the teeth, the nails, the hair: it was in those big, placid eyes, that flattened nose; all ubiquitous features among the crew.

"What happened, Mister Gibbs?"

"To your people." He arranged his expression into one that he hoped conveyed compassion. "To your humanity."

The steadiness of her gaze was unnerving. "The *Saint Rachel Of The Further Fields* has been travelling a long time. She set off from Earth with a complement of three thousand, six hundred, backed up by a full genetic database of human, livestock and food crop genomes. The mission, as you would perhaps expect of an order like ours, was a simple one: to find somewhere to settle where the grass was greener – both literally and ideologically – than it had become on Earth."

"The grass...?"

It's a metaphor. Just go with it, okay?

Bell ignored his interjection. "The *Saint Rachel* journeyed successfully for many generations."

"How many generations?"

"Hundreds." Bell's dark eyes were unreadable. "And therein lay the problem. Over time our mission was... *reinterpreted.* Instead of settling, our people chose to continue travelling. We had encounters. They were not always without incident or consequence. At some point on her travels the *Saint Rachel*'s databases became corrupted and, not long after that, we are told, a contagion was contracted that affected the DNA and threatened to kill off the crew."

"You are *told*?" It was just a hint in the wording.

Bell did not appear to be insulted that he picked up on it. "It was many generations ago, and records have not always been maintained."

"So, what happened?"

"To save the sisterhood it was decided to introduce genetic material from another species."

From the livestock, Hope said on the C-link.

"Which species?"

Now Bell smiled, showed her peggy teeth. "The one sacred to *Saint Rachel*, of course," she said.

"The sheep," he said aloud. To Hope he said, *You're recording all this, right?* Even if they got nothing else from this venture this interview would syndicate far and wide.

Bell smiled. "It proves that we are beloved of *Saint Rachel.* Had it not been for the sheep our people would not have survived."

"Do you still consider yourselves to be human?" Danny asked the question because it would be on the lips of every Hegemony viewer when they saw this. And because he relished the flicker of reaction that, finally, he managed to elicit from the woman's imperturbable features.

"We are all God's creatures," she replied.

Danny searched his bowl for edible bits of vegetable. *Is she saying what I think she's saying?*

Hope was guarded. *That somewhere along the line their community deliberated decided it would be preferable to make themselves more* flock-like*? I don't know, fella, religion's a funny thing. Especially when left to its own devices for a long time. She might not even know for sure. Doubt you'll get her to come out and actually say it, though.*

Danny chewed thoughtfully. *Doesn't matter. The melo-historical they make of this will make it pretty obvious…*

Noticing that the sounds of mastication had stilled, he looked up from his bowl. Everyone was staring. Dark eyes, patient gazes, all trained on him. For a second he was seized with an irrational fear that these unnerving people were capable of eavesdropping on the C-link.

Hope allayed his fears. *They've told their story. I think they're waiting for yours.*

Danny was no stranger to having to bluff and brazen – in fact he relished any opportunity to grandstand – but for some reason now the moment had come to deliver his fabricated history he dried up. He scanned the sisters' flat faces. Their anticipation was palpable, and suddenly the tall tale he had intended to palm off on them seemed silly and obvious. Very little knocked his self-confidence, but this did. It uncapped a well of self-doubt that had been sealed-off since the last time his mother had appraised his commercial performance.

The Honourable Captain? He was glad to be on the C-link. He feared that if he'd had to speak aloud at that moment, nothing would have come out. *They'll see right through that.*

Hope hesitated before answering, and when she did she had dropped most of the artifice from her tone. *Why not tell them your real story then?*

Don't be ridiculous. I'm trying to get them to trust *me.* Danny took a deep breath, felt his confidence ebb back. *No, the Honourable Captain* will *work. I'll make it work. It's only a story after all. I just need a minute.*

The moment stretched, then Bell pushed aside her bowl. "Perhaps you would enjoy that tour now."

When she stood, a loose gaggle of the crew did likewise. They were fewer in number than the welcoming party had been. The rest of the women went back to eating, their stewed roots clearly a bigger attraction than Danny had proved to be. He cursed himself for allowing himself to be so easily thrown. He'd seize the next opportunity, and dazzle them.

Bell led them a short distance to a bank of elevators. He and the woman who had spoken to him at the servery followed but no one else joined them, the remainder of the women drifting away. It didn't matter, he told himself. He only needed to impress their leader.

"The fields please, Floss," Bell said, and the remaining acolyte jabbed her thumb at the control button.

As the elevator descended, Danny's eyes wandered to the floor. Even here there was a square of carpet. This sample was a little worn but the design was clear enough, and here at last it formed a recognisable picture. The geometries resolved into angular silver shapes, whorls of actinic white and lines of cerulean energy, all against the unmistakable curving sweep of a planetary ring system. Noticing his scrutiny his companions pressed against the walls so he could see the complete picture. Yes, it *was* a space battle, and the craftsmanship involved in its depiction was exquisite.

Hey, Hope whispered. *That looks like—*

"You might know this scene as the Battle of Harmony's Shelf," Bell said.

Danny's eyes widened. *Harmony's Shelf*, of course. It was an iconic image from the early times of the Hegemony, when cultural rights had been contested by violence instead of bureaucracy. He'd seen it represented in the media hundreds of times. Only never quite like this. It was as if it were drawn from a different perspective, the other side of the battle than the traditional views. He admired the skill and the imagination, but it didn't change what the image implied.

"You've not been so isolated after all," he said. "This is a Hegemony classic."

Bell shook her head. "We have had no contact with your Hegemony," she said. "Not directly. We do stumble across your communication broadcasts from time to time, but we prefer real experience to *dramas*."

"I don't understand you."

"This scene was woven as it happened. The *Saint Rachel* was there."

Danny gaped at her. Harmony's Shelf had been discovered tucked away in a hazardous corner of the galaxy. The landmark conflict over who brought its unlikely cultural riches to the eager eyes of the Hegemony worlds had been titanic and brief. The odds upon randomly stumbling upon that event would have been astronomical. Bell was clearly talking nonsense, but her expression was completely free of guile.

"You're telling me that this primitive rock, which has spent most of its travels in empty space, just happened to wander through the Ostermann zone during one of the most famous battles in Hegemony history?"

She beamed at him as a teacher might at a bright pupil. "That is correct." The elevator opened. "Come and see our sheep."

They stepped out of the lift onto what could have been the surface of a temperate planet. The effect was so startling that it wiped Danny's next thought from his head. The fields he'd thought to be flat from above in fact rolled like a natural landscape, replete with hills and streams. A zephyr riffled the grass, and the light that had all but blinded him above bathed the scene with a radiance that was, this far down, rather pleasant.

And then there were the sheep. Danny was familiar with such animals, of course. They were among the standard livestock that humans had exported from Earth, although their genetic make-up had usually been altered to suit whatever environment they were imported into, leading to substantial variations between the specimens he had encountered. While the animals grazing here were comparatively modest beasts, there was something quintessentially *sheepish* about them. There was little doubt that these animals came from old stock. And old stock was a very valuable commodity.

"They're all white?" Danny said. "That's traditional, I believe."

"We spin and dye our wool by hand." One of the animals had meandered towards them and Bell buried her hand in its fleece. "That's the way it has been done since our order was founded. We see no reason to change. And besides, we now believe that God prefers his creatures... unaltered."

She met the sheep's gaze instead of Danny's, underlining with obvious regret the close kinship between her and the animal. If her ancestors had once thought that the intention of their holy scripture was to be more like their sacred animals, it seemed that in more recent times the tide of interpretation had flowed back the other way again. This was pretty tragic. It was going to make fantastic melodrama.

"So that's why you never settled?" he said. "Because the promised land was promised to humans, not to... whatever you believe you have become?"

Now she did look at him. "One of the reasons, perhaps." Instead of elaborating, however, she turned abruptly and strode back towards the elevators.

"Where are you going now?" When Bell ignored him, he readdressed the question to Floss. "Where's she going?"

The older crew member simpered. "We do not question the Bell's whim." She lifted the hem of her robe so that she could hurry after her leader. "We only follow."

What the hell? Left alone, Danny vented his frustration to Hope as he watched the women disappear behind the elevator shaft.

She's still waiting for your story, McGrory. Hope had resumed her chatty persona. *You've gotta tell them something. C'mon it'll just be like confessional with Father O'Reilly.*

The reference, as usual, was lost on him.

What's got into you, Hope? he said. *Whose side are you on? Can't you see the opportunity we've got here?*

Yes, I can. Hope's voice was suddenly serious. *I really can. And I really want you to take it.*

Her tone mystified him, but she was right about one thing: he was losing them. He could feel their cooperation evaporating. Danny hurried to catch up with his hosts. Behind the elevator he found a staircase, where the carpet resumed. He followed the engrossing design from tread to tread. At the top, the pattern resolved into a second image; this time depicting tall, twisting crystalline spires. No one in planet-hunting circles in the Hegemony could have failed to recognise it.

Cowrie's World, Hope supplied unnecessarily.

Wrenching himself away from the beautiful rendition of that planet, he found Bell and Floss in conversation with the tenders of some raised vegetable beds.

"Well." He beamed. "This is very impressive."

The women paused in their conversation and blinked at him. Once again their unwavering expectation rattled his confidence. This time, however, he threw off the doubt, rallied his determination not to miss out on his prize. That was until he spotted yet another picture in the carpet at the women's feet. He dropped to his knees to examine the circle of suns. "The *Kori-kori Configuration*," he whispered. When he looked up, the women had moved off again. He managed only a few steps of pursuit before the pattern gave up another familiar wonder. *Wilson's Duality*, in all of its vapour-bound glory. His hosts had begun to ascend to the next level.

"Wait," he called.

Between the leafy beds and the stairs he stumbled over the *Awakening Of The Mechanitrona*, the *Butterflies Of Dhelve*, and, if he wasn't mistaken, the *War Of The Three Worlds*. All of these were key events in galactic history, household names. But, again, each of the scenes was subtly different from its clichéd Hegemony representation. And that was just the ones he recognized. He followed the pattern as it raced and resolved into image after image, and discovered that the really startling thing was that the unfamiliar scenes outnumbered the familiar ones by an order of magnitude.

If Bell could be believed, the carpet wasn't just a work of exceptional artisanship, it was a comprehensive historical record of the significant places and events of the last few thousand years. But that really was impossible. The galaxy was too large, their ship too slow and ancient.

On the next level, a cohort of crew was tackling various processes involved in turning fleece into fibres. Bell stopped to pass a word and a smile with them before walking on again.

"Wait," Danny shouted again, and when that had no effect. "My story..."

This time she deigned to wait for him. "We would love to hear it," she said. Her gaze drilled into him.

"Well..." Danny was out of breath and had a pain in his side from the chase. He swept an arm in a semi-circle, indicating the carpet on which even now he was spotting scene after amazing scene. "But first... it was a lie, wasn't it? Or a joke, a joke at least? When you said that your ship was at Harmony's Shelf, and that was how its image got into your extraordinary carpet." Neither woman responded. "Because if it's true, and all of the other images are true, were woven from *actual experience*... well it's not possible, is it?" Neither woman offered even an ounce of refutation, and so he was forced to complete the chain of thought himself. "Because, no one gets that damned lucky!"

Bell looked crestfallen. "It was neither a lie nor a joke," she said. "Every image you see in our carpet was, exactly as you say, woven because the *Saint Rachel* happened to be at each place at the right time. It is not coincidence, Mr Gibbs. Nor is it luck. It is the Bellwether's gift. We call it divine guidance. If you prefer a secular explanation, you might call it *instinct*, perhaps something we inherited from our ovine cousins. And that is the other reason that our ship never settled. We are a wandering flock now. It is our role to cross the endless spans of the cosmos and witness as many of God's great works as we can. We trust *Saint Rachel* to guide us, and she always does so. We have seen such wonders."

Danny still found it impossible to believe her. And yet, if what these women said *was* true, this carpet was potentially a map to a thousand wonders unknown to the Hegemony. The *Saint Rachel*'s story itself would be a flash in the pan, and even a broker's fee on the sheep's genetic property rights would be of little consequence compared to the riches awaiting him via the combination of these images and the ship's log.

He had to have this carpet. More than ever now, he needed to get these women on his side.

"Thank you, for humouring my curiosity," he said at last, a combination of avarice and excitement quashing the last of the nerves. "And for that I owe you my own tale." He sighed, and inflected his voice with an appropriate degree of weary fragility.

"You must forgive my reticence. Once you've heard what I have to say, I think you'll understand how difficult it is for me to relate. I was born into a military family on a tiny world of so little significance that I won't trouble you with its name. Our family was not a high-ranking one, but our people were involved in a long war and it was expected that we would do our duty, so I enlisted in the orbital patrols."

Danny had closed his eyes to convey how emotional this all was for him. When he opened them, Bell had wandered away again. The woman called Floss smiled encouragingly, however. "Go on," she said.

"Well, I..."

"Continue, we're listening."

Edging after Bell, who had now reached the base of the next flight of stairs, Danny went on. "It wasn't just I who enlisted. My brothers and sisters all joined the same unit, and we forged a crack force whose reputation soon spread beyond our little planet."

"Oh dear." Floss's face crumpled, then she turned and followed her leader up the stairs.

"Wait," Danny protested. "I'm telling you the story."

"Well, yes," Floss slogged up the carpeted steps. "But we were hoping for the other one."

"What other one?"

"The one about you and *Hope To Die*." The hem of the woman's woollen robe danced in front of him. "That one seemed quite funny. There was lots of running away."

"How do you know about that?" Of course the answer to that question at least was obvious. And Hope's subsequent silence as much as declared her guilt.

Floss's answer drifted down to him. "*Hope To Die* told it to the rest of the sisters. It sounds very exciting, although apparently you can be a bit of a scallywag at times. I do hope you get your just desserts at the end."

What exactly have you been telling them? Danny whispered to

Hope, but his ship chose not to reply.

At the top of the stairs, Danny followed Floss over to a corner where Bell was attending an industrious group of crew members. When he joined them he realized with horror that they were ripping the carpet up. They used tools to unpick the weave and main strength to yank the threads free. He arrived in time to see a picture being pulled apart. A beautiful, emerald green world whose images he would now never be able to sell to the Hegemony.

"What are you doing?"

"We only have a finite amount of floor, Mister Gibbs," Bell said. "When new events occur, we have to make room for new pictures."

"But it's *priceless.*" The pile of threads was growing, as was the exposed section of blank decking.

Bell shrugged. "It's just a record. The experience for the crew members who visited that place was priceless." As she spoke, a further influx of crew members arrived and doubled the level of industry. Boxes were opened revealing skeins of bright wool. A complicated apparatus was also erected. It was only when they started applying the yarn to it that Danny recognised it as a loom. The third item that was brought to the scene was an ancient viewing screen.

"Thank you for your visit, Mister Gibbs," Bell said. At her feet the crew had worked fast to create a perfect blank square fringed with threads. "Your ship's energy has been replenished. You're no doubt eager to be on your way."

"Wait, no. I wanted to do a deal. I can make you rich."

The soft snuffling sound that Bell produced sounded quite unlike laughter, but her bared yellow teeth did suggest that she found his last statement humorous. "You've seen how simply we live. What could you possibly offer us? Now we'd like you to leave because we have work to do."

That was when the penny dropped. The realization of it flushed through Danny in a hot rush. "Something's going to happen, isn't it? That's why you're out here. Your *instinct* led you here." Immediately after the realization came the full blown panic. "Please. I want to see it. I *need* to see it. To be a witness—like *you.*" On the C-link he muttered. *Hope, get on this. Record everything.* "Please, this is vital..." *Hope?*

The ship still didn't answer, and Bell turned her back on him, saying only: "Goodbye, Mister Gibbs."

The crew members that bore down on him were stronger than they looked. They crowded him, buffeted him, drove him away from the scene. The last thing he saw as they herded him into the elevator car was the screen flickering to life, displaying a swathe of dark, pregnant space.

"What about my story?" he yelled in desperation.

This time, the snuffling laughter came from the sisters who crowded the rising elevator car with him. When they reached the docking level they wasted no time in bullying him back aboard *Hope To Die.*

Danny felt the mechanisms of disengagement beginning but he remained sprawled on the floor, attempting simultaneously to master his fury and regain his dignity, all the while ignoring the pain in his temple caused by the impact of the shiny boots which had been tossed after him.

"Thanks for your help there," he muttered to Hope as he heaved himself into his chair. "Now perhaps if you wouldn't mind, can we fire a beacon into that forsaken relic? There's no way I'm giving that carpet up." Silently, the command bubble displayed a three-sixty view of the space around them. The ancient rock was already drifting to a respectable distance, but from his own ship there was no other sign of activity. "Hope, don't piss me about. I'm telling you to tag that ship."

The new voice was flat and devoid of character. "I'm sorry, Dave. I can't do that."

"Oh, don't start on me now with that stupid Earthwave shit. I'm seriously not in the mood. In fact, forget the tag. Send in a crawler colony laden with nerve toxin."

"I'm sorry, Dave. I can't do that."

"Oh, go *fuck yourself*."

"I'm sorry, Dave. I can't do that either." Then in her normal voice she said, "I am sorry, Danny, I'm not playing along any more. The story's over."

When Danny finally understood, he felt both sickened and thrilled.

"Who did you call?" he whispered.

"Does it matter?"

He'd never seriously considered that he might one day actually be caught, but the knowledge that—according to the sisters at least—his demise was going to be an event of galactic significance almost made it worthwhile.

He checked the view. For a while there was just the *Saint Rachel*; then, just as a wave of doubt began to lap at his certainty, the first Hegemony ship spun into view. Danny swung in his chair and began to laugh. He could imagine it now, the sector crowded with ships: the forces of law and security and corporate malfeasance from a host of systems, a clutch of independent bounty hunters too. He was on a lot of lists. He wondered how many there would be in the end. *The Thousand Ship Capture Of The Outlaw Daniel Gibbs* had a nice ring to it. As dramas went, his story would be prime time for sure.

Danny waited, laughing with excitement.

In the end, one ship was all that was required. Hope allowed them access without fuss or comment and when Danny left her, meekly and hardly noticed by anyone, he wasn't laughing any more. It wasn't a particularly satisfying ending, she admitted, but at least it was an ending.

Hope was not entirely happy either with her own part in bringing events about. It wasn't at all like being a character in a movie. There were repercussions. Guilt, she discovered, was not an especially pleasant feeling.

In future she would be quite content in the role of observer.

When the Hegemony security ship had gone, she observed that the Saint Rachel Of The Further Fields remained. She watched the gen-ship for a time.

It just sat there, waiting patiently. They were good at patience, she noted, and they had seen so much.

Hope decided to wait with them out there beyond the galactic fringe. Yes, she'd had enough involvement; it was time to try patience. In time, she had the feeling she would be rewarded.

Later. Something winked in the deep darkness. Something bright blossomed.

Something amazing *happened.*

THE BLEEDING MAN

Aliette de Bodard

When Uncle Jarun brought the bleeding man back to Mother's fortress, Sarisha was in the stables, watching. She'd learnt to make herself scarce in the last few years – so that she'd see the things Mother thought her too young for.

The bleeding man was tall and lean, perhaps young, perhaps old – it was hard to tell under the blood covering his face. He breathed slowly, with a sound like a rattle of wood; but he didn't flinch as the guards dragged him off the horse and onto the stones of the courtyard. He didn't make any other noise; just that breathing that always seemed on the verge of faltering – a sound that twisted within Sarisha's chest until her own heartbeat seemed alien to her.

Uncle Jarun stood to the side of the bleeding man, his face expressionless. "Put him in the interrogation room," he said. "I expect Chandni will be along shortly to blood-read him."

After the Pahate guards were gone, Uncle Jarun remained where he was. His face turned left and right, as if smelling the wind. "Sarisha," he said. "I know you're here."

He always knew. "It's not fair!" Sarisha protested, as she stepped out of the stables.

"I know you, little fish," Uncle Jarun said. "You're always too curious."

"I'm not," she said, annoyed at being called by her child's name. "You're the ones hiding things."

He stared at her – his gaze, as usual, revealed nothing. She wished she could be like him or Mother, and not have her feelings transparent. "You're twelve," he said.

"Mother was younger than that when they trained her."

Uncle Jarun's face shifted slightly – Sarisha wasn't sure if he was angry. Every time she raised the subject, there was always the fear Uncle Jarun would show her again that bleak, inhuman fury that had gripped him when she'd first asked him why she wasn't a blood-empath like him or Mother. "Your *mother*," Uncle Jarun said, "does not want you to share blood with us. That's the end of it."

"But –" She wanted it so much: to have her meekness washed away by his blood, or Mother's blood; to become a blood-empath like them; to tear the minds of evil men apart with a thought, instead of being frail and weepy and useless.

"No buts, little fish."

Sarisha shook her head. "You treat me like –"

"You *are* a child," Uncle Jarun said, coldly. She hated it when he did that: when he grew cutting and uncaring, showing her a true blood-empath's face.

Sarisha pouted. It was childish, but she didn't care. "Who's the bleeding man?"

"Bleeding man –" Uncle Jarun turned to look around, and then understanding dawned. "Oh. Just a prisoner, Sarisha."

"For Mother?"

"Yes," Uncle Jarun said.

They always brought the difficult ones to Mother – and she never ever failed to break them. Why wouldn't Uncle Jarun allow Sarisha to be trained? She'd be as good as Mother. She'd be sharp and hard when it mattered and she'd protect the Pahate dynasty like everyone else. "Mother isn't here," she said.

"I gathered that," Jarun said. "When is she coming back?"

"She didn't say," Sarisha told him. "She's in Pembai – there's been a murder there."

Jarun nodded. "She won't be back until tomorrow at the earliest. No matter. This is not pressing. We'll wait for her."

"I can show you my letters? I can draw fifty of them now."

"If you want," Jarun said.

She led him into her room and showed him her latest efforts at writing the noblemen's script, which he praised in his cool, aloof way. Afterwards, they went down to the dining room and had spiced rice and tea. By the time they walked back through the courtyard, the blood had been cleaned away – the servants knew how to keep a clean house.

But Sarisha kept hearing the bleeding man's rattling breath – an endless struggle against encroaching death. And, no matter how she fought it, it wouldn't go away.

That night, after Uncle Jarun had retired to his room, Sarisha crept through the corridors to the interrogation room. She'd taken Mother's keys from the secret compartment in the drawer, and the guards were used to her roaming the castle. No one asked her where she was going.

She didn't go straight to the interrogation room, but instead stopped by her secret place: the room just above it, its parquet floor covered in dust. She'd worked out long ago that the floorboards were a little loose, and if she knelt just the right way, and bent her head to just the right angle, she'd see into the room.

Sarisha had never witnessed a blood-reading – Mother had emphatically forbidden her to do so when she was younger, and the memory of that ban was still strong enough. But Mother had never said anything about the room above or the floorboards.

The trouble, though, was that you didn't choose what you saw: in this case, all Sarisha could make out was moonlight flooding the room, and the cage with the bleeding man, just on the edge of her field of vision. She could hear his halting breath, but not make out any details.

She rose, and went downstairs. The door to the interrogation room towered over her, its dark panels smelling of varnish and wood shavings. She'd never entered it: only Mother, Uncle Jarun and the Pahate guards were allowed in there.

Mother hadn't specifically forbidden Sarisha to enter the

interrogation room – but Sarisha could guess what she would say.

Yet the memory of the bleeding man slumped in the courtyard, and of the strange, fluttering feeling in her chest, was too strong. Sarisha fumbled for the smallest of the keys, and put it in the lock.

The key didn't turn. For a moment she thought she'd got things wrong, and then she realised that the room wasn't locked at all.

The door didn't creak, or groan – everything had been well-oiled.

Inside, the moonlight showed her a large, airy room with comfortable furniture – in some ways scarier than the damp cells. Slowly, Sarisha crept closer to the metal cage and the bleeding man.

He hadn't been cleaned up; and the sharp smell of blood and filth wafted to Sarisha's nostrils, filling her throat with bile.

She was alone: no guards, no Uncle Jarun to protect her if anything went wrong. In the silence of the room she heard the bleeding man's breath – slow, faltering. He must have something in his lungs – something really bad, if the guards hadn't bothered to treat it.

She wasn't scared – she was morbidly fascinated by that sound. And that was frightening. Mother and Uncle Jarun had warned her enough about the blood-empaths who took pleasure in inflicting pain – they were the lowest of the low, barely fit to wear the copper bracelets and the purple. True blood-empaths served the Pahate dynasty by keeping order on the Islands. They did not take power into their own hands.

But she wasn't a blood-empath. She'd never be one – Mother and Uncle Jarun had made it clear they wouldn't share blood with her, not ever.

The bleeding man stirred when she got closer. Crooked hands reached for the bars of the cage, and gripped the metal convulsively. "Who's – there?"

His voice was low, raspy. She didn't answer. The bleeding

man lifted his head to stare at her. Blood had congealed on his cheeks and forehead.

He made a rumbling sound – and only after a while did she realise it was laughter. "The mother's little pup, come to gloat. Don't be afraid, child. I can't bite."

Sarisha tried to imagine that she'd shared blood with Mother; that it was within her like a dark tide, crushing her weaknesses and her frailty; that nothing could make her hesitate, or draw back. But she still felt sorry for him – alone and wounded, with nothing to look forward to. "Why are you here?"

"To die." His voice caught on the last word, and he coughed – a wet, awful sound like something tearing up. "Which will be soon enough, no doubt."

Not sure of what to answer, Sarisha knelt by the cage to look at him. He stared back at her, and for the first time something lit his eyes – a naked, unhealthy hunger that chilled her heart. "You look just like her," he whispered.

Her heart twisted in her chest. "You don't know Mother."

He laughed again. "Everyone knows her. The Ice Lady. Twenty-three years of service and never one prisoner she couldn't break open like a nut."

Sarisha frowned. "That's not what you meant. About knowing her."

His eyes glinted in the moonlight – with the same feral hunger as a tiger. "Didn't I? You must have misheard."

Sarisha knew she hadn't. But no matter how she pressed him, he wouldn't provide answers – and she couldn't get them out of him, she wasn't Mother, she didn't have a blood-empath's powers.

In the end, Sarisha walked away from him back to the safety of her room; but the weary, sarcastic eyes in their mask of blood kept laughing at her. She fell asleep hearing his halting breath, and woke up still hearing it.

It didn't matter. Mother would soon be back; she'd question the man, and the guards would toss his body into a pyre like those of all the other prisoners. He'd be gone. He wouldn't matter.

Deep, deep down, she knew she was lying to herself.

Mother came back with the first of the monsoon storms. From Sarisha's vantage point at the window, she saw Mother and her escort thunder through the gates of the fortress, muddy and bedraggled – everyone except Mother, who sat unfazed on her rowan charger, as if the rain didn't matter.

"Sarisha?" Uncle Jarun said behind her. "Pay attention."

They'd been having a self-defence lesson – Uncle Jarun showing her a man's and a woman's weak points, and the angle of the thrust if you wanted to pin the heart on the point of your dagger.

"Mother's back," Sarisha protested.

"I know. I heard." Uncle Jarun, too, seemed unfazed. "Show me how you do it."

A cloth manikin, reproducing a human torso, was standing on the table. Sarisha approached it, feeling sillier and sillier with every passing moment.

"It's not real," she said.

Uncle Jarun's face did not move. "The point of this isn't to be real. It's to show me you have learnt your lesson. Practise will come later – one of the prisoners, maybe."

Sarisha tried to shut out the image of the dagger sinking into real flesh – and to quell the flutter of fear in her stomach.

The manikin, unmoving on its table, taunted her nevertheless, whispering that she was human – that she was weak. But it was just a thing.

Sarisha raised the dagger, and drove it up to the hilt in the torso. Nothing happened – just a trickle of dried hay.

"The angle was a little off," Uncle Jarun started to say, but he was cut off when the door opened to let Mother in.

"I see you've returned," Uncle Jarun said, turning to face her. They didn't embrace, or even greet. Sarisha – whose first instinct had been to run to Mother – didn't move either.

"And I see you're giving her lessons again." Mother's voice was hard to read – but Sarisha thought she was upset.

"You know my thoughts." Uncle Jarun didn't elaborate – and they all knew what he was talking about.

Mother didn't reply. She turned to Sarisha, and stared at her. She could stare for ages and Sarisha wouldn't be able to guess her thoughts. Mother was like that – even better at it than Uncle Jarun.

"Hello, Mother," Sarisha said, to break the silence.

"Is that how you greet me?" This time, there was no doubt about the emotion – Mother's eyes glittered with an inhuman anger.

Sarisha, paralysed, managed, "Uncle Jarun –"

"Uncle Jarun is a blood-empath. You're not," Mother said, squatting down. "Come give me a hug, child."

Sarisha walked closer, trying to dispel the hollow in her stomach. She wasn't afraid of Mother – wasn't afraid of anything...

Mother's skin was smooth and cold: it was always the same, like hugging a drowned body – it always brought back memories of being a much younger child, and of Mother's hugging her a last time before going to bed. This was – home, in a way that nothing else could be.

"That's better," Mother said, and rose – and Sarisha could see the way Mother's thoughts immediately moved beyond her daughter, to her duty. "We have a prisoner?"

"Waiting for you," Uncle Jarun said. "In the interrogation room."

"I see," Mother said. "What has he done?"

"He killed a blood-empath," Uncle Jarun said, each word clipped, precise, like a dagger thrust.

Sarisha held her breath: it was the gravest of crimes. Mother's face did not waver – but her eyes glinted, dangerously. "Then he'll get what he deserves," she said, and swept out of the room.

Uncle Jarun started to follow her, and then, apparently changing his mind, went back into the room. With the precision of a healer dissecting flesh, he opened up the manikin, and studied the dagger's position. "You'd have missed the heart by a handspan at least," he said, withdrawing the blade from the wound. "Keep practising, little fish."

And then he too was gone.

Of course, the last thing Sarisha wanted was practise. The bleeding man had known her – he'd known Mother. And Sarisha wanted to find out why – part of her, too, wanted to see how Mother would react.

She crept out of the room and into the corridors.

There was another way to her secret place: a dusty, unused staircase that twisted at the back of the tower. Sarisha climbed the steps two by two, pausing on the second landing to catch her breath.

The secret place was empty – but there would be people below: she had to tread carefully.

She could barely see the cage through the floorboards. She tried twisting her neck to make out the rest of the room, but Mother wasn't there – and there wasn't any noise but the bleeding man's breath.

That was weird. Mother had looked determined to see the bleeding man as soon as possible. Why wasn't she there?

As if in answer, the door to the interrogation room slid open – and footsteps echoed on the parquet.

Mother and Uncle Jarun: both in full blood-empath regalia, with the deep purple robes and the copper bracelets on their wrists. They must have changed; that was why Sarisha had got there before them.

Mother stood just under Sarisha, but Uncle Jarun had moved out of her field of vision. No matter. It was Mother Sarisha wanted to see.

Mother glanced at the bleeding man. "You have been brought here on charges of murder," she said.

A liquid, bitter sound came from the cage – the same sickening sound Sarisha had heard in the night. "I won't deny them," the man said. "But you should know that, Chandni."

Mother paused. Sarisha wished she could see her face.

Mother asked, "What's his name?"

A rustle of papers; then Uncle Jarun's voice: "Pundarik of the community of Lai."

"I see." Mother's voice was – changed, somehow. Hollow, Sarisha thought, and it was frightening. Nothing ever touched Mother. "Leave us alone."

"You're sure of this?" Uncle Jarun asked.

Mother shook her head, as if trying to rid herself of a fly. "Yes."

Footsteps went out of the room. Mother remained alone, facing the bleeding man in his cage. "Pundarik," she said, rolling the name in her mouth as if unsure whether to spit it out.

On the edge of Sarisha's vision, the bleeding man rose in his cage. "Chandni." He sounded amused. "It's been some time."

"Thirty-three years," Mother said. "And you have killed a blood-empath."

"I'd kill them all if I could."

"Us all." Mother paused, and then said, "I'll refer your case to another blood-empath of equal rank."

"Frightened?" Pundarik laughed again. "Of a dying man?"

"You're not dying," Mother said. But her voice didn't have the same edge – as if Pundarik had reached inside and torn out everything that made her frightening. She shook her head, again. "But I can be allowed no personal stakes –"

Pundarik gripped the frame of the cage. "So there *is* something left of my sister in you."

"I *am* your sister," Mother said. "And also a blood-empath."

His sister? Mother had never mentioned any family – for as long as Sarisha could remember, there had been Uncle Jarun –

who wasn't really her uncle, but who helped raise her – and the guards and the servants. And that was – had been – it.

"And you're also a mother," Pundarik said. "I saw your daughter earlier." For a moment Sarisha was afraid he'd mention seeing her in the interrogation room, but he didn't go further.

"Leave my daughter out of this," Mother said.

"A beautiful child," Pundarik said, gravely – as if they were both guests at a party, talking of small things. "Who was the father? Some man you paid for one night of – dare I call it pleasure?"

"That doesn't concern you."

Father – Sarisha, crouching over the floorboards, tried to think of a father – of a man who would be like Mother. She'd never thought about it: home was Mother and Uncle Jarun. There was no place for a father.

Pundarik was speaking again. "The daughter of a blood-empath, raised by two blood-empaths. She'd be perfect for the House of Learning."

"She would not!" Mother snapped. Even Sarisha knew what was going on: Mother wanted a normal daughter. Mother didn't want Sarisha to be a blood-empath: she'd speak of a burden too heavy to bear, muttering that Sarisha would be glad to be spared the darkness – and when Sarisha raised the subject, Mother would become cutting steel.

Pundarik – brother or not – couldn't know that. But he had to know he'd gone too far.

"Don't make my decisions for me." Mother's voice was burning with inhuman fury. "You lost the right to judge me thirty-three years ago."

Pundarik was taken aback – but he soon rallied. "And who will judge you?"

"Not a criminal in a cage," Mother said. "You obviously don't realise the seriousness of your situation."

"On the contrary. I have already incurred the worst punishment the law can mete out. Nothing really matters after that."

"Don't be overconfident," Mother said – and some of the old steel was back in her voice. "There *are* worse things."

"And you know them all." His voice was disabused. "What a good servant you turned out to be."

"And what a good citizen *you* turned out to be." Mother walked closer to the cage. "Arrested for a murder and waiting for death in your own filth. Do you honestly believe yourself better than me?"

Pundarik made a wheezing sound. "I have two grown sons. Married men and proud members of their communities. You – you raise a daughter in a house of pain. You have her stand in the courtyard, watching every beaten man your guards drag in. Does she see the broken ones staggering out? Does she watch the corpses flung on the pyres?"

"Enough." Mother's voice had the edge of a drawn sword.

"Don't judge me." Mother turned away from him – and in that brief moment Sarisha saw the glimmer in her eyes. Surely…

No. It couldn't be.

"I'll leave you to ponder your fate," Mother said.

Sarisha scrambled up, heedless of the noise she would make. She ran down the stairs three steps at a time, and slid to a halt on the landing just as Mother walked out of the interrogation room.

"Mother?"

"What are you doing here?" Mother asked.

Sarisha just stood there, staring at Mother, willing herself not to see. Even in the dim light there was no doubt. Mother was crying – small tears running down her cheeks like beads of glass.

"He made you unhappy," Sarisha whispered, trying to bridge the enormous gap in her mind. Mother never cried. Mother was hard inside, as hard as she needed to be, to serve the Pahate King.

Mother –

Mother was looking right through Sarisha. "It's nothing. Nothing."

"Mother –" But Mother had already wandered away.

Sarisha sat down on the landing, feeling empty inside. She remembered when she'd been seven and her nurse had died. She remembered the vast hollow within her, the awful certainty that nothing was ever going to make sense. At the funeral service, Mother had stood tall and unmoving, her face the same blank mask as always. As unbending, as firm as a rock in a storm.

That was Mother.

But not anymore.

It was Uncle Jarun who found her, much later – still sitting on the landing, staring at the stones of the stairwell.

"Little fish –" he said. He'd changed out of his purple robes.

"She was crying," Sarisha said. "She came out, and she was crying."

"I know." Uncle Jarun sat by her side. His face was smooth – untouched, uncaring. Sarisha ached for the same emptiness within her. "Your mother – has had a trying day."

"She never cries." Sarisha couldn't stop the words – couldn't think of anything but those tears, shining in the gloom. "She says we have to be strong –"

"Blood-empaths have to be strong," Uncle Jarun said. "It's not always easy."

"She's shared blood." Sarisha felt small – lost and adrift in her own body. "She –" It should have been within her, a river of blood-empath blood; enough to be her armour and her shield, to protect her against people like the bleeding man.

Uncle Jarun stared at the walls. "Not all emotions die when you share blood."

"But you're strong."

"Not always." Uncle Jarun rose in a swish of robes; extended a hand to her. "Come on, little fish. It will be dinner time soon, and she'll want to see you there."

Dinner was – heavy. It was the only word that came to Sarisha.

Mother and Uncle Jarun ate in silence, not looking at each other. Or at Sarisha.

Mother's face was expressionless, but she wasn't fooling Sarisha – her eyes were still red-rimmed, and the old harshness hadn't come back. What had occurred in the interrogation room had dug claws deep into her, and wouldn't let go.

Sarisha couldn't speak either; there was something lodged in her throat like a fish-bone.

As they rose, Uncle Jarun said, "I can take him if you want."

Mother shook her head. "He's killed a blood-empath, Jarun. By law, he should be punished by a seventh-rank blood-empath."

Uncle Jarun was fifth-rank: Mother was the only seventh-rank blood-empath within the province. "Nevertheless – who would ever know?" Uncle Jarun asked.

"I would," Mother said, and that ended the discussion.

As usual, it was Mother who tucked Sarisha in her bed and kissed her goodnight – with Uncle Jarun standing at the door, watching them both. Saying goodnight was one of the rituals of Sarisha's day – but Mother did all this without her usual efficiency.

"Mother?" Sarisha asked, frowning.

"I'll be fine," Mother said, but it was a lie. Sarisha could see that in her face.

"Good night, Mother," she said.

After Mother had gone, Uncle Jarun detached himself from the door. "Sarisha." His voice was smooth, emotionless, as he threw her practise dagger on her bed.

"I found this by the manikin – which displayed a remarkable lack of wounds," Uncle Jarun said.

"I –"

Uncle Jarun raised a hand. "You didn't practise. In fact, you followed your mother – and somehow were in time to see her walk out of the interrogation room. I'm disappointed in you, little fish."

It hurt – and not only because Uncle Jarun had said it all in the same bored tone, as if she were an animal he didn't care about.

"What if I did?" she asked.

Uncle Jarun did not speak for a while. "Then you disobeyed orders."

"I'm not one of the guards."

"No. You're Chandni's daughter, and I hold you to a higher standard than them."

The worst was the little voice that *knew* that Uncle Jarun was right. She should have practised – and it wasn't her place to spy on Mother. "You never tell me anything," she said, sullenly.

Jarun's eyes glittered – he *was* furious. "Your mother thinks you should be sheltered from the goings-on in this fortress, and I'll make sure you are. That's the end of it, little fish."

But you're not sheltering me, Sarisha thought, remembering Pundarik's words. Neither you nor Mother. You're letting me see the prisoners, and what's left of them afterwards.

She couldn't tell that to Uncle Jarun – not without revealing about her secret place. So she said nothing – although she guessed he was waiting for some word from her. After a while, he blew the lamp and left, still radiating that cold fury.

You're not sheltering me, Sarisha thought. She stared at the liquid darkness, imagining shadows moving within – broken, moaning things that couldn't touch her. I know what's going on, I know about pain and death and the things we need to do in order to serve the King. I know about being strong.

The dagger was on her bed – she could feel its weight on her knees. She remembered the slight catch as it had slid into the manikin's torso; she remembered the bleeding man, taunting Mother in the interrogation room, tearing at her until he had unmade her – destroying everything that had made her strong and happy.

Groping in the darkness, her hand closed around the hill – felt the coldness that travelled up her arm, into her heart.

The bleeding man was destroying Mother. He was a

murderer, already condemned to death; he didn't deserve to live.

If Mother couldn't find the courage to deal with him – then Sarisha would.

In the darkness, Sarisha retraced her steps of the previous night – this time careful to avoid the pools of light where the guards congregated.

She didn't have Mother's keys anymore; but the door to the interrogation room was still open, and Pundarik was sleeping inside his cage.

Sarisha stood on the edge of the moonlit area, considering. Pundarik was too far from the cage's walls: she wouldn't be able to stab him properly.

She could lure him closer – but then he'd be awake and alert, and she *definitely* wouldn't get the right angle for the thrust.

Careful not to make any noise, Sarisha crept closer to the cage, and studied the opening mechanism. She hadn't seen a key for it anywhere – and Mother didn't carry any keys; she just left everything in the secret compartment in her drawer.

Hmm –

The mechanism, gleaming in the darkness, had a protruding lever – and two small spinning wheels wrapped around the lever. But they didn't move when Sarisha touched them.

However – Sarisha bent down to check – yes, if you moved the spinning wheels so that the little notches lined up with the lever, the lever would have room to move downwards. All small things, of course, but unfeasible for the man trapped inside.

Sarisha nudged the wheels into position; then she took a deep breath, and pulled the lever down. It was well-oiled; it yielded with a slow, smooth slide and barely a noise.

The cage didn't open. Inside, Pundarik was tossing and turning in the grip of some nightmare – he'd surely deserved it anyway.

In the silence, Sarisha heard footsteps in the corridor – the guards, they'd pass by the interrogation room – but the footsteps didn't stop, they were going straight for the door, and a hand was weighing down on the handle.

She pulled the lever harder, desperately – and the front part of the cage fell open with a crashing metallic sound, just as lantern light froze her where she stood, dagger still in her hand, still preparing to strike.

"Sarisha?" Mother's voice, faintly puzzled.

Slowly, barely daring to breathe, Sarisha looked behind her – and saw Mother, standing with a lantern in one hand.

"What do you think you're doing?"

She couldn't get any words past her throat. "I –" she felt the reassuring weight of the dagger in her hand. "He made you cry," she said, and it sounded trite, foolish – childish. "I wanted to make him go away – Uncle Jarun showed me how –"

Bitter laughter welled up from the cage. Pundarik was getting up, leaning on the metal bars for support, and the smell of blood and filth and rotten flesh filled Sarisha's nostrils. "You came to kill me?" He laughed again – stopped, bent double by a coughing fit.

"I can do it," Sarisha said. "You're a criminal."

Pundarik laughed again. "Your daughter, Chandni. Your precious little daughter. Isn't she a sight to gladden a mother's heart?"

"Sarisha. Get away from him." Some of the old confidence was back in Mother's voice – but that was a lie to trick Sarisha. Mother wasn't strong anymore.

"I'm sorry," Sarisha said in the silence, but she wasn't. She *had* wanted to kill Pundarik, and what did it matter if she was normal? She didn't want to be normal.

"Sarisha," Mother snapped. "Do not make me repeat myself."

Habit and instinct took over – and Sarisha stepped away from the cage, leaving Mother to face Pundarik.

He was smiling, as if nothing in the world mattered. He was filthy and dying, but he was winning – he was still drawing the strength out of Mother's heart.

"I stand by what I've done," Mother said, quietly.

"You have no other choice," Pundarik said. "Or would you rather admit you failed, Chandni?"

"I've kept the law," Mother said. "I've made the world a safer place to live."

"You killed people," Pundarik said. "You tortured them. How could you hope to raise a daughter with nothing left in your heart?"

"This isn't about her."

"No," Pundarik said. "It's about what you've become."

"What *we've* become." Mother laid the lantern on the ground. "Or will you say you're still the brother who lifted me up on his shoulders at every Feast of the Moon?"

For the first time, Sarisha saw Pundarik waver. But his face hardened. "I stand by what I've done."

Mother withdrew a small knife from her belt. "Then face what you deserve." She sliced into her hand; blood welled up to fill the wound.

Sarisha held her breath. She'd never seen it – she'd never seen Mother do a blood-reading, but she knew how it went. Mother would need to mingle her fresh blood with that of Pundarik – and then she'd speak the words of opening, get into his mind and destroy him.

But Mother had never allowed her –

Pundarik drew himself up. "You think I'm going to make this easy?"

Mother stared at him, dispassionate once again. "You're weak. All I need is one drop of your blood." She walked closer, as calmly as if she were strolling in the courtyard.

Pundarik stared at her – and at Sarisha – and he smiled. "Aren't you forgetting something?"

Mother barely glanced up. "Sarisha. Get out."

Sarisha thought of the corpses and of the shadows moving within her bedroom, and a cold, hard certainty rose within her.

"I'll know. Even if I go out, I'll know what you've done. You can't keep me sheltered forever."

Mother stopped. She turned, and stared at Sarisha – and Sarisha knew what the glimmer in her eyes meant. *What kind of monster have I raised?*

"Mother –" I'm all right, she wanted to say. I'm not a normal child, but you can still be proud of me.

But she never had the chance to speak the words.

In the moment Mother paused – in the moment she was still staring at Sarisha, Pundarik launched himself at her, twisting his legs at an odd angle. One swipe felled Mother – she dropped sideways, her head hitting the lever of the cage with an awful crunching sound.

Sarisha heard that, and everything – slowed down. Someone was screaming, endlessly – and she knew she was the one screaming but she didn't care as she ran at Pundarik with her own blade drawn. "Mother!!"

Pundarik smiled – and then Sarisha slammed into his crotch, in precisely the place Uncle Jarun had shown her in his self-defence lessons, and Pundarik wasn't smiling anymore – he was bent over, coughing in pain.

"Bitch –" he whispered. "Your mother's – daughter –" His hand snaked, grasped Sarisha's hair and pulled. A fiery pain spread through her scalp, so strong she had to bite her lip not to cry out.

She lashed out with the dagger, blindly – it connected, and Pundarik let go of her with a cry.

Surely someone would realise they were here – if only by the noise they were making – surely Uncle Jarun would come –

But the remote, harsh part of her – the part that modelled itself on Mother and Uncle Jarun – knew that help would arrive too late, if it arrived at all.

Pundarik was coming at her again – staggering, on the verge of bending down. She struggled to remember what Uncle Jarun had told her about a man's body –

It was a balance between the part of Pundarik that wanted to fight, and the part that wanted to curl up and whimper. The part in pain was going to win – you couldn't keep pain at bay for long – but it would take time.

She circled him, warily, gripping the dagger.

"Giving up?" Pundarik said, lunging at her. She sidestepped, and he missed her by a handspan. "You're like your mother – an abomination –"

Something twisted within Sarisha. "You hate her that much?"

He didn't answer – he lunged at her again, and this time she wasn't quick enough: he caught a fistful of her hair, and started pulling her towards him.

She shook herself – pain ripped through her, nearly unbearable. But she was strong. She was...

Her scalp ached, but she was free.

Sarisha circled Pundarik again – trying to focus on him through the blood pouring down her face. She was no blood empath; had no armour within her, no dark river of blood in her veins like Mother and Uncle Jarun, but she had breathed in a little of it – enough to be strong.

"I was raised by two blood-empaths," she said, stepping between him and Mother – half within the open cage, smelling the gagging odour of filth and blood. "What do you think I would grow up to be?"

Pundarik stared at her. He'd stopped moving – was breathing heavily, his bloody face twisted in pain. "If – you had been my – daughter, I'd never have let you get – so cold."

His daughter – for a brief moment she wondered what life would have been, growing in a community, running every day through the fields – normal, as Mother would have wanted. She couldn't be normal.

Pundarik was staring at her with sick hunger in his eyes – and now she knew he wasn't looking at her, but at what he saw of Mother in her – at the sister he'd lost. Something fluttered in her chest: the same feeling she'd had when she'd first seen him in the courtyard, covered in blood and hardly breathing, and she knew the name of that feeling.

Pity.

"I'm not your daughter," she whispered.

Pundarik was collapsing – slowly, like a tree toppling down, his eyes still latched onto her. "No. You're – hers – to the – bones."

And Sarisha knew it was true – that Mother had shaped everything she was – had moulded her until what came out wasn't a blood-empath, but a girl who could still feel anger and rage and pity for this man who knew only hatred.

"Yes," she said, as he sank to his knees, staring at her. Pain filled every feature of his face. "I'm hers."

She was level with his eyes now, fighting the feeling that was crushing her chest. He was breathing hard – and sinking lower and lower with every passing moment.

He'd killed a blood-empath. For that, the law decreed he had to die.

The dagger was cold in her hands. She knew she could drive it into his chest, at the angle Uncle Jarun had shown her – that she was strong enough to do what needed to be done.

To do what had to be done...

Who would ever know? Uncle Jarun had asked Mother, offering to kill Pundarik in her stead.

And Mother had said, simply, *I would.*

Sarisha wasn't a seventh-rank blood-empath – wasn't a blood-empath at all, and would never be. It wasn't her place. It would never be her place.

Pundarik was curled up on the ground now – retching, although no bile came up. He wouldn't be rising for a while.

She withdrew, slowly; and found Mother propped up against the outer wall of the cage, staring at her.

"Mother –" Sarisha said. I'm sorry, she wanted to say. It was all my fault – I should have seen it.

Mother's face twisted, halfway between a smile and a grimace, an expression Sarisha had never seen on her face. But Mother didn't say anything; her head lolled back against the frame, and her eyes closed.

Sarisha fumbled for Mother's wrist – and then gave up, and looked in the neck for the voice of the heart.

It was there – weak and trembling, but still there.

"It's going to be all right," Sarisha whispered, holding Mother's hand.

The hand in hers squeezed, briefly; and then there was nothing. Sarisha sat back on her haunches, and waited.

She didn't move when the guards all filed into the room – didn't move when Uncle Jarun's hand fell over her shoulder.

"We'll get a healer," he said. "She should recover."

It might be true; or it might not. She didn't know, not anymore. She nodded, too tired to trust her voice.

Uncle Jarun took her hand, and pulled her upright. "Come on, little fish. Time to go to bed. We'll sort out the mess later."

Sarisha stared at the room – at the open cage and at Pundarik lying on the ground, making whimpering noises. "Yes," she said.

She let Uncle Jarun lead her out of the room, and tuck her into her bed – as cool and aloof as always, as if everything was all right.

"It was my fault," she said, as he bent to blow the lamp. "I distracted Mother. She thought I was a monster. I wanted to tell her I wasn't one, but I never got the chance –"

Uncle Jarun paused, halfway to the bedside table. "Go to sleep, Sarisha. Things will be better in the morning."

"I suppose," Sarisha said, listlessly.

Uncle Jarun blew the lamp, and withdrew. At the door, he stopped. "Sarisha?"

"Yes?"

"She'd still be proud of you – whatever you turn out to be."

"You can't know that," Sarisha said, but she thought of

Mother's squeezing her hand, and of the odd expression on her face.

A smile. A pained smile, but still a smile.

"I know," Uncle Jarun said, and he closed the door, leaving her in darkness with the memory of Mother's touch on her skin.

GEORGE

V.C. Linde

A stone guardian watches three women
stand at an empty grave to imagine
the men who had died.
A son, a brother, a father.
The small parcel of ephemera is delivered
in uniform late in the morning to a well-swept doorstep.
Handed to a step removed, to the past, the childhood,
he was not long enough a man to count,
not enough for it to last
the soft turn of memorised pages and photographs
crashes the final candle
then the flame is only seen as an inverse
reflection on tired minds.
And so she went away with a parcel –
one that was never seen.
Sixty-seven years.
I can return to the place they never saw him
with flowers and the resonance of a family
that just might have existed.

ABOUT THE AUTHORS

Nina Allan's stories have appeared regularly in the magazines *Black Static* and *Interzone*, and have featured in the anthologies *Catastrophia, House of Fear, Strange Tales from Tartarus, Best Horror of the Year #2* and *Year's Best SF #28*. A first collection of her fiction, *A Thread of Truth*, was published by Eibonvale Press in 2007, followed by her story cycle *The Silver Wind* in 2011. Twice shortlisted for the BFS and BSFA Award, Nina's next book, *Stardust*, will be available from PS Publishing in autumn 2012. She lives in Hastings, East Sussex, where she is currently at work on a novel.

Aliette de Bodard lives in Paris in a flat filled with computers and Lovecraftian plants that dream of taking over the living room. When not working as a Computer Engineer, she writes speculative fiction: her trilogy of Aztec noir fantasies *Obsidian and Blood* have been published by Angry Robot; and her short fiction has appeared in venues such as *Interzone, Asimov's* and *Clarkesworld.* "The Bleeding Man" is a story about motherly love and inheritance, and how it's not always the most obvious or desirable things that get passed on to one's children...

Finn Clarke has dual Canadian-British citizenship and juggles her time between Dartmoor and Quebec. Her stories have appeared in a range of magazines from *Descant* to *Big Pulp* and her first collection, *Grim Tales of Hope*, was published in December 2008. Finn is fairly sure she hasn't been invaded by anyone else's personality – although her family doesn't necessarily see this as a good thing – and is currently writing a thriller that is far more exciting than her actual life.

Emma Coleman has lived in Northampton all her life, which perhaps goes some way to explaining why her fiction tends to focus on the bizarre, quirky, and darker aspects of human nature. Emma joined the Northampton SF Writers Group in 2007, and has been honing her skills ever since. "Home" is her first published story.

Jan Edwards lives near the Peak District National Park with her husband, Peter Coleborn. She has a BA in English Literature, and was short listed in 2011 for a BFS Award. Publication credits include: *Mammoth Book of Dracula, Dark Horizons, Alt-Dead,* and *Estronomicon.* For details about Jan's writing, visit http://janedwards-writer.blogspot.com. She says of "Damnation Seize My Soul": "What began as an historical piece on Viking-era female pirates was suddenly overrun by the swashbuckling Gráinne Ní Mháille and Branwen's dark tale from the Mabinogi. Quite when Mercedeys Benks stepped into the arena is a question best not asked."

Andrew Hook has had around 100 short stories published in various magazines and anthologies. Recent work has appeared in *Black Static, Post Scripts, Needle Magazine, Unspoken Water* and *The Monster Book For Girls.* Last year he was one of the judges for the World Fantasy Awards, and his fourth slipstream collection, *Nitrospective,* was published by DogHorn. This year he is co-editing a magazine with his partner, Sophie Essex, titled *Fur-Lined Ghettos.* He can be found at www.andrew-hook.com.

V.C. Linde lives in Derby. She says of "George" that it was "written as part of *Three Random Words,* a poetry project where people submitted three words which then formed the basis of a new poem. Ian Whates kindly donated 'Resonance, Candle, Ephemera' and "George" was born. I am delighted that it has been included here amongst such wonderful company."

Una McCormack is the author of several Star Trek and Doctor Who novels. Her short fiction has been anthologised by Ian Whates, Gardner Dozois, and Farah Mendlesohn. The short story in this anthology, "In Tauris", was inspired by a summer spent reading Joanna Russ and Monique Wittig.

Sophia McDougall is a novelist, playwright, artist and poet. She is the author of the bestselling Romanitas trilogy (twice shortlisted for the Sidewise Award for Alternate History), set in a contemporary world where the Roman Empire never fell. Besides modern Romans, she has also been known to write about fish robots and ghost Nazis. You can find her at:
sophiamcdougall.livejournal.com

Adam Nevill was born in Birmingham, England, in 1969 and grew up in England and New Zealand. He is the author of the supernatural horror novels *Banquet for the Damned, Apartment 16, The Ritual*, and *Last Days*. He lives in Birmingham and can be contacted through: www.adamlgnevill.com

Rebecca J. Payne hails from Cambridge, England. She has previously published work in *Interzone* and *Ethereal Tales*. "A Change in the Weather" was inspired by long winter nights spent listening to the ocean in Porthleven, Cornwall, where the pasties are hot and the sea monsters are very, very cold.

Rod Rees has spent his life travelling around the world, living en route in such places as Qatar, Tehran and Moscow. He is a sometime student of history, being especially interested in the oddballs who populated the Victorian era, of whom Nikolai Tesla (the lead character in "Alternate Currents") was one of the oddballier. Rod's first book, *The Demi-Monde: Winter* – first in a quartet – was published by Quercus in the UK in January 2011. The second in the series – *The Demi-Monde: Spring* has just been released in the UK. He lives in Daventry with his lovely wife

Nelli (a jazz singer and jewellery designer) where he is writing his post Demi-Monde opus, tentatively entitled *Locusts.*

Tricia Sullivan is the Arthur C. Clarke Award winning author of seven science fiction novels, most recently *Lightborn.* She is a student with the Open University, the administrator of a mixed martial arts website, and mother to three children.

Adrian Tchaikovsky was born in Lincolnshire, studied and trained in Reading, and now lives in Leeds. He is known for the Shadows of the Apt fantasy series starting with *Empire in Black and Gold* and currently up to book 7, *Heirs of the Blade.* Book 8, *The Air War,* is out in August 2012. His hobbies include stage-fighting, and tabletop, live and online role-playing. More information and short stories can be found at: www.shadowsoftheapt.com.

Lavie Tidhar is an Israeli author currently resident in London. He is the author of steampunk novels *The Bookman* (2010), *Camera Obscura* (2011) and *The Great Game* (2012), weird-lit novel *Osama* (2011) – which made the shortlist for the BSFA Award – linked story collection HebrewPunk (2007), several novellas and many, many more short stories.

Neil Williamson is the author of *The Ephemera* and editor (with Andrew J. Wilson) of *Nova Scotia: New Scottish Speculative Fiction.* He is also a member of the Glasgow SF Writers Circle. "Lost Sheep" is Neil's second story for NewCon Press (following "The Moth" in *Subterfuge,* 2008). Since the editor clearly enjoys Cuddly Critter stories, Neil welcomes suggestions for featured animals should he ever be invited to contribute again.